Escalation

It happened in
a small New
England town
Vince
xxx.

Also available by Vincent Tuckwood:

Do Sparrows Eat Butterflies?
Karaoke Criminals
Family Rules
Garbled, Glittering Glamours
Team Building
Inventing Kenny
VinceT.net

Escalation

A Novel

Vincent Tuckwood

Escalation
A Novel

Copyright © 2011 Vincent Tuckwood

All rights reserved. No part of this book may be used or reproduced by any means, graphic, electronic, or mechanical, including photocopying, recording, taping or by any information storage retrieval system without the written permission of the publisher except in the case of brief quotations embodied in critical articles and reviews.

Because of the dynamic nature of the Internet, any Web addresses or links contained in this book may have changed since publication and may no longer be valid. The views expressed in this work are solely those of the author and do not necessarily reflect the views of the publisher, and the publisher hereby disclaims any responsibility for them.

Published by:

View Beyond LLC
PO Box 1096
222 Boston Post Road
Waterford
CT 06385-9998
USA

ISBN-13: 978-1466379046
ISBN-10: 1466379049

Front Cover Design: Robert Edmonds, 2011

For all who love, even when
the loving is hard

Sunday

Monday

Tuesday

Wednesday

Thursday

Friday

Sunday

Monday

Tuesday

Wednesday

Later

Sunday

Chapter 1:
Fists

The high school parking lot was dark and empty, silent save for freeway traffic on the far side of town, all roaring, purposeful fury; overnight journeys, too-late commutes, never-ending asphalt.

Thc first fist flew.

* * *

The linebacker came from nowhere. Or so it seemed to Dylan, ever intent on completing the down, arm cocked and loaded, a trap ready to spring on his well-practiced trigger.

Then the impact, crushing and brutal.

Dylan was lifted into the air, spun around and dropped until his face planted in the freshly watered turf.

He tasted fertilizer and lining chalk.

The linebacker was already up and celebrating.

"Yeah!" he screamed, beating his chest with his helmet, "that's what I'm talking about! Yeah!"

Dylan rolled onto his back and watched clouds skittering high above.

Angry? Yes.

Frustrated? Sure.

In the game?

Definitely.

He climbed to his feet and took a moment to let vertigo wash through him and out the other side.

The referee checked him over.
"You all right?"
"Yup."
"How many fingers?"
"With or without the thumb?"
"Wise-ass. OK! Third down!"
Dylan walked to where the line-backer was coming down off his high.
"Hey!"
The line-backer turned, surprised to see the opposing quarterback; wary of retaliation.
"Yeah?"
Dylan smiled and took his helmet off.
"Thanks, man… I needed that."
"Huh?"
"No, really. Thanks."
And with that, Dylan turned and retreated to the hole, readying himself for the next down.

* * *

A cackling shadow little more than a shape against the dark background of the school buildings, spitting out words that Dylan could hardly hear; speaking in tongues.
His vision blurring.
A second fist.

* * *

Ralph nosed at a pile of crap in the gutter, pulling Dylan's attention away from Katie for a moment. He pulled at the leash.
"Ralph!"
He looked back at Katie, whose nose had wrinkled in only slightly-fake disgust, and shrugged.
"Oh come on, don't tell me you've never smelled your own farts?"
Katie punched him on the arm.
"Got ya, didn't I?" Dylan laughed.
She punched him again.
"C'mon, Ralph!"
He pulled the leash and the dog gave up its investigation.

Katie looped her arm through his.
"You know," she smiled, "I'd totally smell yours though."
They dissolved into laughter.

* * *

The shadow urged himself onward in gleeful exhortation.
Playful.
Such fury, alive with anarchic chaos.
Dylan knew this shadow.
But knowing didn't help.
A fist flew.

* * *

"Are you sure?" his dad asked.
Dylan nodded at the open page.
"Yup."
"Then I guess we're decided. Florida it is."
Dylan smiled.
"Florida it is."
"Now you've just gotta learn to play in *real* humidity."

* * *

The shadow lashed out.

As Dylan moved to dodge the fist, he lost his balance, falling backwards, arms wind-milling. When the back of his skull hit the ground, his teeth snapped together, completely severing the tip of his tongue.

A booted foot stomped on his abdomen.

* * *

"This is how you do it, peanut!" Dylan exclaimed.

His younger sister knew what was coming and was already growing embarrassed.

Dylan looked to the door of the supermarket and, when he saw a shopper setting to exit, he grabbed the sampler plate and skipped over to meet her.

"Girl Scout cookie?"

The shopper shook her head. Tried to hurry past.

To which, Dylan turned on the jazz. His blinding white smile, beautiful almond eyes and quarterback's gait.

"Please," he said, "you know it's for a good... no, a *great* cause!"

She paused. Long enough for him to offer the tray. He nodded at the cookies.

"We've got Thin Mints, Dulce de Leches, Tagalongs."

"Well, I guess..."

"Which'll it be?"

She reached for one of the shortbread discs and nibbled at it.

"As good as you remember?" Dylan asked.

She nodded. Of course it was.

"I tell you what," Dylan confided, "whatever you buy today, you can totally keep between the two of us – no-one need ever know."

He winked.

She sighed.

"Oh well, can't hurt I guess."

Dylan turned to his little sister.

"Peanut... This lady has just made a great decision. Can you help her out, please?"

Peanut looked aghast. *How could he have acted like that?*

"Pretty please," Dylan smiled, "with sugar on top? And a promise that I won't give you a big, sloppy kiss in front of your friends?"

The shopper burst out laughing.

"Well," Dylan joined her, "what's a big brother s'posed to do?"

* * *

Dylan curled into a ball, tried to protect his head.

The kicks rained in.

* * *

The quiet of Katie's bedroom; family long-gone to the mall.

Her breath quickening.

"I love you," Dylan whispered.

"I know," she urged, pulling him close, helping him.

"I love you."

* * *

The shadow stalked away across the darkening, empty parking lot, adrenalin howling at the moon, laughter reverberating off the school buildings, a caterwaul of wild abandon.

Dylan lay in the middle of the asphalt.

Dylan lay still.

Still.

Monday

Chapter 2: Eyes Open

Charlene pulled up at the stoplight and indicated to turn onto the high school campus. For the last year or so, a quick loop around the school's interior road had been part of her commute to and from the police department. Thc dctour was only a matter of minutes most days, scanning the buildings for graffiti or signs of forced entry.

The stoplights showed green and she turned through the school entrance, swinging left towards the buildings and the main car park. The campus was deserted, awaiting arrival of buses, cars and the tumult of teenagers.

She got to the corner and turned right, heading along the internal road towards the tennis courts and, beyond, the football field.

As she drove, she sipped at a traveller's mug of coffee; warm and energizing.

She scanned the car park off to the left.

"Wait a minute," she breathed, "what's that?"

* * *

Dylan Ford had been one of the good guys, Baker thought. Everyone knew it, a true New England stereotype. Gifted quarterback, loving family, beautiful girlfriend; every inch of him the classic American dream.

He'd helped Baker out on a school visit to talk about drug avoidance; giving a rounded perspective on steroid use and the choices faced by high-school athletes. This hadn't been a kid swept up by *'Just Say No'* hyperbole, his had been a rational discussion of the pressures and values system that underlay the choice to use banned substances.

That had been what Dylan had chosen to call them: *banned substances*. Not *'drugs'*, not *'roids'*, not anything that would make them seem cool in any way. Simply: *banned substances*. Baker had been worried that such an approach wouldn't connect. But he'd been wrong. And that morning, as he'd scanned the audience of teenagers, from disenfranchised goths at the back, via smiling cheerleaders, to math nerds agog at the possibility of ever breaking the rules, he'd seen what a truly charismatic person held within their potential. They had hung on Dylan's every word.

For just a moment, Baker had been reminded of Bobby Kennedy. Then, too soon, Dylan had retreated from the podium, and it had been Baker's turn to deflate any and all interest; they were teenagers and, for them, that was what grown ups, especially the police chief, were all about.

He drove through early commuter traffic, the town just waking up, dozy heads searching for a meaningful cup of coffee. Normally, he loved the quiet moments before the town came fully alive. But not this morning. Not when he was *en route* to a crime-scene. As he drove, he painted the memory of that high school audience across his misted windshield, seeking any face that might have planned such an attack. He came up empty, unable to identify anything out of the ordinary.

"Like that's a surprise," he sighed to himself.

He arrived at the school just ahead of the ambulance; lights flashing but siren unnecessary in the quiet early morning. The ambulance tailed him around the school buildings and out onto the reserve lot where Baker pulled up behind the single parked cruiser and indicated the ambulance driver should do similar. They both stepped out of their vehicles at the same time.

"Give me a moment, Jimmy?" Baker asked and, without waiting for a response, walked around the cruiser.

As the engines cooled, ticking quietly, Baker heard crows clustered in the trees surrounding the football field on the other side of campus, calling to each other in the hope of finding fresh, dead meat.

Charlene was standing by the body, which she had covered with her coat; only the head visible. She lifted her gaze when she heard Baker approaching, face grey with shock.

"Oh, chief," she said, "it's..."

"I know, I know," he calmed her, "we'll... figure it out."

He dropped to one knee by Dylan's side and looked closely at his face.

"What happened to you, son?" he asked, "who did this?"

A bubble of bloody snot expanded slowly from one of Dylan's nostrils.

Baker stood.

"Okay, Jimmy," he spoke over his shoulder, "he's all yours."

The cawing crows echoed in a moment of stillness.

* * *

It took an hour before the first phone-call came in.

Caller ID confirmed his suspicions: *Simpson, Curtis*.

Lead reporter for *The Daybreaker.*

Even in these days of mass-market internet and cable news, it was the local guys who had their fingers in all the right wallets in all the right places. Someone at the hospital, no doubt. A porter. Or an orderly. Or a nurse.

When it came to the gossip of criminal acts, decency was more often viewed in the rear-view mirror than in the caring of this community; his disappointment was familiar, even though ultimately a waste of energy.

"Everything's reality TV," he opined to no-one. He lifted the phone from its cradle.

"Baker here," he spoke calmly, like nothing untoward had ever happened in this small New England town.

"Hi, Jack," a voice spoke.

"Curtis," Baker responded, "good morning."

"I heard," Simpson said.

Baker really wasn't in the mood to play *'dodge-the-bullet'* but he had little choice; this was an open case.

"Heard?" he said.

Simpson sighed.

"Great headline," he said, "almost a classic: *'Beaten quarterback near to death.'* Like I say, a classic."

Baker rubbed at the bridge of his nose.

"Curtis, you know the drill," he spoke calmly, this being a long-rehearsed dance. "I'm unable to discuss the details of any open case. Should there be anything to share, we will arrange a press conference."

"Sure, sure," Simpson empathized, "but... Hell, Jack... This one, it's..."

"I know, Curtis. I know."

"You know what they're going to say, don't you?"

Baker did. It had been in the pit of his stomach since the first call from Charlene that morning.

He knew what they were going to say, all right.

"Just don't put words in their mouths, Curtis. Please. This... isn't about that."

There was silence at the other end of the phone. Baker looked up at the ceiling, traced the irregular patterns on the sound-insulating tiles.

"I don't think I'll need to," Simpson said, "do you?"

Everything's reality TV, Baker thought as he stared into space.

"Curtis," he said, "I've got to go. And do me a favour, OK? I haven't had chance to speak to Dave and Lilly yet – can you keep it quiet 'til I have?"

A moment.

"Sure. They won't hear from me."

"Thanks."

He put the phone back on its cradle without waiting for a response, knew it would only be a matter of time before it would ring constantly. And now the clock was running down on whether he could get to Dylan's parents first.

Standing, he automatically checked his badge, belt and gun, before heading out of his office, passing Charlene on the way.

"Where are you going?"

"Out to the Ford place," Baker said, "I want to make sure they know what they're in for. You know how to get me."

"Sure."

The phone rang and they both turned to look at the handset. Baker sighed.

"You know the drill, Charlene. Keep it tight."

She nodded and he nodded right back.

It had begun.

Baker turned and headed out to his car.

Chapter 3:
Early Morning Call

Baker drove through slowly-waking streets; folk emerging in the Spring sunshine, checking for newspapers, walking the dog or simply revelling in a morning that didn't carry the deep chill of a Winter so recently departed. Few of them noticed his cruiser, those that did nodding in taciturn New England greeting. Baker returned the acknowledgement but little more, his mind working over words.

* * *

At the Ford's house, the garage doors were still closed. A good sign.

Baker stepped onto the sidewalk, hitching at his trousers, tapping his sidearm out of habit.

Swallowed once, calmed his thoughts and walked up the path to the front door, where he rang the doorbell before retreating a couple of steps.

He placed his gaze off to one side, so as not to be staring at whoever answered the door. Any police officer knocking on the door at this time of morning would be shock enough, let alone the chief, without focused intent to amplify the impact.

He heard the deadbolt being clicked back. The door opened.

"Jack? Er… Hi," Dave Ford said, an immediate question on his face.

"Morning, Dave. Can I come in?"

"Er… Sure."

Dave stepped back, gesturing for Baker to enter, and the two men walked down the hallway towards the noise of a bustling family kitchen.

Lilly was working scrambled eggs in a frying pan as Baker entered, her back to him.

"Who was it, hun?" she asked without turning.

"Lilly," Baker said, calmly.

She glanced over her shoulder. As soon as she made eye contact with Baker, she dropped the wooden spoon into the pan and turned. Slight tremors of adrenalin shivered through her at the sight of this unexpected visitor.

"Peanut," she said to her daughter without turning, "please go and get dressed for school."

"Huh?"

"Please… Go and get dressed for school, sweetheart," Dave repeated the instruction.

"Oh… OK! Want me to wake Dylan up?"

Both Lilly and Dave looked to Baker, who shook his head slightly. A momentary frown ghosted Lilly's face, but she stayed with the moment, swallowing down her fear.

"No, sweetie," she said, "he hasn't got early class today. Let him get some more shut-eye."

And with that, Emily danced across the kitchen, humming to herself as she skipped up the stairs.

"Dylan's in hospital," Baker said immediately, "he was beat up last night at the school. Charlene spotted him this morning."

Lilly crumpled onto one of the wicker seats at the kitchen table. Dave stepped towards her, passing Baker, but then paused.

"How was…"

"We don't know much more than I've just told you. I came straight over, after talking with... Curtis Simpson over at *The Daybreaker* has already got the story. I've asked him to sit on it at the moment. We probably have until…"

"Is he…" Lilly's voice choked before she could finish her question. Dave stepped to her now, a hand going to her shoulder and squeezing reassurance.

"We should get to the hospital," he said.

Baker nodded his agreement.

"Is he..." Lilly fought to speak her question, "is Dylan dying?"

Dave shuddered.

"I... I don't know," Baker said, "I got over here as soon as I could. Jimmy Thompson took him to hospital..."

"Please, Jack?" Dave nodded at Baker's radio.

"Too public," Baker said, as he retrieved his cell-phone from his pocket. The station was on speed-dial.

Frozen in place, they waited for the call to connect.

"Charlene," Baker broke the silence, "any news on Dylan Ford yet?"

He stared into space, fighting hard not to catch Dave or Lilly's gaze as he took the news on board.

At the other end, Charlene finished speaking.

"Thanks... I'll be back soon enough. Have the calls started yet?"

He listened. Nodded.

"Calm before the storm," he nodded in agreement. "Okay. Bye."

He pocketed the phone and turned immediately to face Dylan's parents. When he spoke, it was directly to Lilly.

"He's not critical, though they're monitoring him closely. He's broken up pretty bad. But, by the sound of it, they've not found anything more than that. X-ray showed some internal bleeding, but it's under control."

"Then he's going to be okay..." Lilly's relief flooded her.

"Too early to say that, Lil," Dave spoke, "too early, right Jack?"

Baker nodded.

"They'd have told us if there was anything worse. Sometimes... things emerge over time. But they're monitoring him. That's a good thing."

He looked up at the ceiling as he heard Emily crossing the landing.

"Can someone take her for you?"

Dave shook his head.

"School-bus is due in about ten minutes," he said, "I'll go wait with her."

"Good," Baker nodded. "Want me to stay with you, Lilly?"

As her daughter's footsteps thundered down the stairs, Lilly stood to her full height, fixing Baker with an icy stare.

"No, Jack," she spoke through clenching teeth, "I want you to catch the bastards that did this. We'll be fine if you just do that."

Emily burst into the kitchen.

"Ready!" she yelled.

Baker cracked into a grin that felt pasted on his face.

"Aren't you just!" he exclaimed, content to lose himself in a moment of childhood's joy. "You want a police escort to the schoolbus? Blow your friends' minds?"

"Cooool!" Emily smiled and then her face crunched as she sniffed the air.

"Mommy! You're burning the eggs!"

Lilly responded as if being awoken from a nap, shaking her head suddenly. She walked back to the range and moved the pan from the heat.

"Silly me," she play-acted to the extractor hood, tears lurking just below the surface of her words.

Baker took control, bowing his head and swinging his arms towards the front hallway.

"After you, milady Peanut," he spoke to the floor and, every inch the regal princess, Emily walked past him, backpack over one shoulder, cares far off in the cloudy future.

Baker took a step after her and then turned back to the kitchen. He fixed Dylan's parents with a level gaze.

"I will. I promise I will."

Then he turned and followed the child out into the front yard.

Dave and Lilly hugged for a moment.

"You get showered," Dave said, "I'll be back soon."

"Jesus, Dave… I hope he's OK."

"Me too, sweetheart. Me too."

Chapter 4:
This... Isn't About That

That morning's conversation with Simpson nagged at Baker. The way Simpson had already guessed how the town would react to the news, and how Baker would immediately be under scrutiny.

"This... isn't about that," Baker had said.

And while he still believed that would prove to be the case, he couldn't deny that Mason's unfinished business was at the root of the nagging.

This was the lever Mason had been looking for.

It really was.

* * *

"If we could have some quiet, please!"

The town clerk watched, frustrated, as the bluster and noise continued unabated. She was out of her depth; more used to meetings with no more than five people in attendance beyond the committee.

Mason watched her losing control.

Time to tame the beast, he thought and bent close to the microphone, knowing that his voice would drown out everything else.

A squeal of feedback as his face drew level with the microphone, drawing a split-second of silence into which he dived feet first.

"The meeting will come to order," he spoke assertively, "we will have quiet."

There was a moment where the whole room seemed to stare at him; a tableau of short-circuited emotions and debate. Adrift, people began to sit and, despite some small conversational accompaniment, Mason's order was ultimately obeyed.

He lent back in his chair. Budget meetings. He hated them. Especially when they were as charged as the proposals on the table this year.

"Thank you," he said, slowing his tone to maintain control and order in the room. "Folks, there's no getting away from the facts. We're in the hole to the tune of four-and-half million dollars."

They were hanging on his words now, just as they always were when the town got out of control; his the steady hand on the rudder, the calm at the storm's centre. As always, the velvet glove was his humour.

"The savings we need are not going to come from cutting subsidies to squirrels in the park," he smiled, painting sympathy across his face, "we have to get real."

A few bodies tensed at his dismissive reference to proposed cuts to the Parks and Recreation budget, but the silence largely prevailed. Having taken the attention of the floor, Mason kept going.

"The board of education has offered some limited cuts, but I just can't see how we can maintain current staffing levels."

He looked to the left of the auditorium, to ensure no-one doubted he was talking directly to Superintendent Jansen.

"We need to find at least three bodies from education."

* * *

At the back of the meeting room, Baker grimaced at the political hyperbole and gamesmanship.

Mason and his tin-pot theatrics, he thought.

He knew what was coming. Knew it all too well.

* * *

Mason continued, walking through each department's proposals, highlighting how they were short and what sacrifice would deliver a balanced budget for the town.

He looked down his list.

"And last up on the chopping block," he smiled a little at this, "sorry, turn of phrase. Police department. Is Jack here?"

He scanned the room until he saw Baker's hand go up at the back.

"Hi, Jack," he smiled in what could easily be mistaken as genial welcome.

"This is a pretty fair proposal, we could all learn from it," he told the town council before turning his attention to the wider audience.

"We live in a safe town," Mason continued, "we are decent people who respect each other and care about our communities. And on the few occasions that we fail in that civic duty, the good men and women of our police department are there to help us get back on the straight and narrow."

This brought an unexpected ripple of applause from the audience, who were dancing nicely to Mason's tune.

Yeah, right, Baker thought, *without us, this place would be a regular seventies Harlem.*

"Now, one of the areas that Chief Baker and his staff have handled so well is the most recent spate of teenage high-jinks. I for one appreciate our beautiful downtown area without graffiti highlights."

His smile was all teeth as he built the case.

"And, thanks to the support of his officers, we've seen a marked drop-off of casual violence at the high school. In the months since we removed the dedicated security guard, there hasn't been…

He glanced down at his notes for pure effect.

"… a single incident reported by Principal Sturmann."

Here it comes, thought Baker.

Mason turned his head to the schools' Superintendent.

"I think it's time to reconsider security at the high school, don't you Jansen?" he said. "Things seem to be under control and, as you're looking to make cuts, it would seem that shifting security obligations to the police budget would make sense."

There was a moment of quiet. Mason let it hold, though not for so long that the plain facts could seep through the audience's sheep-like torpor. He looked towards Baker at the back of the room.

"Jack? Please work with Superintendent Jansen to detail your proposal for managing high school security. I look forward to seeing first draft," he looked at his watch, "next Friday?"

Baker stared at him for a moment, then nodded. This was neither the time nor venue for the conversation that needed to happen.

"Thank you," Mason's self-assertion cascaded across the audience, who had yet to wake up to the implications of what had just happened, "and that concludes the budget review. As you can all see, we have some more homework to do before specific budget details are in hand, however I'm sure we'll all enjoy a good and open debate of what's been discussed this evening, so please raise your hand and we'll call you to the microphone in turn."

Mason sat back, a satisfied chess player seeing mate in the next few moves.

* * *

The debate ranged from the contentious cuts to the Parks and Recreation budget – how it might affect the attractiveness of downtown to the seasonal tourist dollars – thru the impact that cut-backs to infrastructure spending would have upon the renovation of the riverside walkway. From there, on to the proposals to cut staff from the schools, though the latter debate spiralled into a spirited argument weighing the relative importance of Spanish, Music or the elite program for gifted kids.

Everyone had an opinion, it seemed, and was intent upon airing it.

Baker knew that the specific shift of responsibility for school security wouldn't even be raised; Mason had a way of making sure his *fait-accomplis* seldom did.

He left the room to the debating public and headed towards the car park, passing the offices where he'd fought to block the decision which had been forced tonight via public misdirection and political sleight-of-hand.

Putting police in schools was the wrong move. He'd told them. Showed them. His case had been solid, based in hard data from across the country.

But he had been fighting ideology.

Tonight, ill-informed belief had won out.

Baker had long lamented a town council that wanted nothing more than to reserve the town for elders and betters, to minimize the presence and impact of younger generations. Over the past decade, the department had been forced to implement constraint upon constraint, all levelled at removing kids' rights.

Skating ban.

Mall patrols.

Weekday curfew.

These were good kids, Baker knew, from good homes. This wasn't the inner city. But the town council was stuffed with members who lived in a fantasy of *ye-olde-worlde* New England; all picket fences and lemonade on the porch. Few of them actually lived anywhere near downtown.

The curfew had been an especially draconian response to the actions of a lone graffiti artist; a move that Baker had resisted. Everything, from his gut to the research he'd done, told him that they should have expected escalation; increased constraint forcing increased rebellion.

They'd lucked out, their graffiti artist growing bored, finding something else to occupy his or her time. Nothing to do with the curfew, Baker knew; *everything* to do with the curfew from Mason's pulpit.

Baker's point had been disproved; his argument undermined.

Within weeks, Superintendent Jansen had hired a high school security guard, Bill Tanner, to prevent a small run of what he termed *'canary-in-the-coalmine'* violence. To Baker's eyes, the symptoms had been little more than run-of-the-mill schoolyard bullying.

As for Bill Tanner's previous experience? Stacking shelves at a local home improvement superstore, family connection to the town council; or, in other words, the *usual*. Basic training had fallen to Baker and his team, who had taken the security guard under their wing, ensuring he didn't light any unintended fires in his day-to-day.

All the time, Baker had been fighting Mason and Jansen as they persisted in their attempts to formally place school security under the arm of the police.

He'd hoped that the calm status quo, Bill doing enough to keep things level, and his own team staying at arm's length would become the *de facto* solution.

But the last round of budget cuts had seen to Bill Tanner's position; partly a reality of fiscal mis-management, and partly a chess-move by Mason.

The status quo had held.

And then, at that night's town meeting, Mason had made his final push.

And the responsibility for school security had been publicly passed to the town police department, with no additional funding, putting Baker on a hook with which he fundamentally disagreed. The town public, in the shape of first selectman Mason expected a proposal the following Friday.

That night, Baker stepped into the car park, packed beneath a curfew-silent night sky, feeling the hook in his cheek and Mason's hands on the reel.

* * *

Now, as he drove away from Lilly and Dave Ford's house, he felt that hook dig deeper. Mason would demand an officer in the school; that order rumbling like a distant train approaching on rickety tracks. Inevitable.

Chapter 5:
So Much For Promises

Baker headed back downtown, thinking a million thoughts none of which coalesced to more than fleeting ghosts.

That this had been a simple case of high school tribalism, he had little doubt; sooner or later, they would scrape enough surfaces to come up with a jealous boyfriend or hallway vendetta. Despite this, the night at the town meeting kept playing over and again. Mason's control of the situation, his calculated manipulation of a budget challenge into a concerted effort towards making the town an occupied territory.

Lilly Ford's face danced across the windshield.

I want you to catch the bastards that did this, she'd asked.

And he'd committed that he would.

And the town would hold him to that commitment. Bring the bad guy to justice. That's all they wanted: *the bad guy.* They would remain largely oblivious to the notion that decisions they made on how the town was managed, the frustrating environment they created for energetic youth, and the desirability of so much money in so few square miles, all might play into a decision to step outside of the law.

There was no shared culpability once the crime was committed.

They would call for the metaphorical head of the bad guy.

And, of course, Baker would deliver.

Of course he would.

Mason would ratchet his choke-hold a little tighter, while everyone looked the other way.

He glanced at the clock on his dash. Nine-fifteen.

Picked up the radio and opened a channel to the station.

"Charlene?"

"Chief?"

"Did you get breakfast yet?"

"First thing this morning, chief."

"I didn't," he watched Dylan's beaten body float where his mother's face had been moments earlier, "it's going to be a long day."

"Sure is," Charlene agreed.

"I'm stopping at Annie's place on the way back," Baker said, to himself as much as to the radio, giving himself a badly needed sense of direction, "want me to get anything for you?"

She thought for a moment.

"No, I don't... No, wait, coffee sweet. Make it a large one, chief, OK?"

"Sure," he said, "be back soon."

"Okay," Charlene was gone, leaving only slight static.

Baker placed the hand-piece back on its clip, shaking his head to clear the random thoughts. That done, he checked his rear-view and signalled for a u-turn.

* * *

Reported in the online section of *The Daybreaker*:

High School quarterback beaten, near death (Posted at 9:25 a.m.)
Police fear explosion of violence at unprotected school.

Dylan Ford, the popular high school quarterback, was discovered badly beaten on the High School campus around breakfast-time this morning. At present, the identity of the assailant is unknown.

Sources suggest that Ford, currently undergoing assessment in St Luke's hospital, has sustained extensive injuries, some potentially life-threatening. His parents are at his bedside in ICU.

The latest attack comes only a few short months since the controversial decision to remove security from the High School campus, and can only serve to reignite calls for Police Chief Jack Baker to take meaningful action.

Baker, who had previously assured residents that the security of children and teachers would not be affected by the decision, declined to comment on the subject earlier this morning.

Dylan Ford, the hero of the recent play-off with…

* * *

Baker stepped into Annie's Place, the popular diner just off Main. Already clearing out after the morning rush, several booths were available. As always, though, Baker chose the counter; a reliable source of unexpected conversation and general information of how things were going in the town.

As he crossed through the noise, bustle and orchestrated chaos of breakfast, something tickled at him, though he couldn't identify the source.

It was always this way when he was beginning to work on a case, things bubbling just below his conscious mind, connections and ideas. He'd learnt long ago to just let the pot boil; sooner or later, it would begin to blow the lid off.

"Hi, Annie," he greeted his old friend as he approached the counter.

"Jack," she welcomed him, "breakfast?"

"Sure enough."

He sat on one of the stools, rearranging the cutlery and napkin out of habit.

"Anything other than the usual?" Annie smiled.

He shook his head, returning the smile, and she quickly wrote out his order.

"Coming right up," she said, "coffee's on its way."

And she was gone, ever efficient, genial and welcoming.

Baker stepped back into his whirling thoughts while he waited for his coffee. Restless, he pulled his cell-phone, checked it was on. He considered calling the hospital but decided against it and pocketed the phone; Charlene would call him if there were any developments.

He couldn't imagine what the Fords were going through right now. Sure, he'd worked his share of violent cases over the years, but none had been perpetrated on him or his family. He'd been lucky, as had most of the residents of the town; this was generally a safe and quiet place, violence an aberration from normality, happening elsewhere, read about or watched on the news and then forgotten.

Not for the first time this morning, he spoke a silent wish for Dylan's speedy and full recovery.

"Guess you've got a lot to think on," Annie woke him from his reverie.

"Huh?"

"It's bad news," she nodded, "sure enough. He's a good kid."

"Huh?"

Annie raised a cynical eyebrow at him.

"Come on, Jack," she said, half-smiling, "don't play dumb with me. I've known you too long."

"I'm not…"

She nodded, connections clicking together in her head.

"Wait there," she ordered, putting his coffee down in front of him.

All of a sudden, his stomach was fluttering with a rush of adrenalin. He breathed deeply, sipped at his coffee. It scalded is lips. He hardly noticed.

Annie returned and handed him a piece of paper.

"*The Daybreaker*," she said handing him the printed article, "online."

He scanned the piece.

"Shit," he sighed.

Mason could have written this, he thought, *it's got his fingerprints all over the pen.*

"Hadn't read it, huh?" Annie looked long at his face.

He shook his head. Breathed deep, scanned the room quickly over his shoulder. Though no one was staring, he felt all eyes upon him.

"Interesting angle, don't you think?" Annie asked.

He looked her directly in the eyes.

"This isn't about that," he said, "I told Curtis this morning. Security wouldn't have made a blind bit of difference."

Annie nodded, keeping her peace.

Baker put the paper down and stared at it, anger brimming.

"He couldn't even wait until lunchtime," he hissed to himself, "couldn't wait…"

"Jack," Annie interrupted him.

When he didn't look at her, she placed her hand on top of his and rubbed at it.

"Jack," she repeated and this time he looked up at her.

"You didn't do this," she said, "you hear me? You did not do this."

He breathed slowly, bringing himself under control.

"Thanks, Annie," he said finally.

"Stay focused, Jack," she said, "Lilly and Dave need you clear headed to deal with this. Let Mason and his cronies play their games. None of that's going to help Dylan recover or get justice. No-one's going to blame you."

They'll sure try though, Baker thought, saddened by how Annie was falling straight into the pattern he'd predicted.

"How bad is it?" Annie asked quietly. "Dylan, I mean."

He shook his head.

"Bad enough," he said and then nodded at the printed page, "but not nearly as bad as Curtis is painting it. They're monitoring him but not overly concerned. Lilly and Dave have gone down there, Emily's at school."

"Anything I can do?" Annie offered.

"Thanks, Annie, but no. Nothing at the moment."

"Except for your breakfast, right?" she smiled at him.

Somehow he found a smile to return to her.

"That you can," he said, "that you surely can."

She turned and walked back towards the kitchen to check on his order.

Baker looked at the paper. Re-read the article. Thought of Dylan Ford's broken body.

And wondered again at how the words read as if Mason had authored them.

Feeling eyes on him from all directions, he decided to nip this particular bud before it could swell and resolved to visit Mason's office immediately upon leaving Annie's Place.

Chapter 6:
Fait Accompli

"Good morning, Jack," Brenda Song greeted him.

She doesn't know yet, he thought, scanning her face. He smiled a fixed welcome.

"Hi, Brenda. Is Mason in yet?"

"Sure. You know him, up with the birds!"

Baker didn't let his smile ebb.

"Any chance I can get some time with him?"

Brenda scanned her computer screen.

"Urgent?" she asked.

Before he could answer, Mason's office door opened and he stepped into the reception area.

"Jack," he said, stepping forward, offering a hand.

"Mason," Jack shook.

"Come on in," Mason gestured to the open door, "We'll be a few minutes, Brenda. No interruptions, please."

Brenda nodded, checking back over Mason's calendar, assessing the amount of damage she'd have to control.

* * *

Mason closed the door and, stepping around Baker, crossed to his desk.

"Sit, Jack," he said without turning towards the other man, "no ceremony here."

Baker sat in the all too familiar seat.

"It's a bad business, Jack," Mason continued. "The Fords are highly respected in this town. And Dylan? Well, I think it's safe to say he's much loved by all, not just ditsy girls with stars in their eyes."

Baker sat still, listening. This was classic Mason, all theatrics and bluster. He wondered how long it would be until the selectman actually asked how Dylan was doing.

"Such violence," Mason warmed to his theme, "no-one deserves such violence, but the Fords least of all. His poor sister…"

He scanned down at a scrap of paper on his desk; checking.

"Emily… What must she be thinking at the moment…"

Peanut, Baker thought, *she doesn't get called Emily very much.*

"Such, such violence," Mason shook his head in resignation.

Baker started a countdown to the first jab.

10…9…8…

"I hope you'll put your best man on the investigation, Jack. You've got my every support to bring the vicious hooligans who did this to justice."

7…6…5…

"Are there any leads as yet?" Mason paused, considering. "No, I would imagine it's a bit early to expect that."

4…3…2…1…

"And it's not as if we'll have any insight from the school…"

Zero.

"A pity that Bill Tanner's not still there. He would have been able to give some insight, I'm sure."

The game was on, then.

"Curtis Simpson already ran a piece in *The Daybreaker*, " Baker said, refusing to play mouse to this cat, "I asked him not to, but he went ahead anyway. I'd already got to Lilly and Dave, so they were warned. Peanut… Emily is at school. Dave and I walked her to the bus."

He made a mental note.

"We'll put a call in to the principal there, make sure she's looked after today. Besides, news like this won't spread so fast at middle school."

"No. Not exactly Justin Bieber, is it?" Mason smiled.

Baker let the attempt at a joke pass. Now wasn't the time for distractions.

The silence held for a moment.

"People will expect action," Mason said to himself, looking up at the ceiling. He levelled his gaze upon Baker.

"We must be seen to be doing something, Jack. We can't just let this float. The Fords are highly respected and..."

Here it comes, Baker thought.

"... people are already jittery enough since you pulled Tanner out of the school. They know it's a powder keg, Jack... Ever since our friend the graffiti artist went underground, it's been getting ready to blow."

Baker couldn't help it and rose to the bait.

"Mason, I don't..."

"They're scared, Jack. Tanner gave them a sense of security. When you took him out of there, you just invited this to happen."

Baker's fists clenched involuntarily.

"We must be seen to act, Jack," Mason nodded, "we have to win back the trust that *you* betrayed."

Somehow, Baker managed to overcome his anger, finding the calm centre of this particular storm. He breathed once, twice, swallowed and then spoke.

"What do you suggest, Mason?" he asked.

Mason looked at Baker long and hard, weighing up whether this was supplication, submission or a simple stand-off. He stood and crossed his office to look out the window; sunshine flooded downtown.

Baker watched the show, already able to guess the punch line.

"The people will want action," Mason thought aloud, "but the investigation will take time. Time we don't have if we're to avoid panic."

Baker couldn't help but smile at an unbidden image of residents running through the streets, tearing at their hair and screaming about the impending attack waves of hostile teenagers. He managed to hide the smile just as Mason turned.

"I want a police officer in the high school immediately, Jack," Mason's tone invited neither challenge nor question, "we must be seen to act."

Like clockwork, Baker thought, heart sinking because he knew he wouldn't be able to refuse.

The bottom line was that he *had* taken Tanner out of the school, and had been seen to do so. Much as he wanted to believe that Dylan's beating wasn't to do with that decision, some part of it was, at least in the collective town mind. Mason and his cronies had made sure that their fingerprints weren't on that particular budget decision, leaving it for Baker to present it to the public, at town meetings, and in the pages, virtual and real, of *The Daybreaker*.

Knowing he couldn't refuse wouldn't stop him speaking his mind, though.

"It's the wrong thing, Mason," he said.

Mason looked at him, unsurprised to hear a challenge.

"Really, Jack?" he said. "Lilly and Dave Ford might disagree with you. We *must* be seen to act."

"It's wrong," Baker held his position, "it won't help."

Mason just stared, his face curiously expressionless.

"You're going to make things worse, Mason," Baker said and, knowing the conversation was over, stood to leave.

When he reached the door, he turned. It took all of his control not to step back into the futile discussion. He fixed his gaze on Mason, who looked at him as if surveying a butterfly on a pin.

"In case you were wondering," Baker said, "Dylan's pretty badly beaten, we're waiting to hear how bad it is, but he should pull through. Lilly and Dave are with him."

Mason nodded.

"I'll…" he began but Baker shut him down.

"No, Mason. Don't call them," he said "they don't need it right now. Give them some space before you put your foot in their mouths."

Baker left Mason behind and stepped out into the reception.

"Thanks, Brenda," he said as he passed Mason's assistant, "sorry if I screwed up his schedule."

He'd never been more pleased to step into bright morning air.

Chapter 7: Damage Control

Finally, it seemed that the initial rush of calls was easing.

Charlene leant back in her chair, breathing herself into calmness.

This job, she thought, *it'll be the end of me*.

She'd caught herself two or three times wondering how the caller even had the temerity to be asking questions about Dylan. In each and every case, she'd sensed little more than a nosey-parker seeking an inside line or scuttle-butt.

A couple of rich suggestions for potential culprits, of course. Her favourite had been from Leary, the old guy out on Woods Road, who'd been certain that this was a hit by Boston gangs to prevent the high school from going any further in the north-east championship. Leary had been adamant that Charlene put down the phone and get straight on to the FBI. She'd had to work hard not to laugh, cry or even scream down the phone at him.

Still, there had been several points where she'd asked herself if she was losing her mind.

The phone rang and she glanced at it; *Baker, Jack* on caller ID.

She pressed the speakerphone button.

"Hey, chief. What's up?"

He was silent for a moment, though she could hear him breathing.

"Are you okay?" she asked.

"I'm fine," he said, "just got through speaking with Mason. You know how that goes."

Charlene nodded to the empty room. She'd seen Baker's end of that conversation many times, often having to ease him in the aftermath.

"Any developments?" she asked.

"Nothing major," Baker said, "or unexpected. *The Daybreaker* ran a piece."

"I saw that," Charlene trod carefully, "and... er... even if I hadn't, enough of the interested parties who've been calling all morning have pointed it out for me. How does the short end of the blame-stick feel?"

Baker laughed.

"You've got such a way with words, Charlene."

"Oh yeah, I'm a poet *and* I know it!"

"Anyway, now it's out, can you do me a favour? I helped Lilly and Dave Ford get their youngest off to school this morning. I don't think the jungle drums will reach her there, but better to be safe than sorry, can you give Principal Miller a call?"

"Get her to wrap Peanut in cotton wool?"

"Kid gloves, right."

"I'll get on it soon as we're done here."

Baker paused.

"What?" Charlene asked.

"You know, I was just wondering what to do next, that's all. There's a thousand conversations and none of them the most obvious to go for first."

"That's just Mason, Jack, got you rattled. He has a way of doing that. Best thing you can do is put him to one side and focus on what needs to be done right now."

"Yeah," Baker agreed, "the politics can come later. Today's all about letting people know what's happened."

"And what hasn't," Charlene added, "sooner you get that done, sooner we can get on and investigate."

Baker paused again.

"Thanks for that, Charlene. I'd been running through the investigation in my head but it's too early. I'll head over to the high school, speak with Walt Sturmann, put a game plan together. There's going to be a lot of shocked kids looking for direction."

"Right," Charlene said, "want me to do anything about *The Daybreaker*?"

"I wish we could," Baker sighed, "but Curtis is going to do what Curtis is going to do and we aren't going to stop him. Best we can do is get things calmed down while we find who did this."

"Sure enough," Charlene said, "I'll get onto the middle school now."

"Okay, bye."

Silence returned to the office while Charlene looked up and then dialled Wendy Miller's number.

As it connected and began to ring at the far end, an image of Suzy flickered through her mind. Though the memories didn't intrude as much now that a few weeks had passed, they were still surprisingly regular, and no less painful for the march of time.

She closed her eyes, visualized a blank page. Now wasn't the time to lament lost-loves.

She heard the far end click as Missy Clark, the middle school secretary, answered.

"Johnson Middle School?" she said.

"Morning, Missy… Charlene Goodlow from the police department here."

"Oh, hi Charlene."

"Can I speak with Principal Miller please?"

"Sure," Missy said, "about the Dylan Ford business?"

Another one, thought Charlene.

"Police matter, can't say more than that," Charlene demurred.

"Oh, I understand. But you don't need to worry, we picked up on the news in *The Daybreaker* this morning. Principal Miller's done a wonderful job, she spoke with all the staff at morning recess. Put them all on watch. Emily's not going to hear it from anyone here."

"That's good to hear, Missy," Charlene said, pleased that they were already ahead of the game, "still, I'd like to speak with Principal Miller if that's all right?"

Missy's voice was colder when she replied.

"Sure. I'll put you through."

The phone went dead for a moment, then Wendy Miller's familiar voice came on the line.

"Morning, Charlene," she said, "I hear that Missy's update wasn't good enough for you."

Charlene could almost see Wendy wink at this. She chuckled down the phone.

"Take it she's not listening in, then?"

"That's right," Miller aped a movie-security chief, "this is a secure line and we are clear to discuss matters of national security."

They both laughed at this.

"How's Emily doing?" Charlene asked.

"Fine, just fine," Wendy's voice was calm now, in control, "Missy filled you in on what we've done, right?"

"She did, sounds like a wonderful job, my friend. But..."

"Worried she'll find out from one of the other kids? Cell-phone or the like?"

You're way ahead of me, Charlene thought, *like always.*

"Uh-huh."

"No need to worry," Wendy smiled, "didn't you know today was *'Surprise no cell-phones-face-to-face-day'* here?"

"You took their phones?"

"Sure," a small laugh, "I'm a regular ten-cent dictator."

Charlene smiled.

"Sheesh!" she laughed, "no matter what happens in life, I want *you* on my team!"

"Why, yes," Wendy added, "yes, you do."

Charlene played along.

"Got something more to tell me?"

"Of course! I'm glad you asked! I've texted with Lilly and Dave. Emily will be going home with me for the afternoon until they're able to come pick her up."

"Don't want her going home to an empty house?"

"Sure," Wendy laughed, "but this way, we also avoid any unexpected sympathy from well-meaning school-bus drivers!"

"You're a machine, Wendy," Charlene said in admiration.

"Nah," Wendy countered, "I'm just a Mom who happens to do this job. Gives me an instinct for damage control. Emily will have a wonderful, unexpected play date with Sonny."

A silent moment; the unspoken, with all it's automatic inference.

You don't have kids, do you?

Charlene's smile dropped a little; hyper-sensitive, thanks to decades of insinuation, assumption and labels.

Again, Suzy ghosted behind her eyelids when she blinked; the ever-present ache reminding her of its teeth.

The moment was stretching. Charlene scrambled to get things back on track.

"You've done a fine job this morning, Wendy," she said, "we couldn't have asked for more."

"Thanks," Wendy said, "I would ask how Dylan's doing, but I'm sure you've had enough of people wanting the inside scoop, haven't you?"

Charlene paused. Wendy had always been able to read between the lines.

"Yeah," she sighed, "it's been hectic."

"Sure. How are *you* doing?"

"Me? Just another day at the office, you know how *that* is."

"Not even close. Middle school isn't exactly the 'hood."

Charlene smiled, suddenly tired.

"No. Lucky for you."

"Have you heard much from Suzy?"

"No, she's..." Charlene spoke before she realized what Wendy had asked, "what makes you..."

"Come on, sweetie, this is me you're talking to: *damage-control-Mom*, remember? If you don't want to talk about it, that's fine. I'll be here when you do."

Charlene felt an unanticipated tear form in the outside corner of her eye, wiped at it absently with the heel of her palm.

"Thanks, Wendy," she said, "I appreciate... It hurts, though, you know? I thought I'd be over it by now but..."

"You miss her. Why's that such a surprise to you?"

Charlene sat for a moment, gathered herself.

"It always surprises me how long it takes to get over a broken heart," she said, closing the door on the pain.

"Well, I've got to get back to business. Thanks for your concern, Wendy, I really mean it."

"Welcome," Wendy said, and there might have been a note of dismay which was lost across the phone line, "let's talk soon, though."

"Sure," Charlene said, "soon. Thanks. Bye."

"Bye."

Charlene ended the call and put her face in her hands for a moment, shuddering as Suzy's betrayal surged through her like a thrumming electric current. Eventually, as some slight feeling of calm returned, Charlene lifted her gaze to the ceiling.

"Get it together, Goodlow," she spoke to the empty office, "get it together."

She stood to get a coffee.

As she was pouring, a sudden thought hit her.

I sure hope Missy wasn't listening in on that.

This brought a small laugh for her and she returned to her desk, mentally preparing to write up her initial report on finding Dylan Ford's body that morning.

Chapter 8: Please Do This

On the way to the high school, Baker's train of thought was interrupted by a warning light on the dash.

He turned in the direction of the nearest gas station, driving to the west of downtown, half-observing people going about their business, moving from shop to shop, heading for a coffee from Starbucks. Things were quiet. Calm. Unchanged.

Dylan Ford's broken body would attest differently.

He shook his head which, despite his best attempts, rang with the sound of Mason's voice. There was a sword dangling above Baker's head, suspended by the single, silken thread of his own opinion of right and wrong. That thread was strong for sure, though Baker knew that in this situation it was likely to break.

He let the metaphor drift from his head as he turned into the gas station.

Waving to the cashier for approval, he set the pump to automatic, and went in to grab a coke and some beef jerky.

"Beautiful day, isn't it?" the cashier said as he rang up the purchases.

Hasn't heard the news, Baker thought, allowing a reflexive poker mask to cover his face and normalize his voice.

"It is that," he said, "blue skies all the way."

He paid for his snack and bid his farewell.

On the forecourt, he saw that George Liu's car was now opposite his own at the pump. Liu, a prominent Asian-American business leader, atypical for this small New England community, was hooking the nozzle into the Mercedes' tank. As he turned back to the pump, he saw Baker and waved.

"Good morning, Chief Baker," he smiled a welcome.

In that smile, Baker knew all that he needed to know.

Here's a man who has heard the news, he thought.

"And to you," Baker deflected, "are you well?"

Liu nodded as he glanced down to set the pump to automatic.

"I am," Liu said, looking back up at Baker.

No, you're not, Baker thought, reading something in the man's face.

"I was sad to hear the news this morning," Liu continued, "Dylan Ford is a good boy."

"It was a shock," Baker agreed.

He liked Liu. How he cut to the chase and didn't appear to want to play any games. Having a good chunk of downtown owned by such an honest tycoon was, in Baker's experience, an anomaly in the region; the town was very lucky.

"Do you have any leads?" Liu wasn't prying, just genuinely interested.

Baker shook his head.

"Too early yet," he said, "we've been notifying people all morning, mostly handling the fallout from the piece in *The Daybreaker*. We'll start asking questions this afternoon."

Liu smiled at mention of the local newspaper. A couple of years earlier, when he'd moved to buy the old bank building on Main, he'd been the focus of the paper's intense suspicion for a month or so. When the deal had gone through fairly, cleanly and, above all else, at benefit to the town, there had been calls for an apology from the paper. An apology that, of course, never came.

"It is what we should expect from a free press," Liu sighed.

"Doesn't exactly help us with a quiet investigation, though."

"No. That is true."

"It's not just that," Baker continued, a thought finally coalescing from the fragments, "if it were just Curtis Simpson acting out his Washington Post fantasies, I could handle it. But what if it makes things worse… what if…"

Liu nodded, encouraging him to continue.

"What if this is some sort of rivalry between high school cliques, some…"

"Gang-war?" Liu put the unspoken words on the end of Baker's sentence.

"I won't call it that," Baker said, "it's too easy, paints things too black and white. We don't have gangs in this town, we have kids without enough outlets for the energy they have to burn. And a town council that wants to…"

He stopped. He'd begun to warm to the familiar theme, dropping his more usual political circumspection.

"Sorry," he said, "it's just a word that hooks me. And if we focus on it, it'll be a huge distraction from solving the attack on Dylan. This wasn't anything to do with a gang."

Liu nodded his understanding and the two men were quiet for a moment.

The fuel pump to Baker's car clicked the end of its cycle. As he bent to remove it, Liu spoke.

"I appreciate your sensitivity, Chief Baker," he said, "and understand your wish not to focus upon labels. However, I do worry about the adolescents in the town. Something is… is brewing here."

Baker replaced the gas nozzle in its cradle and turned to face the other man. Here was the ghost of concern he'd seen beneath Liu's greeting. Baker's instinct told him to listen hard.

Locking eye contact with Liu, he didn't even need to speak to encourage him forward.

"Jason… My son…" a flicker of shame entered Liu's eyes, "Jason has changed recently."

"Changed," Baker spoke quietly.

"Yes. You have met him, I think?"

Baker nodded that he had. He knew a lot of kids in town, but those of prominent community figures had a way of sticking. Jason Liu was a quiet kid, stereotypically respectful of adults and authority. Once past formality, with enough digging, there was a warm smile to be found.

Sadness creased Liu's eyebrows momentarily.

"He no longer speaks with me," Liu lamented, "he is such a good student, however I fear he is slipping. It is hard to tell, he is a closed book. What has become of my son?"

Bullying, Baker thought immediately. It had all the hallmarks.

"If there are... gangs... I am sorry, I must use that language," Liu continued, "I do not want Jason at their mercy. He is a good boy, studies hard. But... I do not need to tell you how a Chinese boy can be an easy target here. Especially one whose father..."

Baker nodded. Liu didn't need to finish the sentence.

"I will not have him being a target because of my success, Chief Baker."

"George," Baker said, "Principal Sturmann would have picked up on anything like that. You would have heard something; Jason is an honour roll student."

"I know," Liu shook his head, this was a familiar path of thought, "there is no logic to it. All I know is that my boy has changed in the past year and I can not get close enough to know what I can do to help."

The pump filling Liu's car clicked off with a noise like a pistol crack in the quiet forecourt, giving both of them a start. Liu grabbed it with a suddenness that surprised Baker, as did the way he slammed it home into its cradle before resealing the filler cap.

All this stress just below the surface, he thought waiting for Liu to turn back to him.

When Liu did turn, his face was set, lips thin slivers pushing down against each other. His voice was filled with undercurrents as he spoke.

"If there *are* gangs, if they are hurting my boy, I will accept no excuse for inaction. I expect you to do whatever it takes to make sure the high school is safe for good students like Jason. Anything less is unacceptable. You will have my support in whatever way you need, however you must act quickly and firmly."

Baker was stunned at the strength of Liu's composure and momentarily silenced.

"I love my boy, Chief Baker. You must do whatever it takes to fix this. Please..."

Finally, the stress eased out of Liu a little and his voice deflated.

"Please do this."

He offered his hand to Baker and the two men shook a farewell.

Liu was quicker into his car and Baker watched the Mercedes ease into light downtown traffic, before turning at the end of the block.

While the handshake had been one of social courtesy, he felt an emergent commitment to George Liu; he was sure that the change in Jason Liu was connected to Dylan Ford, that solving one would undoubtedly help solve the other.

A moment later, he closed the door of his cruiser and exited in the direction of the high school, his head filled with thoughts of high school bullies and their ease in taking aim upon a quiet Chinese kid with great grades.

In his mind, he felt a burgeoning checklist for discussion with Walt Sturmann, not least of which was how ready he was for the draconian solutions first selectman Mason had in mind.

Chapter 9:
Built On Sand

Baker pulled into the high school car park. Mid-afternoon sunshine flooded the area and it could have been a millions miles from when he'd entered that morning, leading a judiciously silent ambulance.

Buses idled, awaiting the imminent arrival of their passenger students.

Baker skirted the short-term parking area adjacent to the school entrance, mostly for disabled badge holders, but decided against parking there. His cruiser, while obviously police issue, was unmarked and he would be able to park at the back of the lot without drawing attention. There, he could clear his head of the day's conversations, all whirling replays and snapshot vignettes, before he spoke with Walt.

He parked in the far corner, switched off the engine and watched the idling buses. He let his thoughts drift, though they were overshadowed by his growing certainty that Mason would expect an officer to be placed in the school as soon as possible; maybe even the next morning.

If that were to be the case, who would he…

The answer was obvious. Though the police department wasn't exactly over-staffed these days, thanks to the relentless paring back of budgets and avoidance of tax increases, it wasn't a financial choice.

Charlene was the obvious candidate, even without other constraints.

Another pre-emptive conversation started to emerge, jockeying for space in amongst all the others dancing across the windshield.

Muffled by distance, the dismissal bell sounded across the high school campus and Baker turned his attention to the exits.

Things were blissfully still for a moment.

Baker breathed silently.

One of the main doors swung open almost violently, before it locked out in its open position. Three kids ran out of the door, seemingly one form with six arms and six legs. They sprinted for a bus off to Baker's left. Soon the exterior of the school was all opening doors and moving teenagers; some fast, some slow, some cool, others nerdy. This was high school in its natural state, only…

Baker closed his eyes for a moment and then reopened them, purposefully focusing on the air above the school buildings. It was an old trick learned in basic training: using peripheral vision to assess movement at night-time, working with nature not against it. He calmed himself, breathed into that spot of air, consciously relaxing his sight, letting awareness drift to the periphery without looking.

He didn't know exactly what he was looking for. Certainly, he expected no sudden revelations of culprit, motive or identification. But there may be something, some hint.

Gradually, he became aware of the energy flowing amongst these kids; *the vibe*, as they might have said back in the Sixties. He let himself drift.

There's tension here, he thought, *different to normal.*

He fought against a cynical impulse to deride his own assessment; hadn't their quarterback hero been beaten near death this morning?

Float, he thought, *float.*

There was something in their clusters… Something…

But it was gone. His very conscious self-talk had exploded the moment.

Baker shook his head and stepped from the cruiser.

As he crossed the car park, it was his turn to play someone else's centre of attention. It felt like a thousand eyes turned to watch him as the students noticed his approach. They watched from the doors, the buses, the cars that surrounded him.

Like prairie dogs, he thought, *tension's got them on high alert.*

He tried to catch someone's eye, to gain an opening to acknowledge their concern, neutralize the suspicion. None of them would give him that opening, though, averting their eyes as soon as he looked at them.

Oh, Charlene, he thought, *this is going to be one tough nut to crack.*

And, in that moment, he knew that he'd grown resigned to following Mason's orders and compromising his own opinion. The thread holding the sword had snapped.

He swallowed his dismay and refocused on the task in hand, meeting with principal Walt Sturmann.

* * *

Baker was welcomed into the principal's office with a shake of the hand and a clap on the shoulder. After the ill-defined tension of the students, he wasn't sure quite what reception he'd expected from Sturmann.

"Sit, sit, sit," Sturmann smiled, indicating the chair across from him, "Coffee?"

Baker held up his hand, shaking his head.

"No, thanks... If I have any more caffeine, I'll bust through the ceiling."

Sturmann sighed heavily.

"It's a bad day, Jack," he said, "the students are... They're feeling it. Dylan is their hero. One of their own."

"Indeed," Baker agreed, "have you heard anything from Lilly and Dave?"

Sturmann shook his head.

"I wouldn't have expected to," he said, "I doubt I'm the first person that comes to mind for them at the moment."

"Right," Baker said, "anything from the students? Any leads?"

Sturmann looked shocked for a moment, before gathering himself to reply.

"Sheesh! You don't waste any time do you?"

Baker paused for a moment, he'd seen Sturmann on the defensive too many times to be surprised, and knew he'd be wise to tread carefully.

"Trails go colder the more time goes by, Walt, you know that."

Sturmann watched him.

"And one of your students undoubtedly knows something about what happened to Dylan?"

Sturmann shook his head.

"You're certain it's one of the students, then?"

The question took Baker aback and he froze for a moment. To have his assumption so clearly called into the open. He really hadn't considered any other scenario than one of high school rivalry or bullying.

Could someone from outside the school have done this?

His gut screamed no, but he pushed that down so that he could at least try to keep objectivity at the root of his thoughts.

"Thank you," he said.

Sturmann's face was a question-mark.

"I had made that assumption, yes," Baker answered, "and it's just that, an assumption. So, thank you for bringing it to my attention."

"For what it's worth," Sturmann said, "I think it's one-hundred-percent accurate. One of the students did this."

Baker's eyebrow raised.

"The trick," Sturmann continued, "will be to work out which one it was."

"Any ideas?" Baker asked.

Sturmann shook his head.

"I've spent most of the day fielding calls from concerned parents, buried by them actually, they're all well-meaning but you think they'd have some idea of what I'm up against…"

He stopped. Caught himself.

Baker had heard Sturmann's habitual *poor-me* many, many times before. Like an illusionist, it always proved better to misdirect.

"I was watching the students as they got dismissed just now," he said, "there was a tension about them."

Sturmann nodded.

"And that's a surprise? They're in shock about Dylan!"

"Pretty much what I told myself," Baker responded, "but I was hoping for a little bit more, maybe someone separating himself from the others, some secret huddles or something."

"Oh, come on Jack," Sturmann admonished, "they're a little more subtle than that. That's what no-one in this town seems to understand. These kids are not all primary colours, it's not black-and-white."

"This isn't a Disney children's special, Jack!"

Baker bit down on his immediate retort. After the day he'd had, and more importantly those to come, seeding any ill-feeling here would prove counter-productive.

"I know, Walt," he said, "I'm sorry. It's just that sometimes it's the earliest, simplest things that can crack a case. I know you've had a hard day, it can't have been easy dealing with the fall-out."

Sturmann nodded.

"But we'll get through this, Walt," Baker said, meaning it, "so long as we work through it methodically and in-step."

The principal was quiet for a moment, looking into space, just missing Baker's gaze.

"Who are you putting in?"

Once again, Baker was stopped dead.

"I..."

"Mason called at lunch-time, told me you'd be putting an officer in the school."

Was that before or after we met? Baker wondered, then caught himself. When it came to Mason and his grand schemes, involvement of those directly affected was often unnecessary.

"He's... That decision hasn't been made," was all he could offer in response.

"That's not what Mason said," Sturmann countered, "he said within the next day or so he'd make sure the kids were protected."

Sounds right, thought Baker.

"What did you say to that?" he asked.

"You know how he gets, Jack. I tried to say no, but he was adamant and Mason... Well, you know he gets what he wants."

Baker could hear their conversation as if he'd been on the call. Sturmann saying little, Mason asserting his *fait-accompli* solution.

He would gain nothing by prevaricating.

"Charlene Goodlow," he said, "she's the only one who can do this, and do it well."

Sturmann nodded. He didn't really know Goodlow but trusted Baker's judgement.

"When?" he asked.

"When would work for you?" Baker responded with a question.

"I..." Sturmann paused, face flushing red, "I don't think I really matter in this one."

Baker paused, feeling all his unease welling at this indicator of the flavour of Mason's call to the principal; Charlene had called it earlier, Mason *did* have a way of getting under peoples' skin.

"Here's what I think," he said, forcing his tone to remain calm, open and honest, "I'm asking Charlene to support you in keeping things calm here; a reasonable short-term response to the violent beating of one of your students. But it is just that: *short-term*. I refuse to police the high school."

"You'd tell Mason that?"

Baker remembered too many bitter discussions, tasted them all again in that moment.

"I have done already."

"Yet it's still happening."

"Yes," Baker said, "yes it is. For now."

He shook his head.

"Walt," he said, "I don't want this getting side-tracked into Mason's other games. Justice for Dylan, protection for the other kids. Nothing more nor less. That's it."

"Well, we *all* want that!" Sturmann protested.

But only some of us are willing to stand for it, Baker thought, the impending conversation with Charlene beginning to weigh heavily upon him.

"Understood," he said, voice dropping in volume, "but here's the thing that you and I know, and that first selectman Mason chooses not to see. This will escalate, Walt. You know it, I know it. We lucked out on the graffiti. I'll go to my grave and still tell you that Bill Tanner was nothing to do with that. You saw it first-hand, he's a nice guy and all, but he wasn't doing much more than treading water."

Baker noted the look in Sturmann's eyes; there would be no challenge to this assertion.

"But whatever's happening here, Walt, even if it's just a one-off, putting an officer right in the middle of it has every chance of blowing the whole thing sky-high."

Sturmann remained silent but nodded his understanding.

"Frankly, it's why I'm putting Charlene in. She's seasoned enough to deal with the tension, I've seen her do it. And it's also because she's a woman, simple as that. The last thing we need is to exercise Mason's fantasies of putting an alpha-male into the ring with teenagers. Even then, this has every chance of getting out of hand."

"I..." Sturmann started but Baker was ready to leave, he wanted to speak with Charlene.

"I need you tight on this, Walt. You've got to be helping us, because if you don't things are going to go very bad, very quick. I've seen it happen before and won't let it happen on my watch. Charlene will be under strict orders, she's not investigating while she's here, and she's not your own private security firm. She's monitoring the situation and providing calm."

Baker stopped. The look on Sturmann's face had just crossed into that of a rabbit in the headlights. There was little more to be gained from discussing the matter further. Sturmann would, or would not, be an aide to Baker's intent, but it was pretty clear that he would follow rather than lead. And if that was the way things were to be, then Baker would work within those constraints.

The bottom line was that this would fall on Charlene's shoulders.

And with that, he stood.

"Let's stay close on this one Walt, okay?" he urged.

Standing, Sturmann nodded.

"Sure," he said, offering his hand to Baker.

They shook.

"What time are you here until tonight?" Baker asked.

"About six. Why?"

"I'll give you a call when I've spoken to Charlene. Confirm arrangements."

Baker turned for the door, increasingly keen to be away from the other man. Sturmann stepped around his desk to follow.

As he laid his hand on the door, Baker looked over his shoulder.

"And one other thing," he warned, "I already had an unwelcome surprise this morning from Curtis Simpson at *The Daybreaker*, so I'm asking nicely that you don't speak to Mason or anyone else until I've confirmed that Charlene's briefed. Please."

The tone of Baker's voice stopped Sturmann in his tracks.

"Sure," the other man whispered, his voice suddenly dry.

"Thank you," Baker said and, after shaking Sturmann's hand curtly, stepped out of the office into the now-empty high school halls.

Chapter 10:
Safe Haven

In the end, Baker decided to sleep on it.

Despite Mason's inferences and assumptions swimming in the air around his head, little would be served by jamming all action into this day. In fact, it was more likely to be a fool's whim to move from decision to action while Dylan Ford's parents learned the full scope of their son's injuries.

And part of him, whispering constant rejection of Mason's plans, understanding that any further action would be an insult to Dylan.

As he pulled in through the back entrance to the station car park, he saw Charlene driving out the front, her shift over. He clicked the radio.

"Charlene?"

"Yup?"

"Anything I need to know?"

"Nothing that we haven't already covered, chief," she paused, and Baker watched her scan the street for oncoming traffic. "What's new from your travels?" she asked.

"Ditto," Baker laughed, pleased that the day was at least a little nearer its end, even if he still had paperwork to go through.

"Nothing from Mason?"

"Nothing from Mason, though…"

Charlene waited at the other end of the connection; Baker watched her watching traffic.

"Though?" she repeated, encouraging him along.

He really didn't want to cover it with her now, not when she was heading home; he should be the one to lose sleep tonight.

"Sorry," he said, "I was gathering wool. It's been quite a day."

He hoped the radio would mask how much of a bluff that sounded to his ears.

"Though?" Charlene repeated again.

"Yeah… I dropped in to see Walt Sturmann at the high school."

"How is he?"

"As freaked out as ever," Baker continued, "he's an interesting piece of work. Doesn't matter what we talk about, he always manages to turn it back to himself and how much pressure he's under."

"He should try working for you," Charlene laughed, "I mean, listen to you! You're not even willing to cut him some slack today of all days."

Baker's smile was only whisper thin.

Many a true word, he thought, once again reminding himself that he wasn't the only one dealing with the impact of the news.

"You're right," he said, "thanks for putting me straight."

"What's next?" Charlene asked, and Baker knew that she was already in the process of getting five from two plus two.

"Next?" he joked, forcing a smile to his lips and hoping it would cross over into his voice. "Next, you go home, get some rest, I hit the paperwork, lose sleep over Dylan Ford's beating. Then, we wake up to a new day tomorrow and start the whole damned carousel again."

His smile had failed him, he glanced across at Charlene's car, hoped she wouldn't turn to see him there.

She didn't move.

"Are you okay, chief?"

Am I? he thought as a vision of Dylan Ford's broken body faded across the windshield, obscuring his view of Charlene's car, *am I really?*

"Yeah, I'm okay," he chose honesty, "I've had better days… We'll get through this though, Charlene. Putting today behind us is the first step."

"Okay, Jack. I'll see you tomorrow."

"Yeah," he said, aware of how tired his voice sounded, "tomorrow… And Charlene?"

"Uh-huh."

"Thanks for being here today, you're a rock."

There was a moment of static before Charlene responded.

"Just doing my job, chief. Just doing my job."

"Yeah… Thanks, Charlene. Goodnight."

"Bye."

Baker replaced the microphone on its hook and sat watching, expecting Charlene to pull out into the street. He was surprised when her car didn't move.

Her head tipped back, as if she were looking at the car's roof, contemplating. After a moment, she brought it back to look through the windshield and her hands came up to wipe at her eyes with the heels of her palms. The movement was abrupt, curt.

With her tears wiped away, Charlene pulled into traffic.

It's been a long day for everyone, Baker thought.

He waited a moment before pulling around to the front, stepping out of his cruiser and walking into the station.

* * *

Charlene turned into her street.

She was worried about the chief; he'd fielded a huge pile of crap today, she knew. But even that worry was submerged behind the hairball of entering her empty house, a couple of hundred yards ahead on the left.

Home had become a nest of heartaches.

Months had passed, sure, but there were too many familiar spaces that seemed waiting for Suzy's return, and she was constantly reminded of her partner's absence. Memories danced in amongst dust motes.

It was particularly bad today, the shock of seeing Dylan first thing this morning, delayed by the distraction of well-intentioned nosy neighbours on the phone.

Or maybe it was the conversation with Wendy, her concern for Charlene.

She felt like a drink, though knew that she would likely face more questions about Dylan at any local restaurant than she had done all day on the phones.

No, her house was the only sanctuary she might find in town, the one place she was desperate to avoid.

She meant to pull into the driveway, she really did. Her hands and feet, however, seemed to have lives of their own and before she caught herself, her house was receding in her wing mirror.

"Where am I going now?" Charlene sighed to herself.

At the stop sign, she pulled right, away from downtown and any restaurant she might have chosen to visit.

Aimless motion felt good and began to soothe her.

The attack on Dylan Ford was such a pity, such an unnecessary act of violence against someone who didn't deserve it at all. Not that anyone ever did. But Dylan was a nice guy, every inch the hero *The Daybreaker* had painted him in the early edition.

Who could have done something like this? Who could deliberately attack and beat any other human being? Knocking them to the ground and then kicking and stomping so hard that...

She tried to stop thinking about the state he'd been in when she'd found him that morning. It took a feat of self-control to do so, and she had to dig deep into her reserves.

If she hadn't been there.

If she hadn't driven through her customary morning loop, she wouldn't have spotted him as she'd driven past. It had been the very surprise of seeing what she'd taken for a pile of rags in the middle of the otherwise empty car park that had made her look twice; made her turn her cruiser and drive into the back car park.

If she hadn't stopped to look.

The rags had only resolved into a body as she'd drawn very close.

If she hadn't been there.

He would have laid in the car park until the students began to arrive.

He'd been in such a bad way.

If she hadn't been there.

Would he have died?

Charlene was shivering despite the evening's warmth. She turned the heater to full but it didn't help.

Turning right at the next corner, not really noticing where she'd got to, she drove through a sheen of impending tears.

She wished Suzy were here; a loving heart, strong shoulder.

But she wasn't.

Charlene ached for anyone who could help her deal with this heartache.

Through bleary eyes and the overbearing heat in the car, a sign on the roadside grew coherent: *Hospital, 500 yds*.

Charlene had found her secondary haven.

She shut the heater off and gunned the engine slightly.

* * *

Lilly and Dave Ford were nowhere to be seen in the waiting area. Charlene stepped up to the nurse's station and asked whether there was a room set aside for visiting family members. The nurse on duty hooked a thumb over her left shoulder at a door with frosted glass. Beyond the door, it was dark.

"Are the Fords in there," Charlene asked anyway, certain of the answer she would receive.

"No," the nurse said, looking up and really seeing Charlene's uniform and badge for the first time, "they left about an hour ago. Had to get home for their daughter. Besides…"

"How is Dylan doing?" Charlene asked.

The nurse hesitated. Charlene breathed deep, adopted what she hoped was a more formal expression. She reached out a hand to the other woman.

"It's all right," she said, "I'm Officer Charlene Goodlow and I was on duty when Dylan was found this morning. In fact, I was the one who found him."

The nurse nodded but still looked hesitant to share any details of Dylan's condition.

"Would you like to speak with my boss, Chief Baker?" Charlene played a new card.

The nurse thought for a moment. Took a long look at Charlene's eyes, which were still red from crying.

"You found him?" she asked.

Charlene nodded.

And there must have been something in her eyes because the nurse nodded once and then spoke clearly.

"He's resting. Multiple fractures. Slight bleeding in his body cavity, though that's easing up – his kidneys, it seems. It's too early to tell whether he's sustained brain damage yet. We'll have to wait for him to come back to us before we can run those diagnostics."

Charlene nodded slightly, shocked by the detail even though she'd feared as much since walking to his side that morning.

"This happened at the school, right?" the nurse asked.

"That's where I found him," Charlene responded, "can't say for definite if that's where the attack happened, but it's a fair bet."

"Any idea who did this?"

Charlene shook her head, sensed a similar interest to that which she'd spent the morning fending off.

"It's not right," the nurse continued, "school should be... Should be safe. If we can't trust schools... What does it say about us? About society?"

Charlene shrugged, wanting to be out of the confines of the reception, so rapidly filling with opinion and conjecture.

"Can I see him?" she asked.

The nurse paused.

"Hmmmm," she looked over her shoulder as if checking no-one was watching, "I guess so, but don't disturb him, okay?"

Charlene placed her hand on her heart.

"I swear," she said quietly, "I just want to see how he's doing."

She turned towards the door, which was security locked.

"Which room is he in?" Charlene asked.

"Twenty-two," the nurse replied, "I'll buzz you in."

The lock thrummed for a moment and then there was the metallic sound of the mechanism firing. The door bounced slightly and Charlene pulled it towards her. As she stepped over the threshold, she looked back at the nurse, who was watching her enter the ward.

"Thanks," Charlene said, "this means a lot."

The nurse nodded.

"Just don't disturb him, okay?"

Charlene smiled assent and then walked into the ward, letting the door close behind her.

She walked a little, checking door numbers, until she got a sense of the direction to Dylan's room.

The door was open slightly and, from her position in the ward corridor, Charlene could see the outline of feet beneath clean hospital sheets. A glance both ways along the ward confirmed she was alone and she stepped into the small room.

As she rounded the door, she took in the whole of him.

He was sleeping, back propped up to about forty-degrees. Intubated, one of many machines to the rear of the bed rising and falling to maintain his breathing. His head was bandaged, the left eye completely covered by a very specific, heavy ocular dressing. Intravenous tubes snaked into his arm and, almost absurd, a sterile clothes peg was clipped to his index finger, she guessed to read his pulse.

Everything hummed, whirred, hissed or beeped gently.

Dylan Ford's life, extracted and spread over machine upon machine.

Charlene shuddered as the thought went through her again.

If I hadn't been there, would he have died?

A small sob escaped her, but she managed to keep it near silent.

She scanned the room and spotted a nurse's stool, pulling it to the side of the bed so that she could sit.

She felt like holding his hand, or touching him in some way, but held back, aware of her commitment to not disturb him.

Her voice surprised her when it broke the silence in the room.

"I'm so sorry, Dylan," she whispered, "I'm so sorry I didn't..."

Didn't what? Charlene thought.

"I wish I'd known it was happening. That I could have been there to stop... This."

She was quiet for a moment.

"It's been whirling through my head all day. Someone must have known this was going to happen. Someone... Did *you* know, Dylan? Had things been building up? Maybe you let things slip a little, hoped they'd go away if you ignored them. Isn't that what they say about... about bullies?"

Dylan remained oblivious to her whispered questions.

"I'm here now though, Dylan," she nodded, feeling tears begin to ease out of the corners of her eyes, "*we're* here. And we're going to get them. Whatever it takes, we're going to get them."

She looked at his prone form, his oblivious body, submerged in machines, wires and tubes, his one visible eye closed; just as surely sightless as the one behind the bandage.

Charlene's hand snaked out and gently stroked Dylan's hand.

"We'll get them," she said, "I promise."

She was quiet with him for a moment, then stood to leave the room. At the door she turned and took one last look at his heavily sedated body.

"I promise," she whispered and stepped through the door.

Tuesday

Chapter 11:
A New Day's Dawn

Charlene woke to dawn's light scaling the wall across from her bed. Outside, the birds welcomed the new day, and in the hazy moments before sleep left her, she could believe that Suzy was still lying next to her; her familiar weight, shape, presence and being. How Charlene wished to maintain the warmth this birthed in her belly and heart, even as the sensations evaporated into the new day.

This loss, it left her so, so empty.

She glanced at the alarm clock, an hour or so until she'd normally rise. She rubbed at her eyes, crusted from tears shed at Dylan Ford's bedside, tears for him, for Suzy, for herself.

Just a day earlier, she'd woken with a similarly heavy heart.

And all the days before that, ever since Suzy had decided to leave.

That blazing, hysterical argument; reproach and betrayal. The magnified blast of a thousand tiny pin-pricks of laser heat, each small indiscretion and meaningless disagreement, burning through to the core of what had kept them together in this tight-knit, ever interested New England town.

Over their years together, neither of them had noticed the very core of their bond eroding and, when the earthquake came, they'd had little sense of early tremors, even when the edifice was collapsing; when the damage had been long done.

There had been no rescuing their relationship; years washed away; long-dry riverbeds suddenly flooded.

She closed her eyes, tried to forget the small, mean triviality of their love affair's collapse.

And saw Dylan's still body; the hiss and rhythmic accompaniment of cold hospital machines replacing the imagined sound of her lover's breath.

She thought of her commitment to him.

Turned to look at the alarm clock again.

Decided sleep wasn't returning this morning and, swinging her feet into waiting slippers, headed to the bathroom.

* * *

Baker thought about calling Mason as soon as he was out of bed.

But he held off.

Sleep had done nothing to clarify an alternate path.

He would call Mason after he had talked to Charlene.

* * *

Sitting in her kitchen, drinking coffee, she scanned the door of her refrigerator, a Rorschach hodge-podge of paper scraps, photographs, magnets and reminder slips. Off to one side, small rectangles of magnetic plastic, each showing a word or phonetic, the impromptu poetry created with these rectangles had always been a hit at their parties; particularly with Suzy's artist friends. Often, the morning after the night before had found a profound thought accompanying the morning milk.

Charlene looked at the words now, perhaps even hoping that they had magically been rearranged since she'd last sat here yesterday morning.

But they hadn't.

Charlene's poetry fridge maintained radio silence.

She crossed the kitchen, bringing her coffee with her.

At the fridge, she cleared space enough on the door and began to slide words and phonetics onto her metallic canvas.

Complete, she stepped back, sipping at her coffee.

Shuddered a little, unsurprised to feel familiar tears pricking at her eyes.

Swallowed hard.

I missed you this morning
Your breath did not
Disturb the air
I breathed
I am nought my love
Empty

"Work," she said, turning to walk from the kitchen.

* * *

Later, in the shower, she tried to imagine the water was washing her history away, leaving her open not to fractured, painful memories but instead to experience and potential. Breathing in the steam, the scents of her body wash and shampoo, wanting so badly to believe in a new start.

But as she towelled off, that familiar ache was never far from her.

* * *

Baker watched as Carl left the station. Nothing to report from the night shift and, thank goodness, no sign of any new beatings to be discovered this morning. Allowing Carl to leave before Charlene had arrived to replace him was a risk but Baker needed this time to prepare. Besides, yesterday had been an anomaly – things were typically quieter than quiet at this time in the morning.

Baker sat in his office, letting his thoughts drift to a near-future where one of his team would be based at the high school.

Charlene was the right choice for the placement in the school; he had no doubts on that count. She had the temperament and calm not to get hooked by Mason's political idiocy. Yet he really didn't know what reaction to expect from her. Would she be upset? Angry that he'd chosen to put her in the school? Or would she take it in her stride, hardly batting an eyelid?

He had to guard against transferring his own angst onto her. Had to keep a calm, objective point of view.

Which wasn't always easy around Mason and his political games.

Besides, just because he had a bad feeling about where this was leading, didn't mean Charlene would necessarily feel the same way. Sure, she knew Mason and his ways, but she might just believe that putting someone into the school was a good idea. She'd found Dylan, after all. She'd had to face that discovery alone just a day earlier.

Was that all of why he'd chosen Charlene, anyway?

This was a time of day that allowed only for truths. Alone as he was, the quiet of the station reflecting his thoughts directly back at him, he couldn't avoid the answer.

He'd chosen Charlene because she was the least likely to be damaged by the placement. That was the top, middle and bottom of it.

Charlene had over a decade on the force under her belt. In all that time, she'd rarely if ever expressed any interest in promotion or extended responsibilities; seeming more than happy to serve the community as a regular officer. Simply put, in the cold light of this new dawn, he knew that she wouldn't worry what this would do for her resume, for her seniority. And this was the sort of placement that could wreck a serious career in very short order.

Is that it? he thought, *really?*

And the thought that she might be little more than his token offering to collateral damage chilled him.

He sat frowning in the silence.

There were so few new edges to discover in his self-reflection; little that hadn't been present throughout the long, sleepless night he'd just endured.

* * *

Charlene passed Carl's car as she drove down Main Street. She waved at him but it didn't look like he'd seen her.

The chief was probably at the station early; not too much of a surprise given the day they'd had yesterday. She drove along for about twenty seconds and then thumbed her radio.

"Chief?"

It took a moment for him to respond, the car filling with radio silence and static. Charlene waved at Annie, who was working on the chalkboard menu outside the diner.

"Morning, Charlene," Baker's voice filled the car, making her jump a little.

"Morning," she said, gathering herself, "I just passed Carl on Main. Anything up?"

"No," Baker replied, "I was in early and let him head home."

"No new news?" Charlene asked, not exactly sure what she was asking.

There was a pause and, in her mind's eye, she could see a crease spreading across Baker's forehead.

"Where are you?" Baker asked.

"Just turning onto Daniels. Should be there in a minute or two."

"Oh. Okay. Good. See you when you get here."

And with that, he was gone, silence flooding into the space his voice had occupied. Only now, Charlene had her own suspicions to blend in with the static.

She hadn't liked the tone of his voice; momentarily wondered whether she'd done something wrong, that maybe someone at the hospital had complained about her visit to Dylan the previous evening.

The car slowed a little as she replayed the conversation.

No. His tone hadn't been confrontational or accusatory. He was thinking, that was all.

She turned off Daniels Street and the station came in view, a couple of hundred yards ahead on the right.

Thinking.

No, her intuition flagged for her attention, *that wasn't thinking, that was worrying.*

She slowed as she approached the entrance to the station car park. There was nothing out of order here, the normal vehicles parked in their normal spaces, Baker's cruiser in its reserved spot.

He'd answered her question with a question. And that always meant he was avoiding talking about something.

She felt anxious butterflies flitting around her stomach and swallowed down on them.

Nothing I can do about anything from out here, she thought.

She reached for the key and killed the engine.

* * *

Baker watched Charlene walk towards the station doors, then as she entered, turned his chair to look through the interior windows, across the team room and into the reception area.

When she turned immediately towards his office, Baker looked away hurriedly, before she could spot that he'd been watching her. An embarrassed flush warmed his cheeks as he feigned interest in a sheet of paper on his desk.

It was a flyer for a pizza joint a couple of blocks over.

And he wasn't interested in it.

Charlene knocked at the door and, looking up at her, Baker beckoned her in. He slid the pizza flyer to the edge of his desk and let it float down into his waste-paper basket.

"Morning, Charlene," he said, trying to keep his tone neutral.

She laughed a little at this.

He shrugged.

"What?"

"You," she smiled, "you're like a naughty school-kid."

He shrugged again, surprised to find that he too was smiling.

"I do?"

Charlene put her hands on her hips, staring at him.

"Yes," she said, "you do. And you're working up the courage to tell me something. So, why don't you just come out with it?"

Baker looked at her for a moment; his long-night of envisaging the conversation all for nought.

"Oh, you're good," he said.

"Learned from the best," Charlene smiled back, dropping a little nod at him, "and that's how I know you're still stalling."

Baker laughed. By the time he spoke, though, his voice was calm again.

"I'm placing you at the high school, Charlene," he said, "Mason and crew are demanding police presence and I have no choice."

She said nothing in response. Baker chose to fill the silence.

"I chose you because you're the right person to do this. I need someone who can stay calm and not get sucked into the whirlpool. You're the best I've got."

"And I'm a girl, right chief?" Charlene added.

Baker could feel the flush entering his cheeks again.

"I'm not going to lie, Charlene," he said, "that's part of the choice. The last thing any of us needs is some macho bullshit pissing contest developing between the kids, the police and the town. There's a real chance that this won't make things better, that things will escalate precisely because we put a cop in there. Carl's too young, too inexperienced and well, you know him, he's got a short fuse. And we don't need a short fuse. Not here. Not now."

Charlene was quiet, thinking. This time, Baker let her have the silence.

"How long for?" she asked, finally.

"At least until we get to the bottom of the Dylan Ford attack," Baker answered immediately.

"At least?"

A frown crossed Charlene's face.

"You mean there's a chance this might go longer," she continued, her voice rising, "you're not telling me it's permanent? Surely?"

Baker shook his head. He stood and walked around his desk. He sat back on its surface once he was next to Charlene.

"No," he said, "that's not going to happen."

"Doesn't sound like it to me," Charlene said, all suspicion.

"Look," Baker fired back, "Mason's playing his usual games, he's been angling for us to put someone in the school for months. But that's nothing to do with Dylan Ford or the attack. That's just Mason's B.S. and, frankly, I'll cross that bridge when we get to it. Right now, if we don't calm things down, he'll whip people up until they're demanding we do what he wants. And then it *will* be permanent."

"Calm things down?" Charlene repeated.

"Right," Baker nodded, "that's what I need you to do. Get things stabilized; get the kids back to their routine, help Sturmann keep things calm."

"Not investigate the attack?"

Baker shook his head.

"No. I'll handle that from here. It won't hurt if you keep your ear to the ground, of course, but I need them to trust you, and *that* means you can't be seen to be playing a game behind their backs. These are teenagers. Suspicion of authority and old people is their default setting."

Charlene smiled.

"I'm not *that* old, Jack," she chastised, "sheesh!"

Baker chuckled.

"One for flinching," he said and punched her lightly on the shoulder.

They both laughed a little at this.

Charlene looked at Baker, saw how tired he looked, knew he'd been turning this over since she'd found Dylan Ford in the high school car park. She could make this hard or easy for him.

Do I mind, she thought, *do I really mind being placed at the high school?*

She thought of her house, empty but for the space which Suzy should have inhabited; of that warm morning feeling that evaporated as soon as reality crashed in.

She thought of driving around town the previous night, looking for anywhere that she could escape for even a short while.

And she thought of Dylan Ford, intubated and surrounded by sentinel machines, thought of her promise to him as he lay oblivious.

"It'll just be for a short while," Baker began to reassure her, "I promise. I think we can…"

"Chief," she interrupted him.

"… get the investigation done in…"

"Chief!"

This time he stopped.

"You don't have to sell it any more," Charlene said, surprised at the relief which warmed her belly, "I'll do it."

"You will? We can…"

"Chief," she smiled, "when the sale is made, quit selling."

"I'll do it."

Chapter 12: Nobody Told Me

Mason called at a little after ten. Charlene watched Baker through the window; an animated discussion for sure, though for his part, Baker didn't stand from his desk chair. Charlene could see that he wanted nothing more.

Trying to keep himself calm, she thought, suppressing a slight smile lest he look in her direction.

Eventually, he put the phone down, springing immediately to his feet. He crossed his office; Charlene pretended to pay attention to her computer's monitor.

Baker wrenched the door open.

"Charlene," he said, still carrying frustration in his voice.

She looked up, wearing a poker face.

"Uh-huh?"

"And you can quit that," Baker said, "you know Mason was just on the phone, I saw you watching. I don't... We don't have time for games."

She shrugged off her mask.

"What did he want?"

"What do you think? You. At the school. End of story."

Baker lent back on the doorframe, tipping his head backward until its crown touched wood. He blew a breath out towards the ceiling.

"I told him you'd be there from tomorrow."

"Tomorrow?"

"Yup."

“Want me to call in today, get the lay of the land?”

Baker thought for a moment and then shook his head.

“Won’t make a difference,” he said, “things seem pretty calm today. No sign of anything new. Sturmann would have called if there was. Talking of which…”

He turned abruptly and began to walk back towards his desk.

Charlene stood and followed him.

“Talking of which?”

He stopped. Turned.

“Sorry,” he said, smiling guiltily at her and tapping his forehead “thousand things going on up here at once. I promised to call Walt once I’d spoken with you. And if I don’t, you can bet Mason will.”

Charlene nodded.

Baker scanned the pin-board above his phone, looking for the list of town numbers. He dialled the high school and waited for the connection to go through.

“With any luck,” he said to Charlene, “yesterday was it. Some petty rivalry brimming over. We catch the kid that did it. Slap his wrist. Job done.”

“Bit more than a slapped wrist, though?” Charlene asked.

“Sure, I guess…”

At the far end of the phone line, the call was answered.

“Good morning,” Baker said, all attention on the phone, “it’s Police Chief Baker here… Yes, a fine morning… Is Principal Sturmann available please?”

Charlene stood for a moment, waiting to see whether Baker would indicate she should stay.

“Thank you,” Baker said into the phone. He was silent for a moment.

“Hi, Walt... Good morning to you too. Listen, I just wanted to…”

Baker looked up, seeming to notice Charlene there afresh. He gestured for her to step out of his office with a little nod of his head.

At least he didn’t shoo me away, Charlene thought, stepping out of the office and closing the door behind her.

* * *

So, Charlene thought as she sat back at her desk, *it starts tomorrow.*

She didn't know quite how that made her feel; aside from the timing, nothing had changed since Baker had informed her of the decision earlier that morning.

She settled back in her chair.

I'll play this by ear, she thought, *what will be will be and all that.*

"I should speak with Lilly and Dave Ford," she said to herself, reaching across the desk to grab a notepad. She began a to-do list:

- *Lilly and Dave*
- *Principal Sturmann*
- *Loose ends - Paperwork!*

She was shaken from her focus on things still to-do by the trill of the station phone, and answered after the usual three rings.

"Hello, police department, Officer Charlene Goodlow speaking. How may I help?"

"Oh…" A male voice, hesitant. Probably expecting a man to answer. "Is Baker there?"

Charlene didn't appreciate the brusque, matter-of-fact tone.

"Who is this?" she asked, keeping the smile in her voice while wracking her brain as to the identity of the caller.

"Curtis Simpson," the caller said.

Of course, Charlene thought, *our local newshound.*

She decided to have some fun.

"Oh, hi Curtis! What would you like to discuss with him?" she asked, voice dripping with mock-insouciance.

This actually threw Simpson for a moment.

"I…" he began and then paused, "I hear on the grapevine that he's going to put a cop in the high school."

She had a feeling she knew who was at the root of that particular vine.

Careful, she thought, *you know this game, it's called fishing for a lead.*

"Those grapevines," she said, "they can be very fruitful, can't they?"

"Would you know anything…"

"I mean, turn your back for one second and all sorts of new growth is sprouting."

"I… Would you…"

"Of course, the problem is that ultimately, you end up with a hangover, regretting the fact you ever had anything to do with it. Wouldn't you say?"

"Erm…" Simpson squirmed, fighting for a way to regain control of the conversation.

Charlene sat, smiling at the sound of his struggles.

"Who's he going to put in the school?" Simpson asked abruptly.

Charlene was very, very careful not to change her tone in any way.

"He's on the other line at the moment," she said, "would you like to hold?"

"Sure," Simpson responded, "that's fine."

She heard the resignation in his voice, she'd successfully maintained her façade.

She hit the hold button, letting him disappear into pre-recorded muzak.

She scanned her list. Thought for a moment. Added a bullet:

- Talking points for press

Charlene stood and walked over to the window of Baker's office and tapped the glass. He'd obviously finished with Sturmann and now looked up from his paperwork, face a question.

"Curtis Simpson," she mouthed, holding up two fingers in a peace-sign, "on line two."

"Simpson?" Baker asked, voice muffled by the wall and glass.

She nodded and pushed her fingers towards him.

He sighed over-extravagantly and picked up his handset before stabbing at a button. The hang-dog look on his face was classic and Charlene turned away smiling.

The doors of the station lobby opened and sunlight poured in, framing the young lady who entered. For a moment, Charlene could only see her as a silhouette.

"Can I help you?" she asked, stepping out into the lobby.

"Please," the teenage girl said, "please..."

Charlene's internal alarms began to chime. Something wasn't right here.

Then, as she drew closer, she realized why. Tears were streaming down the girl's cheeks.

What's happened to her, Charlene thought, mind racing with buzz-words; words like *assault*, *abuse*, and *rape*.

"Are you okay?" Charlene asked.

"Ummm... No, not really," the girl said, beginning to gather herself.

Charlene looked over the girl's shoulders and between the closing lobby doors. There was nobody else outside.

"Has something happened?" she asked.

The girl remained silent, walking forward seemingly on auto-pilot.

"Who are you?" Charlene walked backwards, tracking with the girl.

"Is the police chief here?" the girl asked, pulling her hand through her blond hair, getting it out of her face. She drew a forearm across her eyes, dragging tears across tanned skin.

Charlene's stomach gave an unexpected bump; in that casual gesture, the girl had looked vulnerable, and so, so beautiful.

"He's on the phone," Charlene answered, fighting her impulse, "would you like to wait for him?"

"I... I don't know... Would it be all right?"

Charlene smiled, bending slightly to look the girl directly in the eye.

"Of course," she said calmly, through a smile, "that's no problem."

She indicated a bench.

"You can wait there. Can I get you some water, cup of tea maybe?"

"Water, please," the girl said, beginning to calm now.

"I'll be right back," Charlene said. Scanning towards Baker's office, she saw that he was still on the phone and likely would be for quite a while.

She fetched some water and brought it back to the girl.

"Here you go," she said and sat down on the bench, turning slightly to face the girl, who took a deep swallow of the water.

"Thanks," she said, "needed that."

Charlene decided to nudge the conversation forward.

"What happened?" she said, quietly.

The girl shook her head.

Charlene breathed for a moment, struck both by the girl's beauty and a visceral reaction to the thoughts that tumbled through her mind; possible scenarios and causes that might have brought the girl here.

She kept quiet.

"Nobody spoke with me," the girl said eventually and Charlene worked hard not to interrupt.

"The whole day yesterday," the girl continued, "nobody told me anything. And..."

Her breath began to hitch and Charlene automatically put a hand to the girl's shoulder.

"It's okay," she said.

The girl shook her head violently.

"No," she spat, "no, it's not. He's..."

Charlene rubbed at the girl's shoulder; unaware that she was doing so.

"Who?" she said.

The girl swivelled sideways, and her shoulder pulled away. Suddenly conscious of her hand floating in mid-air, Charlene let it drop to her lap. She was blushing slightly, but she couldn't tell whether it was empathy for the girl's tears or embarrassment. Both, probably.

"I'm Katie," the girl said, "Katie Browning..."

When Charlene didn't recognize the name, the girl – Katie – continued.

"Dylan Ford is my boyfriend," she said.

"Oh," Charlene breathed out on a sigh, slotting all the puzzle pieces together at once, "I'm sorry."

"Sure," Katie's bottom lip quivered a little as she fought to contain a sob.

"Nobody told me anything."

"Nothing at all?" Charlene asked, hardly able to imagine what it must have been like for this teenage girl to know her boyfriend had been attacked but nothing more, "didn't his parents… Didn't Lilly and Dave…"

Katie shook her head.

"They were at the hospital all day," she said, "and I was at school."

"Did you speak to them at all?"

"Yes," Katie breathed quietly, "last night. They told me I couldn't visit with Dylan. Not just yet."

Tears were sliding out of the corners of her eyes.

"But I…" she continued, swallowing heavily to get the words out, "I went this morning. Mrs Ford was there and… She couldn't stop me when we were face-to-face."

Charlene didn't respond, just let Katie process her train of thought.

"Oh my God," Katie breathed, "he's so… so… broken."

A flash-frame flitted through Charlene's mind, for a moment returning her to the side of Dylan Ford's bed, looking down at his beaten body, the sights and sounds of machines that were doing the heavy lifting of living.

"It's going to be all right, Katie," she said.

Katie shook her head.

"No-one cares about this," she said, "it's just another nail in the lid. They'll just screw around with us, try and pin it on someone and, as soon as its done, they'll move on to the next thing. We don't count for anything."

"That's not true," Charlene countered, "not at all. We're…"

She bit back on the words; had been about to tell Katie about the placement.

"It's why I came to see Chief Baker," Katie said, voice strengthening as her sadness at Dylan's state migrated to anger, "he *has* to do something about it. He has to. He's the police chief. He *has* to!"

Charlene looked up momentarily.

Baker was standing in the entrance hall; for how long, she didn't know.

"Katie," he said quietly.

Charlene turned back to look at the teenager.

Her response was slow, almost like she were hearing him down a time-delayed line. Her head swivelled slowly to look at him. A single tear dropped from her chin onto her t-shirt. For a moment, Charlene was transfixed by the sight of it rolling on the cotton towards the rounded swell of her young breast. It soaked into the material and Charlene came back to herself.

She stood, took a step towards Baker.

"Don't know how much of that you heard, chief," she said, "but Katie is..."

"Dylan's girlfriend," Baker finished the sentence, "I know. Come on in, Katie."

The girl stood and, led by Baker's gesture, walked through the open door of his office. Baker followed her. Just before entering, though, he turned to Charlene.

"You did a good job there, Charlene," he said, "she's pretty upset. I didn't even think about contacting her yesterday. I dropped the ball."

"Are you going to tell her?" Charlene asked. "About me?"

Baker nodded, smiling ruefully.

"Well, Simpson knows now, and it'll be common knowledge soon enough," he said, "so I think it's fine for her to know. Set her mind at ease. Let her know she's not in this alone."

Charlene let herself breathe.

"Want a coffee?" she asked.

Baker nodded.

"Sure," he said, "then... Do you want to join us?"

Charlene thought for a moment. Though she wanted to very badly, it was better that she maintained some distance.

"No," she shook her head, "probably not a good idea. Let's debrief after you've spoken with her."

Baker looked at her.

"Okay," he said finally.

"Here or Annie's?" she asked.

"Huh?"

"Your coffee," Charlene clarified, "from the machine or do you want me to head on up to Annie's?"

Baker thought for a moment.

“Like *that’s* any choice,” he smiled.

“Okay, Annie’s it is,” she smiled, “I’ll grab some lunch to bring back while I’m there. Want anything?”

“Just coffee,” Baker smiled and turned to enter his office, “see you in a few.”

As the door closed, Charlene breathed out heavily. She hadn’t realized that she’d been holding it in.

It’s been a loaded morning, she thought, *getting out to Annie’s is just what I need.*

She grabbed her car-keys and headed out, leaving the chief to brief Dylan Ford’s beautiful girlfriend.

Chapter 13: What Not To Wear

The house was as empty as ever when Charlene got home. Nooks and crannies burst with yawning silence; knick-knacks colluded to remind her of how it had been Suzy's artistic sensibility that had first spotted them, and then placed them in the ideal setting.

Charlene dropped her purse on the floor and kicked off her shoes, replacing them with familiar slippers, a small oasis of comfort in this house that seemed determined to wrench in the opposite direction.

Tomorrow would see her first day at the school, only two days since she'd discovered Dylan Ford in the back parking lot.

She turned towards the kitchen and caught sight of herself in the hallway mirror. Stopping, she stepped closer, drawn in by her own eyes.

You look tired, girl, she thought, *too tired.*

Beneath the colour rinse, she saw threads of grey; the beginnings of expression lines around the edges of her mouth, difficult to tell whether from smiling or sadness. There were puffy, dark bags beneath her eyes; too, too many tears, for Suzy, for Dylan and, now, for Katie too.

She closed her eyes for a moment and the sight of Katie walking through the doors of the station was waiting for her, a silhouette framed in a rectangle of bright sunlight. She was a beautiful girl. Beautiful.

Charlene shook her head and, opening her eyes, ran her hand through her hair. She had to focus on the job in hand, a blessed distraction from the emptiness of her home.

But first, strong tea.

She smiled at herself in the mirror, struck once again by how tired she looked, and continued on through to the kitchen.

* * *

"You'll be there," Baker had said, "but don't forget *why* you're there."

"Keeping the peace?"

He'd shook his head.

"Supporting the investigation?"

Again, a shake.

"No," he'd said, "there's one reason, and one only, that you're in that school. You're there so that the grown-ups in this town get to continue their delusion that everything's just hunky-dory."

Charlene had sat. Quiet. She'd not heard the chief like this before.

"But the kids?" she'd eventually ventured.

"The kids are just fine," he'd smiled sadly, "over-excited and under-sexed as ever. They're just fine."

"It's the adults we've got to watch out for."

* * *

"What the hell am I supposed to wear?" Charlene said to herself.

She stood in her bedroom, a mug of tea steaming on the dresser, her closet wide open.

The hanging rack was neatly divided, various uniforms to the right, formal wear in the middle and casual to the left.

Throughout all the conversation about her placement, the subject of dress code had never come up.

Typical Baker, she thought, *all male focus on what needs to happen, not how it gets done*.

"So, what do I wear?" she asked the room again.

And was surprised to find another lurking memory of Suzy.

The two of them getting ready for a night out, joking, playing dress-up, Suzy eventually selecting the outfit which worked best on

Charlene, mixing and matching their clothes, sealing the deal with a kiss.

She blinked the images away, only to find her fingers touching one of her regular uniforms.

You're there so that the grown-ups in this town get to continue their delusion.

They'll want a uniform, she thought, *of course they will.*

And she'd need to make a strong first impression. So that the kids told their parents when they got home in the afternoon.

Charlene shook her head.

She wasn't sure Baker was right, that the kids were not the area of focus. Dylan Ford was a popular kid and someone had done this to him. Resilient they may be, suffering from attention-deficit in most everything else, but Charlene didn't believe that they would already have moved on and past the attack. She knew where the chief was coming from, he flew more in political circles than those of law and order and, for him, the adults of the town were the priority, particularly those on the town council.

Mason. Particularly Mason.

She didn't really know him that well, he was an arms-length awareness, appreciated second-hand through the pages of *The Daybreaker* and the chief's frustrations. She only ever really saw him at distance: an overweight, overstuffed ego in a too-tight shirt that pinched his neck and clung to his belly.

She suspected Mason was on a conveyor belt to a heart attack before he was sixty. Just as her own father had been.

Note to self, she thought, *check in with Mom.*

A strong first impression. To keep Mason and the other grown-ups happy.

She pulled the newest uniform from the rail and checked it over. It was so new that the shirt still bore fold marks.

Strong first impression.

She took the uniform with her to the laundry.

* * *

While the uniform washed, she sat at the kitchen table, replaying the brief conversation she'd had with principal Sturmann that afternoon; really little more than a courtesy introduction.

The arrangements, those few that there were, had her arriving at the school at seven-thirty the next morning. She was to park at the rear of the front lot, yes she could bring her cruiser, just not park right in front of the buildings, no need for unnecessary alarm. Principal Sturmann – no offer made that she should call him by his first name – would be in his office behind the school reception. She should feel free to come on through.

Something was nagging at her, though she couldn't quite put her finger on it yet. The conversations were all beginning to blur.

Sturmann wanting to minimize her presence,

Baker insisting she was a reassurance for delusional adults.

Katie...

Try as she might, she couldn't shake the sight of Katie's tear-streaked face, imagining how it must have felt for the teenager to stand at Dylan's bedside, as she herself had. She could see it as clearly as if she had been there. Tears welling in Katie's eyes running down her face to drip onto her t-shirt.

The washing machine beeped the end of its cycle, loud in the silent, empty house, shocking Charlene out of her reverie. She finished the last of her tea in a single long sip and then headed to the laundry.

The image of that tear, rolling down the material towards Katie's breast stayed with her, no matter how she tried to focus on the work at hand.

* * *

After she had dried and ironed her uniform, she laid it out ready for the next day's early start.

She pulled underwear and socks, placing them on top of her dresser.

A belt for her uniform pants.

And the nagging thought slammed into place clearly and totally.

Should I wear my piece?

The thought was strong enough to stop her in her tracks. She felt her eyes widen, her breath speeding up a little.

Her equipment belt – gun, ammo, radio, mace – was standard issue and worn every day. No big deal, not after all these years.

So why had the thought of it shocked her so much?

Was it Baker's talk of escalation and unnecessary policing?

Was it Sturmann's wish to downplay her presence at the school?

She was still for a moment.

"What do *you* think, Charlene?" she asked herself quietly.

And the answer was there.

She would wear her belt tomorrow, but remove her piece and spare clips. They could be locked in the trunk of the cruiser. Sure, it would be a softer introduction to the school than if she went in armed, but her intuition told her it was the right thing to do; like Sturmann, she didn't want to over-state her welcome.

So, a softer, gentler hand of the police would step into the school the next day.

And screw whatever the grown-ups have to say about that, she thought.

She switched off the bedroom light and went downstairs to catch the late-night shows, not quite aware of how the image of a tear on a teenager's t-shirt called from beneath her conscious thought.

Wednesday

Chapter 14: Good Morning, Class

The high school car park was largely empty as Charlene pulled in. Parking near the back of the lot, as requested, she stepped out into warming sunshine. The chill of night still clung to the slight breeze and ground, but it would burn off soon enough.

She put her coffee cup on the roof and walked around to open the trunk of the cruiser. As she unhooked her gun and spare clips from her belt, she couldn't help looking around herself instinctively. She placed them in the weapons box in the trunk and locked everything up tight.

Standing straight, she faced the high school.

Everything was so quiet. A handful of cars, belonging to the teachers she guessed, were parked in a cluster off the left. She knew the area would shortly be in organized chaos as school buses disgorged and older kids drove in.

She breathed in deeply, to her centre, and wasn't so surprised when a yawn followed closely.

It had been a largely sleepless night. Tossing and turning. Thinking about today, about the politics surrounding her placement. And, in the bouts of sleep between the thinking, dreams had come which, although unremembered, had left her anxious in the waking.

"Nothing this can't fix," she reassured herself, grabbing her coffee. She gulped a mouthful and felt it burn a hot streak all the way to her stomach.

"Ow!" she blurted out and, laughing at herself, walked to the school buildings.

* * *

She sat outside principal Sturmann's office for about twenty minutes while he worked on something urgent. Watching the kids begin to drift in. Watching teachers check schedules. Watching receptionists marshal traffic.

Watching.

* * *

Sturmann called her into his office at about ten-to-eight.

"Officer Goodlow?" he said, leaning around the doorframe of his office.

Charlene nodded, standing to face him. She held out a hand and they shook.

"Come on in," Sturmann said.

She followed him into his office and sat in the chair he indicated.

Sturmann spoke to her as he walked to the window of his office, looking out over the final stragglers.

"We've got about ten minutes," he said.

"Ten minutes?" Charlene asked.

"Before the assembly," Sturmann said, turning.

"Assembly?" She was confused.

He nodded.

"I thought it wise to introduce you formally. Called a special assembly."

Charlene thought about this.

"Won't that... erm... worry the kids?"

"No. They're used to it. Whenever we have announcements that..."

"I'm not exactly a simple announcement... Does the chief know about this?"

Sturmann looked surprised at her concern.

"Really, it's not that big of a deal."

Charlene could almost see Baker's ears burning at this. She felt steel coming into her spine, breathed into that reaction.

Keep calm, Charlene, she thought, *everyone's feeling their way through this.*

"Principal Sturmann," she said in as even a voice as possible, "having a police officer on campus is… Look, it's not…"

She wanted to say *normal*, a word that still carried insulting, derogatory meanings for her.

"…typical for us to be here. The kids are bound to be suspicious, wary. We'd be wise to…"

"I think I know my students, Officer Goodlow," Sturmann bit, "and this is the respectful way to treat them. Total transparency."

His face was flushed as he stared at her. And there was something about his eyes.

He's not angry at me, she thought suddenly, *he may be angry but it's not at me.*

What are you scared of?

She decided to defuse the situation.

"Okay," she smiled, "can we… Can we start over?"

He just looked at her.

She stood, walked back to the door.

"Now, I've been sitting outside watching people arrive. You've been finishing something urgent, then you came to the door and invited me in and…"

She turned, still smiling, making sure she got eye contact with him. As she spoke, she put a foot forward like time had reversed five or so minutes.

"… I came in and you suggested I sit in this chair. And I put out my hand and…"

Sturmann had visibly relaxed and couldn't help but take her hand as she offered it to him.

"Good morning, Principal Sturmann," Charlene said, "I'm Officer Goodlow, but I'd really like it if you'd call me Charlene."

Now, he smiled.

"Walt," he said, "Walt Sturmann. Welcome to our school."

Charlene didn't sit, instead choosing to lean on the back of the chair.

"Better?" she asked.

"Very much," Sturmann nodded. He glanced at his watch.

"We should probably get going to the assembly, huh?" Charlene asked.

The relief that filled Sturmann's face made a picture in itself.

"Indeed."

He started towards the door but as his hand reached to open it, he suddenly stopped.

"Shit!" he exclaimed, "shit, shit, shit, shit!"

Charlene watched in surprise; for once having nothing to say.

"I forgot to call the Fords!"

He was beginning to panic and Charlene thought quick for a route to short-circuit the process.

"Lilly and Dave?" she asked.

He seemed to key in on the names.

"Yes... I..." he swallowed, "I meant to check in on how Dylan is doing. I didn't manage to speak with them yesterday, it was a busy, busy day and... Well, things just got in the way."

"I spoke with his girlfriend yesterday," Charlene said, "Katie. She'd been to see him at the hospital. Condition's the same, just needs time."

An image flashed through her mind: Katie by Dylan's bedside, the Fords in the background, and that one tear dripping onto the girl's t-shirt. She forced herself to focus upon Dylan; the respirator tube.

"He's being monitored, hooked up to every machine possible. Doctors are watching for potential long-term brain damage but he's out of the woods in terms of survival."

Sturmann was calming down once again.

Is this what I'm in for? Charlene wondered, *baby-sitting this guy?*

She thought again of Baker's clarification that her placement was all about the adults in the town and not about the kids.

"Okay," Sturmann said, "that's good."

He seemed to gather himself, reaching out and opening the door.

"Let's get to the assembly," he said.

* * *

He's either a gifted actor, Charlene thought, watching Sturmann lead the assembly, *or a wickedly good poker player.*

Sturmann on-stage, in front of his students, couldn't have been more calm and controlled. Standing at the podium, this was his public persona, his audience, his normality.

As he went through brief announcements, Charlene scanned the room, a sea of teenagers in varying states of fashion; teachers at the head of the rows or clustered together in seats near the back.

Baker's words ringing in her ears, she saw more concern on adult faces than those of students.

As she scanned the room, her eyes fell upon Katie Browning. The girl was staring at her and it gave Charlene a little shock. She had an instinct to wave, nod, some gesture to discharge the energy and acknowledge Katie. In the end she simply smiled.

A pause in the rhythm of Sturmann's voice brought her back to the moment.

"... pleased to introduce Officer Charlene Goodlow of the town police department."

He gestured to her and she was surprised to hear a ripple of applause from the gathered school.

What now? she thought, *stand up and take a bow?*

Luckily Sturmann saved her from an embarrassing silence.

"Office Goodlow has been placed here... temporarily, for the duration of the investigation into the attack upon Dylan Ford."

"Speaking of Dylan, I'm relieved to say that he is off the critical list and being monitored for any long-term consequences of his injuries."

I didn't say that, Charlene thought.

The doors at the back of the hall opened and Mason stepped in. Sturmann noticed this and looked about to speak to him. Mason shook his head and waved his hand, the message clear: *I'm not here, just carry on.*

Sturmann paused.

"Erm... We are preparing a gift for Dylan and his family and would ask that any donations be handed in at reception by close of school today."

He paused, back into his flow once more.

"I surprised Officer Goodlow this morning when I told her we would be having this assembly," he said, turning to smile at her, "and

I'm afraid I'm going to put you on the spot and ask you for some words of introduction to the school."

He looked apologetic and, although she was naturally angry at being caught out, she could easily believe that he wasn't lying. She remembered the Walt Sturmann she'd met this morning before he'd put on his game-face.

"Uh..." she began, "well... Sure, I guess."

Charlene stood and walked to the podium as Sturmann stepped a couple of paces backwards to give her space.

She'd done classroom visits; speaking to groups of kids wasn't a new thing for her. But this was bigger. This was a sea of almost a thousand faces, all looking to her next word. She felt her face flush and an impulse to spot Katie in the crowd; at least one friendly face, she guessed.

She thought about Baker. What he would do in this situation.

He'd be honest.

He'd be to the point.

He'd be careful.

Keep it simple, she thought, *simple*.

"Good morning, everyone," she said, leaning close to the microphone.

Feedback howled around the hall, bringing a fresh blush to her face. There were nervous giggles in sections of the audience.

Charlene laughed a little.

"As you can tell, I'm no rock star," she smiled, easing a little, "I've been asked to come here while we work through Dylan's case, to help keep things calm for you, so that your studies are interrupted as little as possible."

She began to ease into her own flow.

"I've been with the police department a little over ten years. I know some of you," scanning the audience, consciously not looking at where she felt Katie's gaze, "and I'm looking forward to getting to know a few more of you."

"As Principal Sturmann said, I don't have a prepared speech, so..."

She looked back over her shoulder at Sturmann.

"... we could take some questions?"

Sturmann nodded.

"Okay," Charlene said, breathing out in relief, "questions?"

In line with Baker's prediction, she half-expected the teachers to raise their arms for attention. But as it was, things stayed quiet and still for a moment, an embarrassed silence growing amongst the audience.

"No?" Charlene asked again.

A hand crept up to the left. A girl.

Charlene turned to face her, smiling.

"Hi," she said, "good morning. You have a question?"

The girl began to speak but Charlene could hardly hear her.

"Can you speak up a little?" she smiled.

The girl stood, now speaking clearly.

"Are you investigating what happened to Dylan?"

"No," Charlene said, finding the answer waiting for her thanks to Baker's intuitive, pre-emptive briefing, "Police Chief Baker is leading the investigation and I'm not participating. We wanted to keep the two things separate. My focus is on you, all of you, making sure that things don't disturb you too much."

She could feel Mason's eyes on her; Katie's too.

She stayed focused on the questioner.

"Make sense?" she asked.

"Yes, thank you," the girl nodded, sitting down.

Charlene felt a small measure of relief.

"Other questions?"

She scanned the room, but there were no hands raised.

"Okay," she said, preparing to hand back over to Sturmann to wrap things up.

There was a little bustle of activity towards the back rows and Charlene looked towards it. A boy raised his hand sheepishly, obviously being urged on by his friends on each side.

Boys, it's always boys, she thought.

"Hi," she said, "you have a question?"

The boy stood, flushing just about as bright red as the fire extinguishers pinned to the walls.

"Erm… Good morning… I… uh…"

Charlene smiled at him. She'd been this gawky, embarrassed teenager too many times not to feel his pain.

"Take your time," she said supportively, noticing the sniggers of the kids sat around the boy.

"Well..." he began, "I was... Where's your gun?"

This brought nervous laughter from the audience and just before it reached her, Charlene heard Sturmann snigger behind her.

Her heartbeat climbed on an adrenalin rush and now she caught Mason in a glimpse, he was scanning the audience with a look of disdain on his face.

Be careful, she thought, *be very careful.*

"If I could..." she tried to speak over the laughter, "if I could have some quiet."

Gradually the room came to some semblance of calm.

She smiled at the boy.

"That's a great observation and question," she said, kicking out her hip to the side of lectern, "you'll see that I'm not wearing my sidearm. For that matter, I'm not wearing a riot stick, or bullet-proof vest."

She smiled and leant forward on the lectern.

"Of course, should you act in a manner that requires any of the above mentioned items, I won't hesitate to use them."

She could sense from the energy that they were unsure of whether she was joking or not. Which was just as she wanted it.

At the back of the room, Mason was smiling.

Keep the adults happy, she thought.

She decided to seal the deal, tapping the back of her belt.

"And in the meantime, I've still got a can of mace on hand, so don't try me, okay?."

She laughed, moving away from the podium with a big, open smile on her face.

Mason nodded once and stepped out of the back of the hall.

Sturmann returned to the podium and smiled at his students.

"I'm sure the staff would appreciate learning some of your techniques, Officer Goodlow," he joked.

"If there are no further questions," he wrapped up, "I believe we're done for this morning. Officer Goodlow will be here for a while, so please say *'Hi'* to her if you see her around the halls."

"Thank you."

The assembly at an end, the hall erupted into the noise of students and teachers discussing the meeting and preparing for the day.

Charlene sat on the stage, smiling at those kids who caught her eye, and hoping that the mace joke hadn't been a step too far.

Chapter 15:
Do We Understand Each Other?

Charlene spent the morning getting settled in.

They'd found an office around the corner from reception, next door to the janitor's storeroom. When someone walked past the open door, the pervasive smell of Lysol disinfectant increased for a moment.

She sat.

She thought.

She looked through the door into the hall.

Got bored.

Wished she'd brought a book.

Mid-morning, she walked around to the reception and asked for some paper, bringing a pile back to the office.

She began a new list:

- *Meet teachers*
- *Visit classes*
- *Bring lap-top*
- *And books!*

Off to one side of the list, she began to doodle.

* * *

At lunchtime, throngs of school-kids walked past the office door, turning to look at her as if she were a new zoo-exhibit. She'd had enough; energized by their movement, she stood and stepped out of the office, closing the door on the largely empty desk.

To her right, the cloud of disinfectant misting the door of the janitor's closet. She turned left.

The kids were all over, heading out into the yard, towards the cafeteria, a mass of burgeoning hormones, fashion choice and noise.

Might as well get the layout, Charlene thought, happier now that she could walk the halls while they were teeming with life rather than silent and empty.

How quickly the memories of her own high school came back, a mirror universe of cinder block walls, painted up pretty, but just as ugly and functional underneath. Ranks and ranks of lockers; many decorated, but just as many left their neutral grey.

No graffiti, she thought disbelievingly, *not yet anyway.*

She headed deeper into the school, past the nurse's office, the library.

Kids gathered in clusters and streams; bubbles of noise and excitement.

It really was so reminiscent of her own high school; she could have been transported back in time, a teenager once again. Or any number of high school movies from *16 Candles* through to *Glee*.

Except she was now an adult. Worse, an interloper; a figure of interest.

Heads turned to look at her. Conversations eased or stopped completely as she walked past.

By the time she passed the library, she was consciously making eye-contact with the few teenagers who wouldn't look away when she tried to do so. She smiled, even though it felt like it was stuck to her face.

Deeper into the school, the gym on the left, echoing to the sounds of a basketball game. She stopped at the door and watched as the coach worked the team. She wondered how many of these players were on the football team with Dylan Ford. If they had any ideas as to who had attacked him.

You're not here to investigate, she cautioned herself, knowing there was no way she could switch off that particular urge. Anyway, there would be time enough for that in the coming days; as her morning had shown her, she would have to ration out the few peaks of interest across many hours of dull boredom.

She continued her tour, walking a few more halls, all as uniform as the ones she'd walked previously. It was like a common dreamscape, recurring over and again; this conditioned, conditioning environment.

And everywhere the curiosity of the school-kids; sidelong glances, rear-view discussions. What were they saying about her once she'd passed them?

She was approaching a T-junction, the left turn of which would take her in the direction of the cafeteria; clanking hubbub echoing down the halls. As she neared the corner, there was a loud metallic clang from around the right-hand corner and she was instantly transported back to her own high school memories.

Someone being thrown against a locker, she thought, walking faster.

The sound came again.

She rounded the corner. There were two boys about ten yards away; one white, larger than the Asian by his side.

"What's happening here?" Charlene asked, hearing her own voice, much more that of a teacher than police officer.

The kids, breathing hard and blushing slightly, gave her blank stares.

Deer in the headlights, she thought.

Charlene looked up and down the hall. The nearest group of kids were a couple of locker sets further along. She looked back to the two boys.

"Okay," she said, "let's start again…"

She paused. Looked at the embarrassment on the boys' faces.

"Were both of you at the assembly this morning?"

They nodded.

"Good. Then you know who I am and why I'm here. Now, I asked a question. What's happening here?"

After a moment, the Asian kid spoke.

"A… misunderstanding," he said.

She turned to look at him.

"A misunderstanding?" she smiled at him. "Really?"

He nodded. The other kid looked sideways at him and, after a moment, nodded too.

Charlene tried to read the energy between these two, but it was difficult.

“A misunderstanding that involved a body hitting a locker?”

This time they didn’t say anything.

She thought she caught a smile on the white kid’s face.

Bullying, she thought, picking on the little kid who’s different, *some things never change*.

“Okay…” she said, looking at them both but focusing on the white kid, “seeing as how it’s my first day here and things seem to have calmed down now, here’s what we’re going to do…”

The white kid looked back at her. Charlene noted a glimmer of defiance in his eyes; he’d guessed what was coming.

“You two are going to shake hands and apologize to each other.”

They didn’t move.

“Want me to say it again?”

Hesitantly, they turned to each other and shook hands, mumbling apologies.

“Good,” Charlene smiled then, speaking to the Asian kid, “where’s your locker?”

He gestured further up the hall.

“And yours?” she asked the white kid.

He pointed in the opposite direction.

“Then aren’t we the lucky ones?” Charlene said, “why don’t you both head to your lockers and we’ll forget that I heard someone being thrown against one.”

They began to move away.

“Oh, and one more thing,” she said, causing them to turn back to face her, “I don’t forget. So, count this as strike one, okay?”

She looked at them, particularly the white kid. She didn’t know if the warning would have any effect after a few minutes had passed but, for now at least, it had defused any tension.

“Okay?” she repeated just to be sure.

“Uh-huh,” the white kid mumbled.

Charlene nodded at him and then turned to the Asian kid.

“Okay?”

"Yes, officer," he said, bowing his head slightly, "Thank you. I'm sorry."

The apology surprised Charlene.

"No problem," she responded instinctively, "just... er... well, don't go getting thrown into lockers again, okay?"

He smiled a little in response to this, glancing at the other kid. In that glance Charlene saw submission to the more dominant boy, fear of reprisal.

"Sure," the Asian kid said after a moment.

The moment had passed, Charlene knew these boys were just itching to be anywhere but right here. She smiled at them.

"Well," she said, "we're just about done here... But, tell you what, why don't I get your names in case you're tempted to try this again?"

She made a show of pulling her notepad.

"You?" she pointed at the white kid.

"Stuart," he responded immediately, "Stuart Foster."

"And you?"

"Liu," the Asian kid said, "Jason Liu."

After noting their names, Charlene held up her note-pad.

"We understand each other?" she asked.

They nodded.

"Good. Then get gone."

She flicked her head to dismiss them and they headed in opposite directions.

Charlene pocketed her pad, turned around and headed back towards her office.

* * *

"Chief? Have you got a moment?"

"Sure. How's it going?"

"Good. Sturmann had me up in front of the whole school this morning. Speech and everything."

"Ugh... Sorry to hear that."

"No biggie. I just introduced myself, took some questions."

"Anything interesting?"

"Not really, one of the kids joked about me not wearing my piece.

I handled it though, joked a little, you know?"

"You're not carrying?"

"No, it's safe and sound in the trunk of the cruiser."

"Not… Not exactly by the book. I should be giving you some sort of warning."

"Except you agree?"

"Sure."

"I'll consider myself warned then."

"Anything else?"

"Well… I had to break up something a minute ago. Two kids. Didn't see what happened, but pretty obvious that this one kid was bullying the other."

"Trouble?"

"Nah… Just usual stuff. But it makes me wonder, what am I doing here? I mean, do they *want* me acting like a hall monitor?"

"I… There isn't a *'they'* here, Charlene. I placed you at the school, you're following my orders. No, you're not there as a hall monitor. You're supporting Principal Sturmann in maintaining calm at the high school while we investigate the attack on Dylan Ford. That's it."

"…"

"Does that help clarify things?"

"Yeah… Thanks, Jack. I'll try and stay away from schoolyard dramas."

"Okay. Anything else?"

"I don't think so."

"All right, are you going to swing by the station later on?"

"Sure. Once the kids are out and I've huddled with Sturmann… Oh, there was one thing you should probably know."

"Yes?"

"Mason showed up this morning. He was at the back of the hall when I was getting introduced."

"Did he do anything? Did he speak with you?"

"Nope, just listened for a while and then left."

"Probably just checking up on us."

"On you, you mean."

"Ha! Yeah, I guess so."

"Okay. I'm going to grab some lunch from the cafeteria. High school food, oh joy!"

"Rather you than me. Enjoy. Bye"

"Later."

Chapter 16:
Surfacing

Sturmann's office was cooled by air conditioning sufficiently that Charlene felt a distinct chill. To her left, out the window, mid-afternoon sunshine blazed onto the school car park. She wanted to be outside, enjoying its warmth; even if there were nearly a thousand kids migrating to buses and cars, yelling, joking, laughing; the orchestrated chaos of high school dismissal.

"What do you think?" Sturmann asked.

She'd lost the thread of the conversation, drifting beyond the glass, away from this refrigerator office, already dreading the return to her empty house.

Gritting mental teeth, she said nothing.

And he fell right into filling the gap.

"I mean, I know it would be a different approach," he continued, "but I think extending the school year could be a good thing."

He nodded at her, seeking her something; most likely her agreement.

"It might work," Charlene answered, a politician's neutral response.

He looked disappointed.

"Well…" he began.

"If you laid the groundwork right," she cut in, keen to minimize the damage from her comment, "so that it wasn't too great a shock when you finally announced."

She smiled at him and it seemed to help him ease up.

"Yes," he breathed out, "yes, yes… you're right. Thanks."

For nothing, she thought and hoped she hadn't just encouraged him to commit professional suicide.

"Now," Sturmann said, coming back to the moment, "how was today? Anything we need to discuss?"

As he asked this last, his eyes were already scanning the pile of paperwork on his desk. Charlene saw tiredness, resignation and more than a little fear in the glance.

Reporting back was second nature for any cop, she could be done and out in the sunshine in a matter of minutes, which would make him happy too; though she doubted *'happy'* was the right term for Sturmann's state of mind.

"Quiet day," she said, "mostly settling in. I walked the halls around lunchtime, making sure my face was seen, getting ahead of any threat response."

"Oh. And… erm… how were the students?"

"Fine, fine," she said, "I broke up a little scuffle near the cafeteria."

"Broke up?" Sturmann's voice was immediately tense.

This is how it's going to be, Charlene thought, struck once again by Baker's prescience, *making sure the grown-ups are all right.*

She went into calming mode.

"Nothing major," she spoke steadily, "in fact, I didn't see what happened, just came in on the aftermath. Got them to shake hands and move along. No drama. No damage. No blood."

She smiled at this familiar phrase, used to describe *'nothing days'* by practically the whole police department. As soon as she did, though, she realized the joke had fallen flat.

"I should hope not," Sturmann said, shocked.

She almost held her hands up in surrender.

"Just a turn of phrase," she said.

"Well," Sturmann responded, "I'm not sure I appreciate the humour. Especially when Dylan Ford is still critical in his hospital bed."

Sheesh, Charlene thought, *lighten up a bit, why don't you?*

"Sorry," she said.

Sturmann looked at her for a moment and then rubbed his face with his hands, before pinching the bridge of his nose between the thumb and forefinger of his right hand, closing his eyes.

Look after the grown-ups, Baker's voice sounded in her head.

"You look like you've had quite the day yourself?" Charlene said, smiling a little.

Sturmann dropped his hand, opened his eyes to look at her.

"Lot of eyes on me at the moment," he said, "sort of attention none of us needs or wants, especially not my... the students."

"It must be hard," Charlene commiserated, "Dylan's such a popular kid and many people are just shocked by what happened to him."

"If only that were all..." Sturmann sighed, then caught himself, "oh... don't worry about me, there's just a lot of pressure on us to perform, especially with the budget cuts and everything. Mason... Well, it's the town council, really. They're just looking for us to show the performance that justifies our budget."

"Lot of pressure," Charlene smiled.

"It is that," Sturmann said, "you know, it's a long way from why I came into teaching. A long way."

"We all face that, don't we?" Charlene asked, "I mean, I came into police work because..."

"You wanted to help people?"

She nodded.

"Just about," she said.

Though she didn't add the end of the sentence: ... *to help people right the injustices perpetrated against them.*

And it was suddenly swelling within her, all of today's sitting and waiting, the fracas in the hall, the thought of Katie's tears and Dylan lying broken and beaten in his hospital bed.

She slammed a lid on it. For the moment.

But the office had lost its chill, now warming about her; stifling.

She needed to get out.

"I guess..." Sturmann began, but Charlene cut across him, making a show of checking her watch, looking out towards the car park and the milling throngs of students.

"Sorry," she said, "I need to get back to the station, and I wanted to watch the patterns of behaviour as the kids are leaving. Watch them when they don't know they're being watched, you know?"

"Oh," Sturmann breathed out, "okay. Same time tomorrow?"

Fighting against the surging emotion, Charlene forced a smile to her face.

"Sure. Though no whole-school meetings, okay?"

Sturmann laughed a little and nodded.

"Tomorrow," he said.

"Yup," Charlene responded, standing, "tomorrow."

She stepped out of the office and headed directly towards the exits, to the car park; desperate to be in the open air, where she could release her emotions into the sky. The beginnings of what felt like panic pushed at her, surfacing as a tightness in her gut and a thrumming in her arms.

She stepped through the doors, into open air and warm afternoon sunshine, confronted with throngs of students. For now, they hadn't noticed her, but that didn't stop her prevailing sense that she could have been a stranger stepping into a western movie saloon; rinky-tink piano cutting to silence, heads swivelling, doors flapping on their hinges.

She swallowed and, working not to stare herself, turned to walk around the outside of the buildings, maintaining an even pace, like she had somewhere to go, but nothing *that* urgent. All the while feeling like she was the centre of attention, watched by hoards of teenagers in transit to school buses and car rides home.

At the corner of the building, she risked a glance back the way she had come; unsurprised to find no-one looking in her direction.

She kept walking, the noise falling behind. Ahead, over at the sports field, she could see the football team practising. People running track around the outside of the field.

She was calming down now that she was out in the open air, but the immediate head-rush of emotion she'd felt in Sturmann's office was still with her, unsettling her.

What the hell was that all about? Charlene thought.

With the buildings to her right, she continued on towards the sports fields. Her internal chatter was near constant, mostly chastising herself for getting hooked over seemingly nothing.

Opposite the gymnasium building, steps led up to a raised area with fenced in tennis courts and Charlene stopped for a moment, deciding whether to take the steps or head towards the sports fields. In the end, she took the steps; there were just too many students and, presumably, teachers out on the fields.

And I'm through wearing a mask, she thought, anticipation of her empty house yawning wide beneath, *too much time on my own today, way too much.*

Cresting the stairs, she walked along the path that skirted the four tennis courts and was surprised to see a lone teenager sitting on the far court, leaning against the net-post. She was clad in the uniform of alternative teenagers everywhere: *black*.

The path wrapped the end of the courts and would bring her directly in front of where the kid was sitting; putting her on parade for this unknown witness.

Yet there was something about this lone figure.

Was it familiarity?

Some resonance of her own high school isolation?

Charlene thought about the day she'd had, about too much time on her own and was struck by how much she wanted a different conversation. Before she could think much more, she stepped through the gate in the chain-link fence. As it closed, the metal hinges screeched.

The kid turned to look over her shoulder.

She was fifteen or sixteen, face scrubbed clean beneath a tight crop of curly black hair. She did little more than glance at Charlene before she turned back to contemplating the bushes beyond the tennis courts.

When she got within ten or so feet of the girl, Charlene spoke.

"Hi," she said.

"Hi."

The girl still didn't turn.

"What are you doing?" Charlene intended polite conversation, but it came out sounding accusatory.

"Nothing," the girl replied, "what are *you* doing?"

"Sorry," Charlene said, "let me try that again. How're you d... Nope. Mind if I sit down?"

Charlene took the girls shrug as permission and sat, crossing her legs as her butt sank into the artificial surface.

She turned slightly to face the girl, who kept on looking at the bushes. Charlene glanced in that direction.

"Botanist, right?" she asked the girl.

"Huh?"

Her quip had had the desired effect; the girl was staring at her.

"Well," Charlene continued, "you seem pretty intensely focused on those bushes, I figured you must be studying them?"

She smiled at the teenager who, after a moment of consideration, seemed to decide to reciprocate. A smile danced around her mouth, momentarily reviving the ghosts of childhood dimples, before retreating, a subterranean animal caught outside it's burrow for too long.

"Goodlow," Charlene said, "Charlene Goodlow."

She offered her hand to the girl and they shook.

"*Officer* Charlene Goodlow," the girl said suspiciously, "right?"

Charlene thumbed her uniform shirt pocket, insignia on the flap.

"Right," she said, "or at least I've been known to play one on television. And..."

She hesitated, breathing for a moment.

"Look, it's been a long day and... are you okay if I drop out of my formal role for a little while?"

The girl appraised Charlene, looking for some underhand play, some hidden motive.

"Please?" Charlene asked, opening her hands almost as if to show there were no cards up her sleeve.

Quiet hung over the tennis courts for a moment, held from being silent only by distant shouts from the sports fields which melded with the receding roar of school bus engines.

The girl nodded.

"Brina," she said, "and, before you ask, yes it's short for Sabrina..."

This brought an unexpected smile to Charlene's face.

"Cute," she said.

Brina smiled, dipping her head.

"Why, thank you."

Charlene had the distinct sense that, had she been standing, Brina would have curtsied on saying this.

"Brina, huh?" Charlene smiled.

"Yup," Brina responded, "and no, I didn't shorten it to piss my Mom off. I've been a Brina long as I can remember."

"I wasn't thinking that," Charlene defended, "I..."

"It's all right. I'm just used to people asking."

"You get asked a lot?"

"Not now," Brina said, "we moved here a year or so back and, for a while, I was the new girl. And... Well, you know high school."

Charlene nodded.

"Poked and prodded like a science experiment, right?"

Brina nodded, smiling again, eyes twinkling with reflected pinpricks of sunlight.

"So, talking of new girls," she said, "how's *your* day been? That was quite the introduction you got this morning."

Charlene looked at the middle-distance for a moment; *this morning* seemed a lifetime ago, finding Dylan's body eons before that.

She rubbed at her face, surprised to find that she was near tears.

"I've..." she began, but a sudden lump clenched her throat.

"Had better?" Brina asked, reaching out her hand to pat Charlene's arm.

Charlene nodded, still unable to speak.

"I know how that goes," Brina said, "it must be tough coming back?"

"Coming back?"

"To high school."

"Oh," Charlene said, "I wasn't here. I'm from out of town. I didn't go..."

"Bet your school was pretty much like this one though?"

Charlene nodded. Hadn't she had a similar observation while walking the cinder-block hallways.

"Yes. Yes it was."

"I thought you did the right thing at assembly this morning, keeping it short."

"Thanks," Charlene smiled, the tears and lump were dissipating now.

"And when those morons asked you about your gun! I could have slapped them! You did a nice job, joking about the mace and all."

"Again, thanks," Charlene dipped her head in her own curtsy of acknowledgement.

"A gun would be..."

Brina trailed off. Charlene wondered what she'd been about to say; decided to hold back from encouraging her on.

It seemed that the thought was to remain silent, though. Brina was back to staring at the bushes. Eventually, she spoke without looking at Charlene.

"Did you *find* Dylan?" she asked.

"Yup," Charlene answered, "he was over in the back car park."

"Was it..." Brina shuddered a little despite the sunshine reflecting off the tennis court, "bad?"

Charlene thought for a moment, leaning her head back to let the sun warm her face.

"I've seen worse," she said, "unfortunately."

She was suddenly tired, looking forward to heading home, if only for the chance to get a long, warm bath; Suzy or no Suzy.

"He's a good guy, Dylan," Brina said, "he didn't... Well, no-one deserves to get beaten up like that, but Dylan... He's a good guy and he didn't deserve it."

Charlene thought about asking whether Brina had any ideas as to who'd attacked Dylan but a little voice inside told her not to. Part of that was Baker's instruction that he was handling the investigation but it was also coming from her read of this moment; though Brina was talking, she would close down the moment Charlene became too direct.

Besides, she was off-duty now.

As if that *ever happens,* Suzy complained in Charlene's head.

"Did you... Do you know him well?" Charlene asked.

"Not so much," Brina said, "well, no more than anyone else in our year. We're not best buds or anything like that. But he's popular, you know, *everyone* knows Dylan. We..."

She smiled at the memory of something, pausing to enjoy it for a moment.

"We call him *'Mister All-American'* because he's such a cliché, you know?"

Charlene nodded.

"Not being nasty or anything," Brina continued, "just that he's the quarterback, acing his grades, square chin, great abs. He's the whole package but he's so damned nice with it as well!"

She blushed a little.

"You sound like you've got a crush on him," Charlene risked the joke.

Brina burst out laughing and it was a moment before she could speak.

"You've gotta be kidding! He's *really* not my type. Besides, there's no way in heaven or earth that anyone could get between him and Katie!"

"Katie?" Charlene said, voice emerging as something close to a whisper. She felt her own blush warming her face, looked back up to the sun to try and replace it.

"His girlfriend," Brina answered, seeming not to notice Charlene's embarrassment, "they're inseparable. Like the perfect couple, you know? She's a straight-A student, blond, gorgeous... could be a model or an athlete or... Well, you get the drift, she's just beautiful and they're like the American Dream made real. Makes the rest of us..."

She paused; Charlene swivelled her head down to look at the teenager.

"Fucking high school," Brina spat, staring at the floor between her feet, "it's all popularity contests, cliques and who's dating who. No-one is... No-one here is real. They're all hiding behind what they think they need to say and do, what they wear, who they spend time with..."

Charlene watched as Brina's face first flushed and then began to contort towards tears. It was her turn to reach out and touch the girl's arm.

"Want to talk about it?" she asked.

The change was immediate. Brina's teeth came together with an audible click and her mouth set firm. She looked at Charlene from under hooded eyelids.

"No," she said, hardly opening her lips, "no, I don't *want to talk about it*. I'm done talking. This place..."

She swept an arm towards the school buildings.

"... ah, what's the use. I'll be gone soon enough."

Charlene stared at Brina; remembered such similar sentiments from her own high school years, born mainly of her struggles coming to terms with her own sexuality and how far it was from the expectations of everyone else's high school experience.

"I couldn't go to my prom," Charlene said, the words emerging before she knew she would speak of a memory so long-buried, "I... erm... I couldn't take my date."

Brina was still for a moment and then, slowly, turned to look at Charlene. She stared for a long moment and, ever so gradually, began to nod understanding.

She stood, grabbing her back-pack.

"I've gotta go," she said.

"Sure," Charlene said, squinting against the sunlight as she looked up at Brina.

"I'll maybe catch you around," Brina said, turning to head towards the gates.

Charlene didn't say anything else. Too much was going on in her tired head, competing and clashing, her own stuff and what she'd sensed in Brina and Katie and Dylan lying on the hospital bed and Sturmann being near breaking point and Mason at the assembly this morning and the question about...

Enough, she thought, *you're not going to solve any of it sitting here*.

She stood, turning towards the gate.

Brina was already long-gone, surprising Charlene by how she'd managed to disappear so quickly.

Charlene walked out of the tennis courts and back towards her cruiser, already calming in anticipation of that bath and glass of wine.

Thursday

Chapter 17:
Can I Get A Witness?

The previous day's pattern continued into the next day: arrive early, settle in, get bored, wander the halls. Baker had warned Charlene of some things about this assignment, and hinted at many more behind his poker player's mask, but he hadn't included that it would feel so empty and pointless.

Several times during the second morning, she found herself picking up her cell-phone, about to dial no-one in particular, just holding the phone like a kid with an empty ice-cream cone.

It did little but compound the sense of an incomplete home she'd left behind that morning.

At morning recess, she'd meandered the campus, hoping for sight of a familiar face; even Sturmann would have been enough. But there had been none, not Sturmann, not Brina.

Not Katie.

Which had been something of a relief.

At two that morning, she'd woken from a dream which had already dissipated into the mist of the early morning; alarm clock ticking on her night-stand. She'd been too warm, sweating. Turned on, there'd been no denying it. And worse, she suspected she'd been dreaming of Katie Browning. As she'd fought to get back to sleep, a sensation of skin and touch had been waiting every time she'd closed her eyes. Her thoughts had whirled with what the dreams might infer.

It's just a dream, she'd repeated over and again, *just random stuff that's helping you process the day.*

It doesn't mean anything.

As she'd drifted slowly back into sleep though, her last thoughts had been that she didn't really believe that.

The forgotten dream, her physical arousal, had sat uneasy in her thoughts all morning, when she'd walked the halls, when she'd absent-mindedly picked up her cell-phone.

It doesn't mean anything, she'd repeated to herself.

At lunch-time, she considered heading out to get a sandwich, but decided instead to brave the school cafeteria once again. She stood in line, tray in hand, in amongst teenagers who watched her warily but wouldn't meet her eye. Made small-talk with some of them. The food had improved since she'd been at school, though in truth anything would have been an improvement on that score, and she grabbed a salad and bottle of water, paid at the registers and headed out to the tables.

She sat in one of the far corners, where she could watch the students not watching her except when they thought she wasn't looking.

After about five minutes of informal surveillance, she saw Brina step into the food service area. She was surprised at how this brought a smile to her face, how much she was looking forward to seeing her emerge. As it was, she was to be disappointed; Brina came out amidst a crowd of kids and left the cafeteria without noticing Charlene.

Amidst the hubbub and to-and-fro, Charlene remained an island.

Her phone rang, bringing blessed respite from her isolation.

"Charlene here," she answered, speaking quietly.

The line wasn't good, crackling with static.

"… endy… ere… I wante… how… you…"

"Sorry," Charlene said, "the connection's lousy, can you try again?"

She thumbed the *off* button with the phone at her ear and then brought it down onto the table before her. Unknown number.

Katie walked out from the food service area, carrying a tray.

Charlene felt a burst of energy, carried over from her sleepless night.

Instinctively, she ducked down a little.

The phone rang again.

"Hello?"

She watched Katie cross the cafeteria and sit in the opposite corner. Sideways on, thank goodness.

"Charlene?"

"Yup," Charlene focused back on the phone, "who is this?"

"Wendy," the voice said, "sorry, the signal in the school can get pretty lousy."

"Oh... Hi, Wendy," Charlene smiled.

"Hi. I was just thinking about you. Been a couple of days since we talked. How are you doing?"

Distracted by Katie, who sat alone in the far corner, Charlene hardly heard the question.

"Huh?"

"Are you okay?"

"I'm fine," Charlene said, though she feared the truth lay in a different direction, "just tired."

"Uh-huh," Wendy sounded sceptical, though Charlene knew that was probably her transferring onto the other woman. "Are you at the high school?"

"You've heard, then?"

"Sure. It's not exactly the best kept secret," Wendy laughed, "and remember, I'm a *principal-at-large*; news travels very, very fast."

A group of boys had drawn level with Katie.

"And what are you hearing?"

"Oh you know, smoke and noise, mainly. Lots of opinion, very little fact. Teachers telling me it's the end of the world as we know it..."

"And I feel fine," Charlene added, watching the boys.

"Not much of that going around," Wendy laughed again, "but it seems like you've managed to help Walt Sturmann calm down."

"Walt?"

The boys were milling around Katie's table.

"Sure," Wendy continued, "he's always been high strung and... well, this thing with Dylan Ford has really got him spooked. It's good that you're there."

"Making sure the grown-ups are all right," Charlene said to herself, watching the boys.

"Well… that's an interesting way of putting it, but I guess you're right."

"Listen, Wendy… I've got to go, is there anything you need?"

"Oh, okay," Wendy paused, thinking, "not really. Like I say, I was just checking in. Let's get together for that drink some time soon, okay?"

"Sure," Charlene said, "speak soon."

She thumbed the *off* button before Wendy could say goodbye, forking a mouthful of salad and chewing it slowly; the taste had begun to fade and the greens were beginning to wilt. She swallowed.

There was a kid opposite Katie, chatting to her. Something about the way he was sitting, leaning forward. He wasn't eating; neither he nor his friends had trays. They seemed to be speaking amiably enough but there was something about them that she couldn't pin-point.

Charlene scanned the other boys, who almost formed a circle around the table. As she looked at them she suddenly caught what it was that had been making her uneasy. Katie was tense in her seat, sitting upright, more so than she had been before the boys had arrived.

She's scared, Charlene thought, *the kid scares her.*

Katie threw her head back in laughter. The boy was grinning widely from ear-to-ear, smiling around at his friends. He looked familiar.

Even though she was laughing, Katie was still tensed, ready to fight or run away. The boy reached out to touch her hand and Katie nearly jumped out of her skin. He made a big show of lifting her hand and then, gently, kissing it.

He's hitting on her, Charlene thought, *with his friends all stood around, no wonder she's tense.*

The boy stood suddenly and made a little bow to Katie before turning and walking away, his friends in tow.

Katie looked around, checking who'd seen the conversation.

Charlene, blushing, suddenly found renewed interest for the depths of her unfinished salad.

After a moment, she risked a glance, but Katie had left.

He was hitting on her! Charlene thought, a little dismayed at the thought that this could happen while Dylan had been so recently taken to hospital.

And even while she wrestled with that dismay, she felt her unease from the previous night's dream scoot over a little to let some jealousy join it.

She began to wonder whether she should have stepped in. Done something to break up the uncomfortable situation.

Really, Charlene... Really?

She rubbed a hand over her face, ended up pushing it into her hairline.

"What am I doing here?" Charlene sighed to herself, "what am I doing here?"

She put her dinner stuff on her tray and made for the trash-cans.

It was only as she was pitching trash that she remembered.

The kid who'd been hitting on Katie.

It had been the Asian kid she'd saved from a beating the day before. What had his name been? Jason... Jason Liu.

"Interesting," she mumbled to herself, and the boy next to her gave her a sidelong, quizzical look. Noticing this, Charlene turned.

"Oh, don't mind me," she said, smiling, "I always talk to myself."

"Er... Sure," the kid said, "whatever."

He turned and walked away.

Charlene looked up at the ceiling, blowing air out through pursed lips.

What am I doing here? She asked herself once again.

Chapter 18: Donuts

Her phone buzzed as she left the school buildings for the day; Baker's number.

She thumbed the green button and put the phone to her ear.

"Chief?"

"Yeah," Baker said, "it's me. Can you come into the station on your way back home tonight?"

Her stomach lurched; this didn't sound good.

She thought for a moment.

"Urgent?" she asked.

"No, not really but I wanted to check in on how things are going."

Charlene listened carefully, he seemed to be telling the truth, wasn't holding something back. Not that she could really tell over the phone anyway.

"Want to talk about it now? I'm out of the buildings, on my way to the cruiser."

"No," Baker said, "face-to-face is easier."

There it was again, that little lurch; she was on edge, her forgotten dreams of Katie, the confusion over what she'd seen at lunch.

"You're getting me worried, chief," she only half-joked.

There was a pause and, after a moment, even past the static and wind rumble in her phone's earpiece, she heard him sigh.

"Nothing to worry about," he said, "for you, at least."

She stopped walking, standing still and looking up to the sky.

"I'll be there in about ten minutes," she said, "and I'm bringing donuts!"

Baker laughed at his end of the call, a single sharp bark. They always resorted to the perennial police comfort food when days got to be hard-going; their own little in-joke.

"Make mine *Pretty-In-Pink*," he laughed, "none of that healthy option crap."

"Sure," Charlene smiled, "be there in ten."

She ended the call.

* * *

Getting the coffee and donuts was interesting.

Lots of teenagers from the high school hanging around both inside and outside the donut shop; as unwilling to meet her eyes here as they had been in the school buildings.

Charlene felt every step of the uphill battle she was waging; those that had passed and, especially heavy, those yet to come.

She stood in line behind a boy, easily identifiable by both his fashion non-choices and the air of disdain with which those around favoured him: *classic dork*. His raggedy hair and coke-bottle glasses; acne blooming on face and neck. Alone in line, avoiding contact with any of the other teenagers in the shop.

Charlene felt his pain, his very singular out-group.

Watched him pay and exit like a chastised puppy, eyes downcast, fingers gripping the paper donut bag until they turned white.

She stepped up to the counter, placing and confirming her order; the only conversation she had with anyone in the donut shop.

What's the world coming to, she asked herself, *when the only people you talk to are wondering how much change you'll leave in the tip jar?*

She paid and left, just another chastised dork, carrying a bag of donuts and two coffees; watched all the way out of the shop by Jason Liu, sitting in the corner, sipping at a coffee, out of her line-of-sight.

When the door closed behind Charlene, he went back to chatting with his friends like she'd never been there.

* * *

Baker was in his office when Charlene arrived at the station. He watched her pull in and step from her cruiser; waved a hello.

In turn, Charlene hoisted the donut bag and coffees above her head slightly, like a champion lifting a cup too heavy for tired arms.

Baker gave her a double thumbs-up and headed out of his office to open the doors for her.

Good to be back home, Charlene thought, smiling to herself.

* * *

They sat quiet together, the first sugar rush of the donuts hitting, coffee warming their core.

Charlene looked at Baker.

"You look tired, chief," she said.

He thought for a moment.

"Yeah," he said, "I'm feeling it today. I…"

He stopped, took a bite of his donut; reflecting on what he'd been about to say.

"There's a lot of interest in you at the moment, Charlene. A lot of eyes on us."

She shrugged.

"That's new?" she said. "We knew there would be, right? It's a big thing to have me in the school. Of course they're going to pay attention."

"Sure," his brow furrowed slightly, "but they're really interested. Mason was…"

Another pause. Charlene saw Mason's bulk at the back of the school hall, his piggy eyes glimmering.

"Status reports," Baker continued eventually, "Mason wants daily status reports."

They were still for a moment, staring at each other over decimated donuts.

Then Charlene burst out laughing; Baker couldn't help but join in.

"Daily?" Charlene managed to say through chuckles. "Really?"

"He's very serious," Baker was all mock-gravitas, "it's his civic duty to protect the children. He would be standing in dereliction of duty if he were to abandon the sacred trust the people of the town have placed in his hands. He swore an oath to protect the town and bring prosperity and peace to the people who were good enough to elect him to the high… exalted… office of… first selectman."

Baker couldn't keep it up and brayed laughter into the room. There were tears dancing at the corner of his eyes. Neither of them could do anything other than laugh.

Eventually, Charlene eased back enough to breathe.

"Where, exactly, did he place the pulpit when he told you all that?" she asked.

Baker thumbed towards his office, smiling now.

"Do you think," Charlene asked, "that he looks himself in the mirror each morning and says *'good morning, Mr President'*?"

Baker laughed.

"No," he said, "I don't think he's that insane. Though he might have primed Mrs Mason to say it."

They both roared laughter again.

When they had calmed down enough to speak, Baker's smile dropped.

"We are going to have to report in," he said, "you know the fuss he'll make if we don't."

Charlene nodded. She appreciated the double-bind the chief was in; not wanting to be in the school, but committed to doing it well.

"Written or verbal?" she asked.

Baker shook his head.

"I don't think it matters," he said, "whatever's easiest for you."

Charlene thought for a moment, seeing Jason Liu hit on Katie in the cafeteria, feeling again the claustrophobia that had claimed her in Sturmann's office.

"Well, it's just high school stuff. I haven't seen anything to suggest otherwise. My reports are going to be pretty much along the lines of *'I kicked my heels and tried to think of something new to kill the boredom'*, so I guess either works," she said.

"Tell him that enough times, and he'll be the one getting bored," Baker smiled.

"What do you think he wants to hear? What's he waiting for?"

Baker shrugged.

"I could hazard a guess, but it'd be speculation," he said, "besides, you know how much I trust politicians. He wants what any of them want: his own way. They're all big kids, when you cut through the bluster."

Charlene smiled.

"So, I'm working the kids while you're keeping the grown-ups, who don't *realize* they're big kids, happy?"

"That's about it," Baker frowned.

"I'm back in high school," Charlene said, "and you're stuck in kindergarten."

She reached out and took another donut.

"What are we doing here, Jack?" she asked.

Saw Katie's tear hitting the material of her t-shirt; felt the texture of a breast from a half-forgotten dream.

"What am I doing here?"

Friday

Chapter 19:
Foot In Mouth

Baker checked his phone. No messages; usually a very good thing first thing in the morning. As he drove into downtown though, headed for Annie's Place, he couldn't shake the feeling that the lack of message was foreshadowing something.

He parked up and walked the block or so to Annie's. People waved at him, nodded acknowledgement.

He couldn't get the anxiety to cease ticking just below his stomach.

Maybe I'm sick, he thought, *maybe that's all it is*.

But it wasn't. He knew it.

He arrived at Annie's Place; opened the door and stepped into the warmth and chaos of breakfast serving.

Some people, no more than usual, turned to look at him.

Annie emerged from the back room.

"Hi, Jack," she called over the packed dining room, "usual spot?"

He smiled, nodding.

"Sure," she smiled right back.

Jack walked towards his seat at the counter as Annie turned to serve a booth in the corner.

As she moved, though, she looked back over her shoulder.

"Hey, Jack," she called, "did you see *The Daybreaker* this morning?"

* * *

The paper was spread across the counter, where successive patrons had read different sections. Even with the disarray though, it was clear what Annie had been referencing.

The headline, in print that seemed to throb and swell as he looked at it:

Gang Responsible for High School Violence – Mason

Baker sat down on the stool, shaking his head.

He remembered the laughter he'd shared with Charlene the previous evening, all at Mason's unknowing expense.

Payback, he thought, *karma's a bitch.*

Annie came over to him.

"Did you read it yet?" she asked.

Baker shook his head.

"Just the headline," he said, "is it even worth reading the article?"

Annie thought for a moment.

"Not really, no," she said. "Is it true, Jack? Is it gang-related?"

He almost blew. In that moment, all of the pent up frustration at Mason and his political gamesmanship, all of it threatening to spew out; he felt it rising like liquid fire up his throat.

He looked at the ceiling, blew a breath out towards the lights.

"No, Annie," he said, "it's not true."

He dropped his gaze to look her in the eye.

"Not in the way you're thinking," he said. "Now, how about I order some eggs and coffee, then try to eat my breakfast in peace? I get the feeling today's going to get hectic.

* * *

He read the piece, of course he did.

It would have been laughable if it hadn't been so pointed.

This was chess all right and Mason was playing for keeps.

The only piece of new news was that Charlene was now placed at the school. Aside from that, it was all opinion; Curtis Simpson toeing Mason's line like a hideously obedient puppy. As he re-read the article, Baker considered that Mason might actually have written it.

The thrust was that the attack on Dylan Ford hadn't been random, that it bore the hallmarks of inter-gang violence, particularly that seen on the West Coast between Hispanic and Black gangs.

Simpson's helpful hand had included a glossary of links for readers to follow to learn more of gang-culture.

Mason even suggested one of these web-sites in one of his quotes, for parents who were: *'worried that their own children might be attracted to join the gangs'*.

The second time through, the article was as disconcerting as the first time. A third reading didn't make it any better.

It was the way Mason was given the whole tail-end of the piece to lay out progress-to-date: the curfew, the graffiti solution and, best of all, the placement of a police officer in the high school:

> "I attended the assembly where Officer Goodlow was introduced to the children. It is clear from Principal Sturmann's remarks that he will not tolerate further violence, and is prepared to use the full power of the law to bring wrong-doers to justice. I support his stance one hundred percent."

Baker couldn't get past that paragraph cleanly, he felt like laughing, crying, screaming, shouting, anything but being forced to accept that Mason could be so blatant; Walt would never have said, or even intimated, any such thing, especially to his students.

His eggs grew cold on his plate as he read and re-read Simpson's piece, Mason's words.

The ink began to swim on the paper.

"Lost your appetite?" Annie asked, passing behind him.

"Guess so," Baker answered, smiling grimly, "this is about enough for anyone to deal with."

"Look," Annie said, coming behind the counter and smiling, fighting to get him to make eye contact.

Eventually, he did.

"You know Mason," she said, "you know he's just making sure he's seen to be at the centre of the universe. That's who he is."

"I know," Baker responded, "but..."

"No buts," she said, "you've got no right to be surprised that this has happened. We even spoke about it a couple of days back."

She was right, of course. Maybe that's why he'd been so hooked by the piece, maybe it was just disappointment in himself.

"I guess," he said, nodding.

"Anyway," Annie continued, voice filling with her smile, "the real point is that there's been no more violence. So whatever you're doing, you're doing it right. Short of heading into the school and beating up a kid, Mason can't change that. And he knows it. You just need to ride the roller-coaster to the end."

Baker smiled at the analogy.

"This is why I keep coming here, Annie," he said, "you're an oasis of sanity in a crazy, crazy world."

She eyed his cold, untouched breakfast.

"Well, it must be that because it sure as heck doesn't seem to be my eggs."

* * *

Baker walked back down the block towards his cruiser, reaching for his phone to call Charlene. As he paged through his contacts, a snippet of Annie's counsel kept repeating.

'Short of heading into the school and beating up a kid,' she'd said.

It nagged at him, triggering some thought deep in his subconscious that he couldn't get into the light.

Highlighting Charlene's number, he hit the dial button and waited for the call to connect.

Short of heading into the school and beating up a kid.

"Hi, chief," Charlene's voice spoke in his ear.

He'd reached the cruiser and now leant on its hood.

"Morning, Charlene," he said, "did you catch *The Daybreaker*?"

"Nope. Something I need to know?"

"Need to know? No, not really," Baker said, "but you should read it anyway."

"That's cryptic, chief," Charlene sounded suspicious, "can't you just tell me?"

"What, and take away one of the things that could distract you from the boredom today?" Baker joked.

"Understood. Anything else?"

"Nope."

"OK. See you later, when I'm ready to file my next blow-by-blow status report."

She laughed and ended the call.

Good job she can't see my face, Baker thought. He wasn't in the mood for laughing.

Chapter 20: Did You Expect Anything Different?

Charlene walked from her cruiser towards the school entrance.

Time to wake up, she thought, *it's a brand new day.*

It seemed like she'd been telling herself that for too long; the house had felt particularly empty last night. Claustrophobic. Sleep had played cat and mouse with her all night and she'd tossed and turned between memories, things to do and concerns about the dreams that may await her.

And the fact that she hadn't told Baker about any of it. Not just now on the phone, nor last night over donuts and coffee.

That one had really eaten at her.

She supposed it was because of their laughter; shared ridicule of less-than-illustrious leaders. That sunburst oasis of interaction, positivity amidst the boredom of patrolling the school and the vacuum of coming home.

Should she have told him? Should she tell him?

What was there to tell?

That she was on the rebound and there was a very attractive girl involved in her professional situation? That she was developing a crush?

One horny dream did not all that infer; it had been a dream, simply that!

This is what happened when you were working through break-ups and change. She'd read enough books to know that.

I just have to get through it, she thought, *I'll wake up one day and all this will be a memory that I can laugh about.*

She walked towards the school where buses and cars were just arriving for the new day.

Time to wake up, it's a brand new day.

* * *

Just before morning recess, she emerged from the close confines of her office. She hadn't yet walked the halls during class; the investigator within wondered what she may discover.

But, as it was, it was nothing.

The halls were as empty as they would have been early in the morning, before anyone save staff arrived.

She passed a mural painted by the millennium's graduating class. It showed sunshine, trees, kids enjoying each other's company.

It showed hope; belief in a better future.

Where are those kids now? Charlene wondered as she walked, *how many of them are pumping gas, working Wall Street, in prison? How many are raising kids too early because they were too sloppy to use prevention?*

She wondered whether the millennium's high school quarterback was still playing football, or whether he'd become trapped in a dead-end job, a loveless marriage and the monthly struggle to pay the bills.

Who had that quarterback been, anyway?

These fleeting moments of being someone, of leading the pack, of rising above. They all passed.

She thought of Dylan Ford, lying in his hospital bed, slowly recovering.

She resolved to visit him that evening.

The bell for the end of class sounded and, almost immediately she saw class-room doors begin to open; heard the same happening throughout the school, echoing down halls.

The silence and calm was obliterated by the gathering masses of teenagers heading for recess.

* * *

Her cell-phone rang as she headed towards the gym complex.

Baker, again.

"Hi, chief," she answered, "forget something?"

She moved to the side of the hall, leaning into the end of a bank of lockers.

Baker was quiet for a moment. When he spoke, his voice seemed calm, but she could tell he was biting back to control himself.

"Mason," he said, "he's..."

"Been shooting his mouth off again?" she finished the sentence.

"No," Baker said, "for once he hasn't. It's *The Daybreaker* piece. It's really got me thinking."

"How so?" Charlene asked. She didn't like the undercurrent in the chief's voice.

Again, Baker paused.

"The way this is happening," he said, "if I didn't know better, I could put two and two together to get way more than five."

Out of habit, she checked to see whether anyone was listening in to her discussion. Glancing behind, she saw no-one and, returning to the front, the nearest kids were at the end of the hall; unless she started shouting they wouldn't be able to hear a thing.

"But you *do* know better, right chief?"

He thought for a moment.

"It's like he's planning the whole thing, Charlene. Like..."

"When did you become the conspiracy theorist, Jack? Can you hear yourself? Mason's not doing anything but using this as an opportunity to put himself front and centre. He's a politician, Jack... That's what they do! They're all just teenagers who never grew up. And I know teenagers, I'm still stuck in high school!"

The line went quiet save for static and clicks.

"You're right," Baker said eventually, "I'm over-thinking this. I'll head over there this afternoon. Ask him to ease off."

She watched the kid from the donut shop walk through the throngs at the end of the hall. He was no less dorky in the light of day, and there was some pushing and joking at his expense.

There's always a victim, Charlene thought, *always someone to pick on.*

The kid looked embarrassed, hurt and, worst of all, resigned to the treatment.

"How are things there?" Baker asked.

"Same as ever," Charlene said, focusing back on the phone, "nothing much happening except me walking around looking for something to do."

"That's a good thing," Baker said, "don't forget that."

"Sure. Well, if you want to quote me to Mason, go ahead. Tell him I'm giving the *all clear*."

"Thanks for the offer," Baker said, "but I think I'll let you save that for your status report."

A warm coal of the previous night's laughter gave off an ember.

All of a sudden, she sensed something at the far end of the hall. She stepped out from the bank of lockers and looked down there, but could see nothing untoward.

The dorky kid had moved on and things seemed pretty calm. There were fewer kids down there now anyway.

She saw Katie drift past the end of the hall, chatting with a girlfriend; she didn't stop, was gone in a moment.

Still, Charlene, couldn't shake the uneasy feeling that she'd missed something.

"You there?" Baker spoke in her ear.

"Oh… Sure," she said, "recess is almost over and I've got some more rounds to do. Need anything else from me?"

"Nope," Baker said, thinking, "thanks for listening. And let's keep hoping that you're this bored every day. Sooner we get you back to regular duty the better."

"Amen to that," she said, "I'll call you later. Bye."

"Yeah, bye."

She ended the call and, holstering her phone, headed down the hall. She'd grown used to the kids half-looking at her and didn't even try to engage them now.

She got to the end of the hall. To the right led back towards the main part of the school. On the left, the sports facilities.

Instinct took her left.

She got to the next intersection and the dorky kid was there, leaning against the lockers, getting his breath. His bag was on the floor, books and other belongings strewn about it.

Charlene rushed to his side and he looked up as she arrived. She saw fear in his eyes, mingling with shame; a horrible sight. His face, already red, flushed even harder, the acne seeming to turn purple as she looked at him.

"Are you okay?" she asked.

"Of course," he fired back, voice trembling with anger and adrenalin.

Charlene held up her hands.

"Helping," she said, making sure her smile held just the right intensity.

He didn't say anything in response.

Charlene looked up and down this offshoot hall but there were no other kids in sight. Who had done this?

The kid's eyes were beginning to glaze over, to shut down as the energy surge left him and humiliation filled the gap, and Charlene silenced her inner investigator, squatting to retrieve his bag and belongings. When she had them all together, she stood and held them out towards him.

He was trembling now, on the verge of tears, the lower lids of his eyes glistening slightly.

Your choice, Charlene, she thought, *start asking questions and have him bawling or let it go.*

As it was, he made the choice for her.

"Thanks," he mumbled and walked back towards the main section of the school.

Charlene watched him until he was nearly at the junction.

"Wait!" she called.

He turned to look at her but continued walking backwards, increasing the gap between them.

He was scared, embarrassed, humiliated and, Charlene knew, this wasn't the first, second or even third time this had happened. This was his life.

"Never mind," she said, deflated by her inability to help him. Or, more accurately, his unwillingness to be helped.

He disappeared around the corner.

Charlene stood for a moment and let the wave of memories rise from within. Her own bitter high school experience, being different, being the outcast, being side-lined and ostracised by cliques who always seemed to be elsewhere from where she found herself.

She'd been the odd girl.

She'd been the dork.

She'd been the homo.

And right now, like him, she would have wanted to be alone.

Alone.

Then why's he walking back towards the main buildings? she thought suddenly.

She looked towards the sports facilities.

He's not walking towards the school, he's walking away from…

Charlene started walking in the direction of the gymnasium.

* * *

But she didn't find the attacker.

The sports facilities were largely empty, save for a class getting ready for a basketball session, emerging in ones and twos from the locker rooms. In the gym, a teacher warming up a whistle.

Charlene walked out of the exit by the side of the gym entrance and headed toward the fields. But these were similarly empty.

Whoever had attacked the kid was nowhere to be seen.

First the Asian kid, now the dork, Charlene thought, *maybe there is something going on under the covers here.*

From where she stood, she could see the tennis courts on the rise overlooking the football field and, just visible, a lone figure leaning against the net-pole.

She headed in that direction.

* * *

"Hi, Brina," Charlene said as she approached the girl, "getting some air?"

Brina looked at her but didn't speak.

Charlene stood, waiting for an invitation to sit.

"Me and my dumb questions, right?" she laughed.

Brina nodded, glancing towards the buildings before checking her watch.

"This is a great place to take a break," she said, "get away from... Well, you know."

Charlene smiled. She did.

"Mind if I sit?" she asked.

"Sure," Brina replied, "it's a free..."

"Country, I know."

Charlene sat.

"Hey, do you know..." she began but suddenly realized that she didn't know the dorky kid's name.

"Who?" Brina asked.

"I don't know his name," Charlene admitted, "I saw him yesterday afternoon at the donut shop and, just now near the gym. He'd been roughed up and I was wondering if you knew him."

"Well, that's not much to go on," Brina smiled, "let me put my psychic waves out into the world."

She held her forehead, thumb on one side, fingers on the other and closed her eyes, holding out her other hand and waving it back and forth.

"Woooooo," she joked.

Charlene couldn't help but laugh.

"All right," she said, "point taken."

Brina looked at her.

"What does he look like?"

"A dork," Charlene said, suddenly catching what she'd said as Brina burst out laughing.

"Nice," Brina smiled.

They were quiet for a moment.

"Seriously," Charlene tried again, "that's what I thought when I saw him at the donut shop. He's just typical, I guess... Greasy hair, thick glasses, zits... Just everything about him is a cliché. He's a dork. There's not much else to say."

She gave a brief laugh at her own inept description and Brina looked at her for a long moment.

"What?" Charlene said.

"Nothing," Brina replied.

It was Charlene's turn to assess the teenager.

"Look," Brina said as she felt the moment stretching, "if you know anything about high school, you'll know one thing: no-one cares about the dorks. No-one notices them. Except for the bullies, who get their groove on by making them feel like shit, and the beautiful people who can use them whenever they need to boost their own egos."

Charlene didn't speak, letting Brina continue.

"So, no I don't know your particular dork," she said, "and you just about described most of the kids at this school. I thought you were trained in this shit?"

Charlene felt a flush entering her cheeks.

"I'm not investigating," she said, surprised by how defensive her voice sounded.

"No," Brina fired back, some venom entering her voice, "but you are on duty, aren't you? Monitoring us? Protecting us? Keeping us in line?"

Off in the buildings, the bell for the end of recess rang. Brina reacted to it like a coiled spring, standing and turning towards the buildings. Charlene stood too and faced the girl.

"I told you the other day," she said, "I'm not here to…"

"Look," Brina stared Charlene in the eye, "this is high school. And you can't change high school. People get picked on. People get treated like shit for being different. People get beat up. That's how it works. If you expect anything different, you're in the wrong place."

And with that, she pushed past Charlene, bumping shoulders as she passed. Charlene counted to ten before glancing back but Brina was already out of the tennis courts and heading back to the buildings; the conversation was done.

This is high school, Charlene thought, *if you expect anything different, you're in the wrong place.*

Chapter 21:
Please, Take A Seat

It sat with him all morning and he knew he couldn't let it stew over the weekend; the storm-cloud of taking Mason to task.

It had to be today.

The call with Charlene had helped. If nothing else, it had calmed him, easing him back from anger which had only swollen after he'd first read the piece at Annie's Place.

He hadn't had to think hard on what had hooked him.

Gangs.

Such a singular label. Applied so easily to explain away any aberration within the normal pattern of things.

There had always been gangs, of course. He wasn't in denial. When people who didn't have something wanted to get it, they formed a gang; seeking out the like-minded.

Except society had, over the years, rewritten that description: … *they formed a gang; seeking out their own kind.*

Their own kind.

'Gang' had become a convenient label for any minority group, an easy out-group terminology. Stereo-typing at its worst. And, in this largely white town, it was such an offensive way of writing off the small but growing minority population.

Which is where the hook barbed into Baker's flesh.

In a long career with the police department, he'd seen practically everything: accidental death, bodily harm, drug casualties, rape, murder. Most of it committed by white on white; a function of demographics for sure, but indicative of the delusion in which this tight-knit town lived.

It's those *other* people that are the problem, not us. Not me. Not we.

Mason was the voice of that *'we'*.

Elected to office, but self-appointed to judge and jury.

When he labelled this a gang crime, he was appealing to his base: the old money in the town, the people looking for someone else to blame for their current ills.

Those people hurt our quarterback.

And it stuck in Baker's throat.

There was *no* evidence that this was anything other than a one-off act of violence. The investigation would succeed. The law would out. But in the meantime, Mason would make capital off the beating, using it to push the town even further towards non-acceptance of difference.

Mason may have been on the wrong side of history but he was very, very good at rewinding the clock.

* * *

Come lunchtime, Baker was very hungry.

He'd been so preoccupied strategizing his planned discussion with Mason that he'd forgotten about the cold eggs at Annie's Place.

His stomach growled.

He left the police department and headed back towards Annie's.

Don't know about third time being a charm, he thought, with a little smile, *but I'll take a second chance at those eggs*.

* * *

Main Street was quiet as he walked towards Annie's. Folk about their business, a little traffic. Another calm day.

Like the one before. And before that.

Like the day Dylan Ford got beaten near to death.

Mason, omnipresent at the back of his thoughts, wanting to draw a manufactured pattern from a single data point.

"Penny for them?" a voice said from his right.

He turned.

"Oh, hi Joe," he said to the real estate agent, standing outside his office. "Sorry, I was miles away."

"You looked it," Joe smiled, "is it this business with the Ford boy? The gangs?"

Baker held his poker face.

"Connected," he said, "though you shouldn't believe all you read in *The Daybreaker*. There aren't any gangs in the schools or anywhere else in town."

Joe looked sceptical. Baker turned to face him fully.

"Come on, Joe," he said, "you know this town better than most. You sold most of it!"

This replaced scepticism with a smile for a moment.

"You know the neighbourhoods here. You know the people."

"True," Joe began, "but…"

"No… no buts, Joe," Baker bit, "just because Muh… *The Daybreaker* wants to whip up some imagined conspiracy about this doesn't make it real. It's… well, it's a cheap shot, trying to get folk to blame a small section of our town for something when there's no evidence."

The real estate agent was silenced for the moment.

"And until I have evidence," Baker said, "no-one can say anyone did anything. That's the way the law works."

Joe raised his hand in surrender.

"All right," he said, anger an undercurrent in his voice, "sorry I asked, Jack. Sheesh!"

Baker breathed.

"No," he said, offering a hand, "I'm sorry. It's been a tense couple of days and the piece in *The Daybreaker* is… well… I guess that'd be repeating myself, wouldn't it?"

He smiled as they shook hands.

"I'll catch you later, Joe," Baker said and walked on towards Annie's Place.

He'd gotten a few yards when he heard Joe call out after him.

"You'll get them, Jack," he called, "I'll keep my eyes open."

"Thanks, Joe," he called back over his shoulder, waving a farewell.

* * *

Annie's Place was full to bursting, the only available seats were at the counter. Annie saw him enter and called out across the room.

"Back again, Jack?"

"You know how it is, Annie," he smiled and shrugged, "I just can't keep away. Besides, I owe my empty stomach some eggs from this morning!"

She pointed towards the counter and he answered with a nod.

He stepped from the doorway towards the aisle that led to the counter and a familiar voice sounded from off to his left.

"Jack," Mason said, "won't you join me for a bite of lunch?"

* * *

Baker sat, the white noise of conversation and cooking that filled the restaurant now fading to a background tapestry.

Mason; all piggy eyes and smiling certainty.

The first selectman offered his hand across the table and Baker had no choice but to shake.

"How goes the battle?" Mason asked light-heartedly.

Baker breathed, conscious to keep an even tone, this being a busy lunchtime seating at Annie's.

"Battle?" he said.

Mason smiled.

"Figure of speech," he said, "how are things, Jack?"

"Good," Baker replied, "did you get a status report last night? I told Charlene about it."

And we laughed at your micro-management, he thought.

"I did," Mason played with the corned beef hash and eggs on his plate, seeming to consider which section his fork would transfer to his mouth, "sounds like all's quiet on the high school front."

"It is."

Annie stepped up to the side of the table.

"OK, Jack, what'll it be?"

Baker smiled up at her.

"What I didn't get around to eating this…"

He paused, aware that Mason was listening carefully.

"Eggs, over-easy, sausage, bacon, home fries," he said.

"Rye toast?" Annie confirmed.

"As always," Baker smiled.

"And anything for you?" she asked, turning to face Mason. "More coffee?"

Mason bowed his head slightly.

"That would be great," he said, pushing his cup across the surface of the table.

"Okay," Annie said, pocketing her order pad, "I'll get your order in, Jack, and be right back with coffee."

She navigated away through the busy restaurant.

Baker breathed deeply.

"Any questions from the status report?" he asked. "Did it meet your needs?"

Mason nodded.

"Absolutely. Officer Goodlow appears highly competent. She did a nice job of introducing herself to the students."

"Oh, were you there?" Butter wouldn't have melted on Baker's poker face.

"Snuck in the back," Mason confided, "more to keep an eye on Walt Sturmann, truth be told; the last thing we need right now is him going off the deep end."

"He'll be fine," Baker said, "he's a little shaken but he knows what he's doing. Charlene is working closely with him."

"Well, these are trying times," Mason said, forking a pile of corned beef hash and egg yolk into his mouth.

"With gangs running around everywhere?" Baker could hold it back no longer; any plan he'd had long discarded thanks to this chance encounter.

Mason chewed, smiling. Swallowed.

"You saw that, did you?" he asked, chuckling.

"I did."

"Yes, well… Curtis has… Well, he has a way of extending the quote, making the source seem…"

"More serious than they are?" Baker asked, sensing Mason was building a wall behind which to hide.

"Extreme, I would say," Mason continued, "no areas of grey for *The Daybreaker*, not in Curtis Simpson's pieces anyway."

His fork moved restlessly around the plate, mixing food, readying the next mouthful.

Annie returned with an empty cup for Baker and a full pot for both. They were silent as she poured; Mason eating another mouthful.

When she'd left, Baker picked up the thread.

"There's no gang in town," he said, "you know that, Mason."

Mason nodded.

"I didn't say there was," he protested calmly.

"You did in *The Daybreaker*," Baker countered, "the whole piece was about this being a case of gang violence, with you the main source!"

Mason put his fork down.

"Chief," he said, "Jack… We are in a diner on Main Street and there are plenty of ears to hear us. Can we keep the volume down? Please?"

Baker sat back a little in the chair; aware that Mason was right, that his voice had been getting louder.

"As I just said, Curtis Simpson has a way of amplifying quotes."

"So you didn't say it was gang violence?"

"That's what I said, isn't it?"

Baker just sat, perplexed within the barrage of information and nuanced behaviour.

"And besides," Mason continued, "even if I had, I would have meant *gang-like* at the most."

This was as close to an admission as Baker was likely to get.

"Gang-*like*?" he asked. "What, exactly, is gang-*like*?"

Mason chewed another mouthful, thinking. He glanced around the dining room.

"You know," he nodded, "when *they* get together, there's just…"

"They?"

Mason scanned the room again and then, after a moment, shook his head.

"Never mind," he said, "the point is that I didn't say there was a gang in town. I will have to have a word with Simpson about stretching my words. Make sure it doesn't happen again."

Annie arrived with Baker's food.

"Here you go, Jack," she said, putting the plate in front of him.

Baker's stomach gave a little lurch; despite the conversation with Mason, he was hungrier than ever.

"Thanks, Annie," he said then, unable to resist, "First Selectman Mason was just apologizing for his quotes in *The Daybreaker* this morning."

"Really?" Annie looked towards Mason, shocked.

Mason's cheeks were flushing red, his eyes tightening, a thin line creasing his forehead. His lips pulled back slightly into a snarl as he spoke.

"I was not apologizing," he said, "I have nothing to apologize for. I was misquoted."

Suddenly, all the tension ran out of his face and it was like the previous conversation hadn't happened at all.

"But then, if that's what you want to believe, Chief Baker, feel free to continue on. There's little I can do to change your mind."

Now Baker knew what Mason was up to. His voice had risen in volume; he was playing to the gallery of patrons in Annie's Place. Baker glanced at Annie and similar awareness was in her eyes.

He's playing us again, Baker thought, *does he ever stop?*

"The bottom line is that I was misquoted in *The Daybreaker*," Mason spoke to the room, even casting a fleeting glance to check people were hearing him, "what we have seen is an act of gang-like violence. Whether that means we have an active gang or not isn't really important, not when Dylan Ford lies recovering in hospital."

There was nothing Baker could do, and they both knew it.

"I should think you of all people, Chief Baker, would be keen to get past such sensationalist distractions and do the right thing for Dylan. Find whoever did this and bring them to justice."

Baker tried to keep eye contact with Mason but the first selectman's eyes were too busy making connection with as many people in the room as possible. He looked down at his eggs; appetite deserting him once again.

Mason turned to look at Annie, who seemed rooted to the spot, incredulous at the game that had just played out. With his right index finger, he drew a quick letter V on his left palm.

"Check please!" he smiled.

Sunday

Chapter 22:
A Much Needed Shoulder

Saturday came and went as every Saturday had since Suzy had left.

Charlene spent the day avoiding; pottering, tinkering, browsing. Empty spaces didn't seem quite as dangerous when she filled them with meaningless action and thought.

She couldn't shake the feeling that she'd missed something. It hung in the back of her mind, in the shadows, sometimes leaning just enough to give its edge a glimmer, yet retreating whenever she looked for it directly.

What had she missed?

*   *   *

Around noon on Sunday, her doorbell chimed through the silence.

Charlene, sitting at the kitchen table, looked up from the newspaper she was staring at but not reading.

And here's me in my jammies, she thought; Sundays, her lazy morning.

She walked through to the front door in time to hear someone knocking the wooden frame and a muffled voice.

"Charlene?" A woman's voice.

She took a sidelong look in the hallway mirror, didn't much like what she saw and decided, as it was Sunday, she had the right not to care too much.

She opened the door upon Wendy Miller.

"Well," laughed the middle school principal, "aren't we a pretty sight this morning?"

Charlene smiled in return.

"Come on in," she said.

* * *

They sat at the kitchen table, sharing coffee and cookies.

A lull in conversation; silence not uncomfortable.

For Charlene, even having another body in the house, somebody other than herself living, breathing, interacting, was an improvement over holes.

"I was worried about you the other day," Wendy said.

Charlene shook her head.

"No need to be," she said, "I'm fine."

"Really?"

"Sure. I mean, I'm still hurting. Suzy…"

Charlene tailed off, looking out through the kitchen door towards the empty living room.

"… There's just a lot of her spirit still here, in the house."

Wendy shuddered slightly and Charlene caught the movement. A sudden, unexpected laugh burst from her.

"Ha! I make it sound like she died, don't I?"

Wendy nodded.

"Well," Charlene reflected, dropping into mock New Jersey gangster, "maybe she is… *You're dead to me, Suzy!"*

They both laughed for a moment.

"It hurts thought, doesn't it?" Wendy said.

Charlene nodded, latent tears rising fast to choke her.

"Uh-huh."

Wendy sipped quietly at her coffee for a moment.

"When did you last talk to her?"

"It's been a couple of weeks," Charlene answered, "I called her… I'd had a couple of drinks and…"

She stopped, blushing.

"You drunk-dialled her?"

Charlene nodded.

"I got her sister," she said, "Suzy was already in bed but she woke her up. We talked for a while but... She told me not to call her again. That she didn't want to talk to me. That she was done with the rear-view."

"Ouch," Wendy reached out and patted Charlene's arm.

"It... It would be easier if I knew why she'd left, what I'd done, but..."

"Do we ever know?" Wendy asked. "I mean, really?"

Charlene was quiet for a moment, thinking.

"She's really not given you chance for closure, has she?"

Charlene shook her head.

"That's why she's..." Wendy nodded towards the rest of the house.

"Yup."

They were quiet for a moment, looking through the kitchen door.

Suddenly, Wendy sniggered.

"Ooh," she laughed, "that was a real Dr Phil moment, right?"

Charlene chuckled, tears of sadness mixing with those of humour.

"Uh-huh," she said, "pretty much."

Wendy looked towards the ceiling, laughing, trying to get herself under control. She flapped her hands at her face like miniature fans. Eventually, she calmed herself enough to speak.

"How about we change the record?" she said. "How's the investigation going? Got any good leads?"

Charlene looked at her.

"I'm not investigating," she said, familiar words locking into place, "I'm only there to help Sturmann keep things calm."

"You're not investigating?" Wendy reflected.

"Uh-huh."

"You? Are not investigating?"

Charlene nodded.

"Yeah, right," Wendy smiled, "like you could ever not be doing your job."

"But my job here is to..."

"Nope. Don't try that. I know you too well."

Charlene sat, chastened.

"So," Wendy continued, "do you have any leads?"

She stopped, sipped at her coffee. Waited.

Charlene considered for a moment. What leads did she have? Really?

"None," she said, "I haven't come across anything that's made me think twice. Couple of minor incidents, typical stuff really, just…"

She thought of Brina for a moment.

This is high school, she'd said, *and you can't change high school.*

"I think it's all a storm in a tea-cup," she said.

Wendy shook her head.

"Lilly and Dave Ford wouldn't want to hear that," she said.

"Ouch. Cheap shot," Charlene fired back.

Wendy held up her hands from where they rested on the table.

"Sorry," she said, "first thing that came to mind."

"No, it's all right," Charlene shook her head as if shaking off a thought, "I have the same feeling myself. Seeing him… How badly he's been beaten up and then being in the school. It doesn't feel right, somehow. There should be more to the case. But I really think it's just a one-off."

Even though I can't help feeling that I've missed something, she thought.

"Kids get picked on," Charlene repeated Brina's counsel, "kids get treated like shit for being different. Kids get beat up. It's just high school."

Wendy was looking at her. Closely, trying to gain her full attention.

"What?" Charlene asked.

"Are you okay?" Wendy asked. "I mean, *really* okay?"

Charlene was quiet for a moment, trying to ignore the unbidden image of Katie that danced through her thoughts.

"Yeah," she said, "I'm fine. I just… I wish I knew what I was doing there, that's all."

Wendy reached out and patted the back of Charlene's hand.

"You're being you," she said, "and that's enough."

Charlene's eyes brimmed with tears. She rubbed at them angrily.

"Thanks," she said, adding, "Dr Phil."

They laughed hard into the silence of the house.

* * *

"Lilly and Dave Ford wouldn't want to hear that."

Wendy's off-the-cuff remark stayed with her all afternoon.

It had been good to see her friend; the house seeming to lose a little of its foreboding emptiness.

But that statement.

It nagged at her.

She thought back over the previous week, of the changes that had been put in motion when she found Dylan Ford lying in the high school car park. Wendy had hit a raw nerve; Charlene had been focused on the school, sure, but she couldn't deny that more of her attention had been to her own stuff. It was the aftermath of Suzy, the break-up, she knew. And while it was an explanation, it wasn't an excuse.

And still that nagging thought that she was missing something.

Later that afternoon, as she bounced around the house like a pinball trying to come to terms with Wendy's comment and her reflection on the week, she decided she would go to visit Dylan again, hoping that his parents might be there as well.

* * *

Much as it had been on Monday evening, ICU was quiet.

She'd fully expected to have to explain her presence again; as she was not in uniform, she'd even gone so far as to put her badge in her jeans pocket.

As it turned out, she need not have been concerned. In the waiting area, she bumped into the nurse who had been on duty on Monday evening.

"Oh, hi," the nurse said, "here to see him again?"

Charlene nodded.

"Yes," she said, "how's he doing?"

The nurse smiled.

"Good. No major changes but he seems pretty stable."

"Can I go in and see him?"

"Sure," the nurse said, "just for a short while though, okay? He can't have too many people around for too long."

Charlene caught the inference.

"He's got visitors?"

"Uh-huh," the nurse nodded.

My lucky day, Charlene thought, *looks like I'll get to see the Fords after all.*

"Thanks," she said to the nurse, "I'll keep it brief."

And she turned to walk through to Dylan Ford's room.

* * *

Throughout the ward, the lights had been dimmed slightly; natural rhythms recreated in electricity, to assist patients in gaining some sense of the passage of time. She walked through the quiet aural cloud of rhythmic, metronomic machines working in each of the rooms and bays.

The door to Dylan's room was closed and she tapped on it lightly before opening it inward. She stepped into the room, readying herself to say *'hi'* to Lilly and Dave Ford.

Katie turned from where she was sitting.

Charlene's body gave an involuntary jump, electricity thrumming through her hands and feet; breath speeding up, she could felt her pulse fluttering in her throat.

Katie smiled.

"Hi," she said.

Charlene didn't know that she would be able to reply.

"Hi," she said.

"Are you okay?" Katie looked at her.

Charlene nodded.

"Just..." she began, getting herself back under control, "just wasn't expecting anyone to be here."

Katie smiled.

"It is pretty quiet. You know they keep a list of visitors at the nurse's station, right?"

"I didn't."

"On the white-board. Only three visitors at a time, so they keep track."

"Thanks. I'll check it out," Charlene said, voice calming now. "How is he tonight?"

Katie turned to look at Dylan.

"About the same," she sighed, "getting better."

She reached out and stroked the back of Dylan's hand.

"I hope."

Charlene stood for a moment, torn between staying and leaving. With the flickering illumination coming of the machines gathered around Dylan's bed and the hushed ward beyond the door, the moment seemed almost sacred. She should not disturb it.

Katie turned again.

"Please," she gestured, "come in."

"Are you sure? I don't want to dist…"

"It's fine," Katie smiled, "I could use the company. It feels like I've been sitting here alone for days, not hours."

Charlene stepped into the room, letting the door close behind her. Katie's eyes reflected the dim light of the room and the dancing twinkles of the screens ranged around the bed. Charlene was drawn towards the girl; there was no denying it. Sensations from forgotten dreams flirted with her and she was powerless to switch them off.

"It's so quiet," Katie continued, "even when other people are here. Everyone whispering."

"Like they're trying not to wake him up?"

"Yeah, like he's sleeping. When Peanut… his sister… When she comes, it's different, I mean she's only eight or nine and she doesn't really know what's going on, just that Dylan's lying here not moving."

"It must be hard on her."

Katie was quiet for a moment.

"On all of us," she whispered.

"It gets lonely," Charlene said, thinking of Suzy, of her empty, aching house.

"Yeah," Katie said, sadness creasing her face to poignancy for a moment.

Charlene walked towards the bed. The opposite side from where Katie was sitting was busy with machines and support equipment. She was aware of charts and records off to one side, would have read them if she'd had a clue what they meant, anything to distract her from the pull she felt towards Katie. Eventually she chose to stand at the foot of the bed, behind Katie's chair.

"How are his parents?" she asked, desperate to speak on safe territory.

"Good," Katie brightened a little, "given..."

"Sure."

They were silent for a moment.

"It's not fair," Katie sighed as she looked at her boyfriend, the age-old teenager's lament rendered apposite by circumstance, "it's just not fair."

Charlene watched as tears began to well in Katie's eyes.

She reached out and put her hand on Katie's shoulder, feeling her own pulse quicken at the touch.

The younger girl leaned into the contact and Charlene, who realized now how much she'd expected rejection, moved her hand back and forth in comforting sweeps.

"It's okay," she said quietly.

"No," Katie responded immediately, voice hitching, "no, it's not. I sit here and watch him sleeping and I hope he's getting better but I don't know... I don't know! They just keep saying he's stable but he... he... Nothing's changing... He's not getting better and there's... there's nothing I can do. There's nothing I can do!"

Charlene squeezed Katie's shoulder, eyes pricking with tears.

"You need a break," she said, all too aware that she must control the attraction until it diminished, "why don't we go grab a coffee?"

Katie looked at Charlene, then turned to look back at Dylan.

"Okay," she nodded, reaching out to his hand once again, "I'll be back soon."

She was still for a moment, touching the back of his hand between wires, clips and needles, waiting for something, some response. Her shoulders slumped slightly as it became clear that tonight, like the days and nights that had gone before, Dylan wasn't home.

Charlene became aware that her hand was still on Katie's shoulder and she let it drop to her side, stepping backwards, away from the bed.

Katie stood, grabbed her purse and turned, wiping at the tears in her eyes.

"There's a coffee shop down near the ER," she said.

"Yeah," Charlene nodded, turning for the door, "I passed it on the way in."

She didn't add that she'd been to the ER many times while on duty, accompanying casualties and victims.

Opening the door, she looked back over her shoulder at Katie who stood, framed in halo by the light from the machines; skin tanned, hip cocked innocently to one side.

She has no idea how beautiful she is, Charlene thought, *she really doesn't.*

She swallowed down the tension that was rising in her throat; though the attraction was natural and unbidden, she was all too aware that it would be just plain wrong for her to act upon it.

Katie's eyebrows raised in a question.

"What?" she said.

"Oh nothing," Charlene shook her head, clearing her thoughts, "when we get down there, I'm buying, no arguments."

"Sure," Katie smiled, "I can let you do that."

* * *

For a Sunday night, the coffee shop was surprisingly busy.

"Twenty-four-seven, three-sixty-five operation," Charlene said to herself.

"Huh?" Katie asked from where she was bending to look at the pastries.

"Oh, nothing," Charlene replied, "just that it's busy in here, that's all."

Katie glanced over her shoulder at the tables and chairs.

"Sure," she said and went back to deciding what she wanted.

It's a good thing, Charlene thought, watching Katie, knowing that it was better to be in a crowded public place than alone together.

"Can I help you, ma'am?" the guy behind the counter asked.

"Sure," Charlene said, "I'll take a small coffee with room, and one of the cinnamon rolls… Katie?"

"Huh?"

Katie looked up, saw that Charlene was waiting for her choice.

"Oh, sorry," she said, "I was miles away. I'll take a small mocha and a slice of the banana-nut loaf. Thanks."

Charlene paid and they stood to one side waiting on their drinks.

"You know," Charlene said, "I kind of like hanging out in hospitals."

Katie raised her eyebrows.

"Seriously?"

Charlene realized what she'd just said.

"No! I didn't mean visiting someone," she laughed, "I wouldn't wish that on anyone! It's… there's just such an energy here. Everyone is moving through, going from here to there. I could sit and watch the whole world pass right in front of me. I know it's a little weird but I tend to think of hospitals as a healthy place; people don't… They don't pretend here."

Katie nodded, though it was clear she wasn't following Charlene.

"Small mocha!" the barista announced.

Katie reached out to take it.

"That's mine, thanks."

They walked to a free table which gave them a view of the coffee shop and, beyond that, the ER waiting area. Charlene, through force of habit, sat so that she could watch it all over Katie's shoulders.

Neither of them said anything for a few moments. They sipped at their drinks, nibbled at pastries.

"You must think I'm mad," Charlene said eventually, laughing at herself.

"Why?" Katie smiled.

"Well… Going on about the hospital like that, and all."

Katie shook her head.

"Not really. I just didn't get what you were talking about. Try me again."

Charlene smiled, sipped at her too-hot coffee.

"It's like," she began and then nodded at a couple sitting a couple of tables over, "look over there, but don't make it obvious or anything."

Katie did so.

"See the guy in the red t-shirt? About fifty or so?"

Katie nodded.

"Look at how they're sitting together," Charlene continued, "see how they're so relaxed with each other. I don't know who they're visiting, what's happened, and I definitely don't know them outside of the hospital; for all I know, they may be on the brink of a bitter divorce. But right now, here and now, they're just being themselves. They're just content being together."

"Does that make sense?"

Katie watched the couple for a moment.

"Yeah," she said finally, "I get it now."

She took a moment to scan the whole coffee shop, her gaze lingering at each table for a moment before moving on.

"You see it, right?" Charlene asked.

Katie nodded, finally bringing her attention back to their own discussion.

"That's amazing!" she said. "That you noticed! I hadn't ever… I never would have thought about that."

Charlene felt herself blushing at Katie's open admiration. She shrugged.

"Goes with the territory when you do what I do for a living."

"Still though…" Katie protested.

"You know, I've always…" Charlene began, all of a sudden feeling an unexpected vulnerability, "I've always been like this. Watching people, watching what's happening with them, how they are with each other."

"Always?" Katie asked.

Charlene nodded.

"As far as I can remember," she said, "I'd sit and watch people when I was a kid."

"You must have loved high school, then?" Katie joked.

"That's… er… not the word I'd use to describe it."

"Really?"

Charlene sipped at her coffee. She could feel the risk of being so open, but was unable to stop; maybe she'd spent just too long with an empty house.

"Really. I was… different, I guess. Always felt like I was…"

Katie nodded encouragement over the rim of her coffee cup.

"… on the outside looking in," Charlene finished.

"Aren't we all?" Katie asked, smiling.

No, Charlene thought, struck again by the teenager's unpretentious beauty, and deflated by her naïveté, *no we're not.*

"Maybe," she said.

Katie put her cup down, placed her hands on the table and sat up straight in her chair, making direct eye contact with Charlene.

"So," she said, "what do you see when you look at me?"

The question rocked Charlene and she could feel the blush returning to her cheeks.

Aphrodite, she thought immediately, *a beautiful, beautiful Aphropdite.*

"I..." she tried to speak but words seemed to have deserted her, "I..."

Across the vestibule, the entrance doors to the ER slid open.

"Help me!" a woman's voice screamed, *"Oh, please! Help me!"*

Every head in the area turned to look towards the entrance; Charlene was already on her feet, running towards the screaming woman.

As she arrived, she saw that the woman was supporting a teenager, his arm draped around her shoulder, the other hanging at his side; there was something wrong with how that arm moved, something *very* wrong.

The woman almost collapsed under the weight of the teen but a guy in a Red Sox t-shirt who had been standing near the door got there in time. He grabbed the kid's other arm instinctively to brace against the fall.

The kid howled, his head raising towards the ceiling.

As she saw his face, Charlene had a moment of pure clarity.

It's not a game any more, she thought, *he's number two.*

It was the kid, the dork, though his face was already puffing around his eyes, she recognized him even at distance. He wasn't wearing his glasses, and she suspected the cuts around his eyes might have come from their shattered edges. He was missing a couple of teeth.

Charlene drew close.

"What happened?" she asked.

The woman who had brought the kid in looked at her.

"It's pretty fucking obvious, isn't it?"

Charlene was taken aback with the venom in the woman's voice. She breathed for a count of five.

Adrenalin, she thought, *pure adrenalin.*

She looked the woman in the eye, nodding slightly. Reached into her pocket and pulled her badge.

"Officer Charlene Goodlow, ma'am," she said, "please accept my apologies."

"Oh..."

Charlene nodded at the boy.

"Can he walk?"

"Just... I think."

"Sir?" she looked at the guy in the Red Sox shirt. "Are you able to support him?"

"Yeah, I've got him."

"Okay. I'm going to get a nurse. Stay here."

She turned to head back into the ER. Katie was waiting just inside the doors. She looked at Charlene, eyes filled with panic.

"It's another one, isn't it?" she asked. "Isn't it?"

Charlene didn't stop walking.

"I don't know, Katie," she said, "it could be."

"But..."

"I can't stop... Go home. I'll see you at school tomorrow."

Katie watched Charlene walk deeper into the ER.

"Another one," she sighed as tears began to well in her eyes.

Monday

Chapter 23:
For All To See

That night, long after Katie had left, long after the parents of the boy, Bobby Kingston, had refused to let them press for his attacker's identity, long after the fog of caffeinated exhaustion had all but erased effectiveness, Baker sent Charlene home.

She slept but didn't rest; mind churning over the snippets of clues that she either did or didn't have, imagined or real. And, a gilded thread woven deep in this confusing tapestry, her raw attraction to Katie, the conflict that this recognition brought to her.

Charlene woke a moment or two before her alarm, head as heavy as it would have been had she drank the night away.

It was Monday and she was beginning her second week in the school.

* * *

Baker couldn't shake the conversation he'd had with the Kingston's the previous night. Their son had lay there on a gurney, floating on pain-killers, in the room but high above the ceiling, plaster drying around stabilizing rods that pinned his fractured arm straight. Baker had been struck by how the bruises on his face and neck had seemed to develop even as he stood there; like a photograph in a dim darkroom.

Another mute witness; one whose parents would ensure he remained that way.

She had nodded at her husband.

"This is so very, very wrong, Chief Baker," he'd said, "but it's happened for a reason. Someone decided to beat my son just like they did Dylan Ford and they had a reason. I will not… let you make it worse by forcing him to turn informant."

There was anger in his eyes. Understandable, Baker knew, yet horribly misdirected.

"I know how you feel but…"

The anger flared.

"*No!* You have *no* idea how I'm… how *we're* feeling! Our son has been beaten up, his arm broken for Christ's sake and all you can do is stand there and ask whether you can question him? He's not your witness, Baker…"

Baker was about to respond when Kingston spat out his final, damning sentences.

"Besides… I thought you had an officer in the school? This wasn't meant to happen again! This is your fault, Baker. *Why didn't you protect him?"*

Mrs Kingston had been crying openly, making no attempt to wipe away tears that coursed down her cheeks.

Driving down his street now, on his way to the office, Baker heard those words again, and again, and again. Over and over in his head; some small part of the accusation resonating with his own self-criticism.

Was I too focused on Mason and his games? he thought, *was I?*

And, despite all his logical analysis, which continued to refute Kingston's claims, he couldn't shake his ill-founded guilt; it's endless questions.

Was he too late putting Charlene in?

Was he wrong to keep the investigation himself?

Was she the right person for the job?

Should he have done it himself?

Would he have noticed something that Charlene had missed?

And on. Question upon question which could never be answered with absolute confidence.

Though his rational conscience was clear, his emotional centre was rioting. And wasn't that what he was reacting to after all? Wasn't he just agreeing with Kingston that something very, very wrong had happened, been allowed to happen, on his watch? Wasn't that it when it was trimmed to a nutshell?

He turned out of his street and headed downtown into what he already knew would be a testing, bitter day.

* * *

At first, he sensed it, more than saw it.

As he turned onto Main Street and headed down the hill into downtown, he had the uneasy sense that something was wrong, but couldn't name it. He scanned front yards, vehicles in driveways, slowing his speed to a little above a crawl. He watched for animals about to cross the road, kids playing behind parked cars, readying to chase an errant ball into the oncoming traffic.

But he could see no obvious trigger for his uneasy feeling.

Movement on the far side of the street caught his attention and he looked in that direction. But it was just Myra Bentley who, ahead of her shift at the Post Office, was jogging up the hill out of downtown, all Lycra and Apple headphones. As she neared him and spotted the cruiser, she gave a wave, which he returned with a smile.

He turned to look back through his windshield and found his answer.

There on the side of the Trinity Building on Main Street, where it rose a single storey higher than the building next to it. In letters at least five feet tall, yellow paint on red-brick background, visible even from here, at least a half-mile away:

WEEZ A GANG BEEYATCH!!!

Baker forced his attention back to the road long enough to pull over. When the cruiser was stationary, he sat, staring at the graffiti. After a few moments, he realized he was still gripping the wheel, his knuckles white with the pressure he was applying.

"Shit," he breathed out as he released his hands.

He stepped out of the car and walked around to the front, sitting back on the hood, folding his arms in a gesture that mixed anger and defensiveness at the same time.

All he could think of was Mason; the *I-told-you-so* that was sure to come his way when all he wanted to do was send one in the opposite direction.

"Shit."

* * *

Charlene was pulling out of her driveway when her cell-phone chimed. She thumbed it into hands-free mode, picking up the call.

"Hello?"

"Charlene?"

Baker's voice.

"Hi, chief," she said, "happy Monday."

"I wish."

She glanced at the handset for a moment as if that would make her able to read the expression on his face.

"What's happened?" she asked.

Baker sighed so loudly that she was able to hear it over the sound of the engine and the noise of traffic beyond that.

"Tell me."

"It's escalating," Baker said, "just like I... Our graffiti artist is back in business."

"Downtown?"

"Uh-huh," Baker was calming a little now, "on the side of the Trinity Building. I could see it from my neighbourhood."

"Shit."

"That's what I said. This isn't just some teenager goofing off, Charlene. This is... Serious."

"Think it's connected to the attacks?"

Even to her ears that sounded as naïve as it was.

"Forget I asked that," she smiled, "do you want me to start digging?"

Baker was quiet for a moment and she could visualize him clearly, eyes looking upward, brows raised, breathing out a stream of air towards his nose; all consideration and weighing options.

"No," he said finally, "keep your eyes open but... We can't make this worse, Charlene, we just can't and... If you're in there asking questions it'll just stir up the nest even more. I'll do the digging. As far as you're concerned, the graffiti didn't happen and, if it did, you don't know anything about it being connected to the attacks."

"Poker face?" she asked, not particularly liking what she was hearing.

"Nah," Baker said, "you don't need to go that far, don't stonewall anyone. Just keep an open mind, discuss it with people if they want to talk about it… Who knows, we might get lucky and one of them might give us a lead without thinking about it."

"Okay. Want me to call in later?"

"Sure," Baker said, sounding like he was back in some semblance of control again, "though make it after lunch, I get the feeling I'm going to be getting this paint removed all morning."

"If only it was that easy, right chief?" Charlene laughed.

"You got that right."

"Okay. I'm nearly at the school now. Speak to you later."

"Sure," Baker signed off, "later."

The line beeped off.

Charlene fought against the urge to turn the car around and head back to Main Street to take a look at the Trinity Building.

Don't make it worse, she thought, deciding to take that caution as watch-words for the day.

Don't make it worse.

Chapter 24:
When Watching Isn't Enough

She sat and watched them for a while; watched them tumbling out of buses and cars, all teenage energy and hormonal propulsion. These back-pack toting cliques, clustering like reproductive cells, moving through the living, breathing organism that was high school.

She sat and watched.

* * *

She watched jostling, bustling throngs moving in their flow, bestowing attention on some, withholding it from others. Chatting, laughing, feigning shock and surprise at some joke or gossip fragment.

This social dynamic moving to its own rhythms and means, propelled by connections that, for any adult, might as well have been extra-terrestrial in origin.

* * *

She watched Brina walk onto campus, solitary and singular, untouched by the masses; seeking no contact. Seemingly spot-lit in different tones, a colder hue than the early morning sunshine. Different, disconnected.

Brina disappeared into the buildings, leaving the buzzing clusters behind.

* * *

She watched Katie.

Her ease. Her magnetic presence.

How eyes flicked to watch her, heads turned; even if the awareness was only subliminal.

Her beautiful face troubled by the attacks; clouded even on this sunny day.

Too youthful to be creased by worry; these scars would heal.

Her smile emerging through her anxiety briefly to land like a beatification.

Oh, to be touched by such beauty.

* * *

She watched Walt Sturmann standing at his office window, watching in turn as his students arrived.

Here was a face that was old enough to wear its concern unvarnished.

Here was a man out of control; the centre, unable to hold.

He held a piece of paper, every few seconds passing it from one hand to the other.

The paper went unread as he watched the students arrive.

* * *

She watched the Asian kid, Jason Liu, make a beeline for Katie, all bravado and confidence, smiling as he stepped up to her.

Something in the movement of his hips.

Something in the way Katie flinched backwards when he spoke; a tiny movement that maybe only Charlene saw.

Something…

* * *

She watched buildings swallow the students until the car park was just another collection of quieting metal, engines pinking as they cooled a little in the morning sunshine.

She watched buses disappear to their next round of pick-ups; for middle school, and from there onward to elementary-level kids.

This carousel of the everyday.

* * *

She watched Sturmann turn from his window with a hefty sigh, finally giving attention to the paper in his hand.

* * *

"There isn't much to go on," Charlene said, "Bobby's parents refuse to let us interview him."

"Really?" Sturmann looked pained.

"Yup. Say they're concerned that he'll get beaten even worse if he talks about it."

Sturmann sat, thinking this over; mouth down-turned, the creases across his forehead seemed set rigid.

"That serious?" he mused.

Charlene nodded.

"Do you think..."

Sturmann didn't finish the sentence; Charlene let him have the space.

"Christ!" he sighed. "If they won't even speak up about... About... What hope have I got?"

Charlene saw the brief expression of despair that fluttered across Sturmann's face as he said this. She wished she had something to offer to balance it out, all the time sensing that nothing she could do or say could ever be enough, that what the man was feeling was far, far beyond the beatings of two teenage boys.

The quiet sound of her breathing caught Sturmann's attention and his game face returned almost as quickly as it had dissolved a moment earlier.

Burying it, Charlene thought, *swallowing it down.*

She thought of her empty house, of driving night-time streets just to avoid the return; paintings and trinkets and knick-knacks attached to painful memories, quiet spaces aching to be filled. She thought of Katie's radiant smile, her ease, a single tear rolling down the curve of her breast.

"Are we done?" she asked, needing to be out of his office.

* * *

She sat at her desk. She checked her emails. She walked the halls. The day passed much like those of the previous week.

Around mid-morning, she realized she was looking forward to lunch.

Her guilty shame at the reason was already beginning to fade.

She wouldn't act upon the attraction.

She'd do no wrong.

She wouldn't make it worse.

* * *

The cafeteria was packed; movement and the hubbub of a hundred different conversations. Cell-phone jingles and over-loud giggling. The organism breathing.

Charlene lifted her tray from the rail by the register and headed towards the seating area. She'd timed her arrival, so wasn't surprised to see Katie sitting alone, yet to attract table-mates. She headed over.

Katie saw her approaching and broke into a broad, welcoming smile.

"Anyone sitting here?" Charlene asked, nodding at the chair.

"Be my guest."

"I'd love to," Charlene said.

Katie looked at her for a moment, her smile faltering just a little before returning.

Charlene sat down.

"Healthy," Katie said, nodding at Charlene's salad.

"Yup," Charlene laughed, "gotta watch what ends up on my hips."

Katie laughed, her previous unease now evaporated.

"I wouldn't know!"

"No. Count yourself lucky, but it'll get you eventually."

"Death and taxes."

"Huh?"

"Death and taxes," Katie smiled, "my dad says it all the time. The only thing we can count on: death and taxes."

Charlene nodded.

"That would be a man's point of view," she added, "for we goddesses, I would add the increasing effect of gravity on our most gorgeous bits, the endless battle against cellulite, and the struggle to keep our skin from turning into burlap."

They both laughed at this.

Charlene opened the sachet of balsamic dressing and dressed her salad.

Katie watched her.

"Do you cook?" she asked.

"I used to, when..." Charlene began, and then caught herself, "I like to when I get the chance."

"That looks really good," Katie nodded at the salad, which Charlene was still stirring and tossing, "maybe you should try eating some of it."

Charlene gave a little jump, like she'd only just noticed there was a salad in front of her.

"Sure," she said and forked a mouthful of greens to her mouth.

"Any news on Bobby?" Katie asked, "any leads?"

Charlene shook her head, indicating that she had something to say once she'd finished the mouthful. Katie sat and waited, watching her chew, smiling wider as each moment passed. As always it took longer to finish than Charlene had hoped and she found Katie's gaze uncomfortable, choosing to look around the room to avoid direct eye contact. When she looked back, Katie was still smiling at her, clearly amused.

Beautiful, Charlene thought, unable to suppress her reactions.

She swallowed the salad.

"I'm not investigating," she said. "I shouldn't really tell you, but I think it's important you know. I'm not investigating."

"Oh, I thought..."

Out of the corner of her eye, Charlene could see the registers. She looked that way now. Jason Liu was paying for his lunch.

"What do you know about that kid?" she nodded in the direction of the registers.

Katie turned to look.

"I thought you weren't investigating?" she said, gaze lingering on Liu for a moment, before turning back to face Charlene.

"I'm not," Charlene shook her head, "I've just... He's..."
Katie's smile had dropped.
"He's what?"
Charlene felt her face flushing, her heart beginning to race. This was jealousy, plain and simple; she didn't like the fact that he'd been making plays for Katie.
"There's something about him," she said, "I don't... I don't trust him. I've seen him hanging around you and... Well..."
Katie was staring at her now, registering the strength of feeling in Charlene's voice.
"He..." she began but bit down on the words.
Without thinking, Charlene reached out and put her hand on the back of Katie's hand, looking her in the eye and nodding.
"He what?"
After a moment's silence, Katie slowly withdrew her hand. She glanced back across the cafeteria and watched Liu walking to join his friends on the far side of the room.
"He... He attacked Dylan and Bobby," Katie said, still watching him as she spoke.
Charlene was shocked to silence and, in turn, stared at Liu across the room.
"I thought..." she began.
"He did it," Katie repeated.
She turned to look at Charlene.
"I just know he did."
"You..." Charlene stared at Katie for a long time. "Do you have proof?"
"I thought you weren't investigating?"
"I'm not. I told you. It's just..."
"I thought I could trust you!"
"You can," Charlene nodded, "always! It's just... you sounded so certain but is it a gut feeling rather than anything specific?"
Katie looked at her.
"Without any proof," Charlene continued, "there's nothing anyone can do, you know that."
"I guess, but..."
"What?"

"Well," Katie hesitated, "you said it yourself. He's been coming onto me pretty hard for a while now, even... even before Dylan was... and this last week he's been doing it more. There's something about it that's just..."

She shuddered.

"Without any proof, I can't..."

Katie slammed her hands on the table, her frustration drawing looks from the tables nearby. She got her breathing under control and the other kids went back to their conversations, doubtless now revolving around Katie and Charlene.

"I know you can't do anything," Katie said through clenched teeth, "I didn't ask you to do anything, did I?"

Charlene shook her head.

Tears were beginning to brim in Katie's eyes; frustration, pain and fear all mixed together in the way her lips tightened.

Charlene felt emptiness in the pit of her stomach.

Once again, her hand travelled with a will of it's own, touching the back of Katie's hand, now rigid with blocked emotion.

"I wish I could make it better," Charlene whispered.

Her hand began to stroke Katie's skin.

"I'd do anything to make it all go away."

The tension in Katie's hand began to ease a little.

"I'm just trying to help," Charlene said quietly, "I care about you and..."

Katie pulled her hand away as if snake-bitten. Her face pursed like she'd bitten into a rotted lemon.

"Ugh!" she exclaimed. "Are you coming onto me?"

The disbelief and disgust was clear in her voice.

"You are, aren't you?"

Charlene felt the bottom drop out of her stomach, panic racing throughout her whole body.

"I didn't..."

"Ugh!"

Katie stood and stepped away from the table, watching Charlene all the time.

"Katie..."

The teenager shook her head.

"No! No, no, no."

"Katie!"

"Don't talk to me again. Understand? Don't ever!"

Charlene watched as Katie turned on her heel and stormed away. She watched her walk all the way across the cafeteria and out through the exit doors. She watched even though Katie had left.

Slowly, she became aware of eyes upon her and glanced around the room. No-one had been close enough to hear the conversation, she was sure, or maybe that was just hope speaking, but she was sure they'd seen the fight. As she looked at them, they returned to their conversations, shame-faced.

All except Jason Liu, who sat watching her from the far side of the room, drinking in the detail of the aftermath.

But Charlene didn't notice him looking in her direction; she was thinking through all the potential implications of what had just happened.

And she was back to watching.

Watching the space where Katie had been.

Chapter 25
We All Have Burdens

She was still shaking when she got back to her office. Closing the door, leaning back on it as soon as it latched shut, she exhaled a noisy stream of air towards the ceiling; the tears were coming. She felt for the door handle but then remembered that it had no lock.

A lump rose in her throat and she was crying; hot, angry, frustrated, embarrassed.

Stupid, she thought, *stupid, stupid, stupid!*

The walls of the office loomed down upon her, making her feel smaller than an ant.

Deeply shamed, Charlene cried alone.

* * *

She was still there five minutes later when she heard a knock at the door, though her tears had long since dried.

Her errant heart gave a little bump.

It's Katie, foolish hope spoke in the back of her mind.

"Who is it?" she asked through the door.

"Sturmann," a voice said.

She let go a breath she hadn't realized she was holding; deflated.

"Just a second."

She opened the lowest drawer of the filing cabinet, grabbed a mirror from her purse, scanned the black bags beneath her bloodshot eyes; relieved that what little mascara she wore was waterproof and had not smeared.

She became aware of the time she was taking, feeling how Sturmann's suspicions might be growing as he stood in the hall.

What did he want, anyway?

She pulled her cell-phone and put it to her ear, even though it was silent.

"Uh-huh," she said, "I think so. Hang on a minute?"

She reached and opened the door. Sturmann was leaning on the wall opposite. She lifted one finger towards him: *wait*.

"Yes... Yes..." she feigned, "a little later on. No, everything's quiet here. I'll call in before I leave."

She ended her imaginary call, thumbing the *off* button and holstering the phone.

Sturmann smiled briefly, a nervous grin that sat uncomfortably on his face.

"Baker?" he asked.

Charlene smiled at him giving neither positive or negative.

"What's up, Walt?" she asked and her question caught him off guard for a moment.

"Oh..."

Sensing his unease, Charlene moved to defuse the situation.

"Still having a happy Monday?" she smiled.

Sturmann's shoulders slumped a little, more resignation than relaxation.

"Yes, a happy Monday," he repeated the familiarity, "week two has indeed opened its arms in wide embrace."

She looked at him. It was almost like they hadn't spoken earlier that morning.

"Has something else happened?" Charlene asked, more to herself than the principal.

"Yes," he frowned, "more graffiti. Several of my staff stopped by to tell me. I don't come in down Main Street, so hadn't seen it myself."

"Oh, that," she said, realizing that she hadn't even mentioned it to him that morning, "the chief will have had it cleaned off by now."

"Yes," Sturmann paused, "but it... With Bobby as well, it doesn't suggest things are calming down."

Charlene thought about her argument with Katie.

"Really?" she feigned. "Things here seem pretty calm to me?"

"I'm glad you think so, I really am. But I know these kids. They're full of anxiety..."

There was a yelp of excitement from further up the hall as a group of girls rounded the corner. Sturmann actually jumped a little and, once again, Charlene saw how quickly he set his game face to *everything-is-under-control.*

The girls nodded greeting at them.

"Hi," Sturmann said, "how are your days going? Good?"

After a round of responses, the bustling group moved passed, pleased to no longer be stuck with the school principal and his captive police officer.

"Full of anxiety, all right," Charlene smiled, once again trying to defuse Sturmann's prevailing tension.

He stared her directly in the eye.

"It's time we talked, Officer Goodlow."

"Charlene, please."

"Charlene," Sturmann said, "it's time we talked."

A note of desperation in his voice.

"My office," he commanded, "now."

And, just for a moment, Charlene felt long-buried guilt twist her stomach, the fear of getting caught, the fear of being different, the fear of being called out.

The fear of being summoned to the principal's office.

And, just as her teenage self would never have had a choice but to respond to the summons, she had none now.

Charlene followed Sturmann towards the administrative offices, blushing furiously; a march of shame becoming intricately woven with her catastrophic conversation with Katie.

* * *

With the door closed he relaxed, if only fractionally.

It was as if the wooden barrier were shielding him from projectiles rather than teenagers; as if he'd up-ended a bar-room table in a wild west movie, dodging from behind it to fire at the bad guys.

The weight of his position sat heavy on his shoulders, especially here in what was supposedly his territory. He was dragged down by much more than gravity, pulled into a hunched position, his chin out and over his chest, his bottom lip pouting outwards. Clearly, he was being brought close to tears by this tension, by the expectations placed upon him.

Is it just his position? Charlene wondered, *is that really all it is?*

She watched him, relieved to have even momentary distraction from thinking about Katie.

Though his office should have represented some small semblance of refuge, a place where he might talk openly, he had fallen silent. A couple of times, he drew breath as if to speak only to exhale slowly, as if he were desperate not to crack, to keep whatever he was thinking behind a veil.

His hesitance raised Charlene's own tension, still simmering from the altercation with Katie.

Did she really need this? Really?

"I…" Sturmann finally spoke, "I wonder if…"

He shook his head.

"You look stressed, Charlene," he finally finished, "how are things going?"

His deflection towards her caught her by surprise and her thoughts surged forward.

What, she thought, *now that I've expressed my desire for a teenage girl whose boyfriend was the first victim of a multiple attacker? Now that I've broken the trust placed in me by my boss and the people of the town? Now that I'm not so sure I'm not going insane? How are things going now?*

"Fine," she said, "although it's… more stressful than I expected."

Sturmann looked at her long and hard.

"Understatement," he said, nodding; eyes searching.

She stared back at him, daring him to push her. She was angry suddenly, resentful of this intrusion. And, if truth be told, all too aware she was feeling ages-old insecurity; her teenage self screaming, *just leave me alone!*

I never thought I'd feel this again, she thought, cringing a little at the shrinking sensation that threatened to overwhelm her.

Sturmann blew air towards the ceiling.

"They want to privatise," he said quietly, almost as if to himself, "want to take us to Charter status."

"Huh?" Once again, Charlene was caught off guard by his sudden change of subject and tack.

"The town council," he said by way of explanation, "well... Mason really... And... Well, Jansen pretty much lives in Mason's pocket, so there's no resistance from that direction."

"Privatise?"

Sturmann looked at her, his face setting with frustrated anger. His upper lip curled slightly.

"If you hadn't noticed, this town is ridiculously debt-ridden. Going to the dogs."

"Wait," she interrupted, "calm do..."

"And there's a certain breed of public figure that just love to use any moment of disarray to line their own pockets. Bring the corporations in."

Charlene hardly heard what he was saying, the emotion on his face was so strong. It was like a red cloud between them; a fog that obscured reasonable discourse.

"... they want to privatise all the schools, take them out of public funding and, more importantly, out of public control. It's an age-old trick, screw the people over while they're looking in a different direction!"

"Really?" she breathed, hoping to at least defuse his anger.

"Are you really that naïve, Officer Goo... Charlene?"

She shook her head, fought to calm her voice.

"No, not really, I mean I see this sort of thing on the news, at the federal and state level but here, in the town?"

Sturmann nodded.

"In my experience," he said, an icy sarcasm in his voice, "politicians are all the same. Out for number one. They'll do anything to get what they want."

Do anything, Charlene thought, head swimming, fighting to be in the moment with Sturmann while still reeling from lunch and the argument with Katie. Her legs were beginning to go a little numb and she felt like she might pass out or puke or do both. She looked over her shoulder, saw Sturmann's desk and moved backwards until she was able to sit back upon it.

"And Mason," Sturmann continued, "Mason's been studying the greats. He's wired for this. He's a dictator. He's Fidel Castro, Hugo Chavez, Gadafi. As far as he's concerned, this town belongs to him and he'll make it just what he wants it to be. And what's the first thing we know about dictators?"

He looked at her, the question in his eyebrows.

Charlene shook her head, reeling.

Sturmann broke eye contact with her, scanned the wall of his office, where his certificates lined up next to year-upon-year of graduating class pictures.

"They dumb-down their population!" Sturmann exploded. "They privatize the schools to control the teachers! That's what he's doing, Charlene! That what he's doing!"

"But… I…"

Her pulse hammered with adrenalin, lights going off in her eyes.

"What? You haven't read about this in *The Daybreaker*?" he smiled sardonically. "Well, that's the second thing we know about dictators: they control the media. And, if you hadn't noticed, Curtis Simpson jumps to Mason's tune."

She thought about Baker's reaction to *The Daybreaker*, his exasperation with the tone and content; a reaction that went back a long time before the attacks on Dylan Ford.

Sturmann blew a jet of air towards the ceiling.

"And this is where you end up," he spoke through gritted teeth, "with police on campus, teachers who turn a blind eye, students beaten as an example, and…"

"Wait," Charlene interrupted, "are you saying that…"

Sturmann stopped, caught himself.

"No," he said, looking at her, "I'm not saying that Dylan and Bobby were beaten as an example to the other kids. I'm not *that* paranoid, Charlene. Those kids weren't attacked as part of some grand plan cooked up by Mason and Jansen. There's no conspiracy, they're not evil, just incredibly manipulative and greedy."

She sat quietly; her challenge had seemed to ease things slightly and Sturmann was beginning to calm down.

"But I tell you what they will do. They'll use any and all of this to reinforce the need to make change in the school system; to privatize. And every one will turn a blind eye."

That's the second time he's used that phrase, Charlene thought.

"You think people know what Mason is doing?" she asked.

Sturmann laughed out loud.

"Of course they do," he said, "he hides things in full sight! It doesn't matter whether they agree with it or not, they see it happening and do nothing. Look how quickly they agreed to put you here, which is what he's wanted since before Bill Tanner was even put in position."

She thought of the former security guard, he was a lovable guy, pleasant to spend time with, polite; had he really been just part of some grand plan?

"But you said the teachers were..."

"Look," Sturmann cut across her, "the teachers see what's going on here, they see the powder keg, they know it's going to explode, and they can't help but notice Mason's intent, he's been a fixture here for the past couple of years, *'just dropping by'* as he says."

Charlene thought back to that first morning, when she'd been introduced to the school assembly. How Mason had stepped in at the back to watch, almost like he'd been invited. How not one head had turned in surprise to see him there. She saw him now, standing at the back of the hall, surveying.

"Have you tried to talk with them?" she asked.

"I gave that up a long time ago. I'm used to not being listened to. I'm a lone voice and they're able to mobilize the whole town against me. I tried but I'm done."

She saw him then, all of him, this defeated, exhausted man, hunched by the door to his office as if skulking out a side exit.

"The teachers here," Sturmann continued, "they know what's coming and, believe me, they're looking out for number one. It's understandable; none of them wants to be the one who ends up on the chopping block."

"That pleasure is reserved for me, and me only."

Chapter 26:
Just Someone To Listen

The cloud stayed over Charlene all afternoon; the mess of her conversation with Katie, augmented by Sturmann's talk of political doom. It was all heavy on her shoulders as she sat doing nothing in her small, cramped office.

When the claustrophobia got too much, she decided to walk the halls. To be moving would at least provide distraction. As she stepped out of her office, she was momentarily disoriented by the noise, the shouts and rumble of teenagers *en masse*.

What's happened now? Charlene thought, certain that this was the next instalment of the campaign which had begun with Dylan Ford's beating. *Only it didn't, did it?* A little voice. *It began with the graffiti, back when Bill Tanner was still here*.

She ran towards the noise, keen to head off the conflagration. This was what she'd been placed here to do: *keep things calm*. All the pent up frustration and energy rushed through her, adrenalin frying her nerves.

She was sprinting by the time she neared administration, its roaring noise.

As she rounded the corner into the open area, it felt like everything stopped moving. She scanned quickly, gaze darting here and there, looking for something, anything. Things slowed down, time drifted.

And everyone turned to look at her.

Everyone fell silent.

It was dismissal. The kids were just heading out to the car park and bus pick-ups.

Charlene stood, breathing heavy, blushing as the masses stared at her.

She realized her hand was at her belt, where her gun would normally have been. She forced her arm to relax and drop by her side. Pulling herself upright. Breathing.

And caught the gaze of Jason Liu who was standing near the exit.

His grin would have befitted the Cheshire Cat.

She turned away hurriedly.

Only to find herself face-to-face with Katie, walking alongside a couple of other girls.

They each recoiled a little.

Katie's eyes widened with surprise and she stopped walking.

"You…" she breathed out.

Charlene couldn't speak.

The other girls took a couple of steps before they realized that Katie wasn't with them. One of them turned back.

"Katie?"

"Uh-huh?"

"Are you…" the girl paused, sensing the charge between her friend and the uniformed police officer, "are you coming?"

There was a moment of quiet, which soon filled with the returning rumble of other students.

Please don't go, Charlene thought, desperately keen to talk with Katie, *please?*

Katie seemed to sense the plea.

"Sure," she said, "I'll be there in a minute. Wait for me outside?"

"Okay," the girls said and continued on, leaving Katie and Charlene still amid the migrating throngs.

* * *

"Can we talk?" Charlene said eventually, the words like dust in her mouth.

Katie didn't reply, her only response a continued, steady stare; eyebrows cinched down, there was anger here.

"Please?"

"I don't..."
"Please!"
Katie stopped to think. Finally, she nodded.
"Okay."

* * *

They made their way back to the cafeteria which was largely empty, save for a few of kids sitting and chatting in small clusters.
Charlene waited for Katie to choose somewhere to sit, letting her take ownership of this conversation.
"Here?" Katie asked, looking back over her shoulder as she indicated the table.
And even through the worry about the situation, even through the near panic that was only slightly easing from her system, Charlene had a crystalline moment in which a single thought spoke.
Beautiful.
"Sure," she said, "if it's good for you?"
They sat and were quiet for a little while, each assessing who would be the first to talk, the potential damage loaded into any words.
The silence was broken by Katie's cell-phone, which she retrieved from her purse.
"Hello?"
She looked at Charlene, rolled her eyes.
"Sure... Uh-huh... Yeah, fine. I'm gonna be a while... Sure... Call you later, okay?"
She nodded and ended the call, dropping the phone in her bag without looking.
"Was I right?" she asked, flint in her voice, "were you coming onto me?"
Charlene flinched slightly at the sharpness of the question. She shook her head.
"No... I... No..."
"You were, weren't you?"
Charlene breathed deeply once, let the air out towards the ceiling.
"I'm sorry," she sighed.

A triumphant expression ghosted briefly across Katie's face, gone almost as soon as it had appeared but long enough for Charlene to catch it.

"What?" she said, feeling her own anger rising, she didn't like how ashamed she felt.

"What?" Katie shrugged.

"That look on your face," Charlene continued, "like you just got the cream."

Katie shook her head.

"I don't… I'm sorry, it's just…"

"What?"

"I've never… Never met a lesbian before…"

Her voice trailed off into almost childlike wonder.

They were quiet for a moment, Katie staring at Charlene with fear of an explosion.

Suddenly, unable to stop herself, Charlene snorted out a laugh.

This brought a smile to Katie's face.

"What?" she smirked.

Making Charlene laugh even harder.

"What?" Katie was giggling now.

Charlene's belly filled with laughter and she roared it out loud, all the pressure and pent up frustration of the past few days stewing down into the explosive rise and fall of her diaphragm. Tears were in her eyes. She wiped at them, saw the kids on the other side of the cafeteria looking in their direction but caring not.

She brought her attention back to Katie, who was dabbing at her own eyes. Gradually her breath came back under control.

"Oh… I'm… suh… sorry," she said, "that was just too…"

But she was off again before she could finish the sentence.

"Too… too… rich! Like I was in a zuh… zoo! The world famous Tasmanian lesbian, known for comfortable shoes, driving a Subaru and shopping at Whole Foods!"

They laughed at this but the manic edge to the energy was easing off.

"Sorry," Katie said.

"No need to be," Charlene shook her head, "I've had a lot worse said to me over the years, believe me."

"But I..."

Charlene's face settled into something resembling calm.

"Can I be honest?" she asked.

"Sure."

"Promise you're not going to go off the deep end again?"

Katie thought for a moment.

"Sure," she said.

"First of all, forget the labels," Charlene said, "I have a heart, I have a brain, I breathe just like you and everyone else on this planet."

Katie looked a little confused.

"We... *I* love like anyone else. So, yes, I find you attractive. You're a beautiful young woman, though I don't think you know yet just how beautiful you are."

Katie blushed and went to speak. Charlene held up her hand.

"I..." Charlene continued, "I broke up with my partner a few months back and I've been..."

What have I been, she thought, for the first time truly stepping out into observation of her self, *what have I been?*

"... Lonely."

"Oh, I'm sorry," Katie said, "that sucks."

It does, Charlene thought, *it sure does*.

"That's one way of putting it," she said, "it's been... bad. The house feels so empty. I..."

Tears pricked at Charlene's eyes afresh.

Katie frowned.

"So you *were* coming onto me?" she said, voice tightening as some of her earlier revulsion reappeared.

Charlene shook her head.

"No! I wasn't... I was..."

Katie stared at her.

Charlene sighed and rubbed both hands angrily up and down her face, wiping away tears.

"Okay," she said, voice firming, "here's the facts. You're beautiful, I just told you that. Of course I'm attracted to you! How can I not be?"

"But..."

"But nothing. I can't stop myself feeling this any more than you could."

"But you're a grown up!"

"Sure," Charlene bit, "like that suddenly changes anything I'm feeling in here."

She patted her chest a couple of times; hard.

"How do you think I feel, Katie? How do you think it feels knowing that I'm falling for you and all the time you're completely unavailable."

Katie's mouth was falling open, like slow-motion shock taking control of her face.

"I'm losing sleep," Charlene continued, "can't focus. I'm..."

Katie stood abruptly.

"This is too much," she said, "too much!"

"Please," Charlene pleaded, standing to look Katie in the eye, "let me explain."

"I don't know," Katie said, shaking her head.

Charlene slumped back into her chair, closing her eyes for a moment.

"I just want someone to understand," she said to herself, voice lost in the dark, "for once, I just want someone to listen."

Hot tears welled, the lump returning to her throat.

Charlene opened her eyes, fully expecting to see Katie walking away. But the girl was still standing there, looking down at her, a halo of cafeteria lights framing her hair.

Beautiful, the thought came to Charlene again.

Then Katie stepped around the table, bent towards Charlene and hugged her side-on, cheek-to-cheek. Katie's cheek was hot, her arms firm yet soft around Charlene's shoulder. Charlene lent into her, breathing her in.

"We can be friends," Katie said quietly, "but that's it. Nothing else."

And she stood and walked away, out of the cafeteria, without once looking back at Charlene.

When the door closed behind her, all the air seemed to leave Charlene's body at once and she was shuddering with imminent tears. She bit down, hoping to hold them in with an effort of will.

Frantically, she looked left, right, assessing just who had been witness to the conversation, scared of what was welling inside her now.

He was sitting on the far left side of the cafeteria, not so close that he could have heard. But in clear line of sight.

Jason Liu, gimlet-eyed, watching Charlene as she began to lose control.

How long had be been sitting there? Had he seen the whole thing?

He did it, I just know he did! Katie's voice sounded through her own welling confusion and shame.

Eyes blurring with tears she stared at Jason Liu.

His right hand lifted, pointed at his own eyes, turned, pointed at her eyes, back at his own, back at hers.

I see you.

You see me?

I see you.

Chapter 27: History Repeating

Charlene couldn't move.

Jason Liu stared at her across the cafeteria, effectively pinning her to her chair as if she were a butterfly in a display case.

Silence; an extended moment.

* * *

He stood. He nodded.

I see you.

He turned and left the cafeteria.

* * *

The air went out of her in a whooping shudder. Tears pricking at her eyes. She sobbed once, head reeling with the day's tension. Her mind screamed that she had to get out of there.

Anywhere, she thought, *anywhere but here*.

She sat for a moment longer, though; unsure whether the tremors running through her legs would prevent them bearing her weight.

The cafeteria, the halls beyond, loomed silent around her.

Wiping at her eyes with the heels of her hand, angry at her tears, frustrated with the situation, she stood; once more the lonely outcast.

Charlene had expected never to feel this isolated again.

* * *

She filed a quick email report for Mason and Baker before leaving the campus: *nothing to report… school calm… Sturmann aware of graffiti and in control*, wincing at the amount of detail that she was choosing to leave out.

And besides, she hadn't lied, anything else was more to do with her than the situation at the school.

What would I have written? She thought, *major crush on high school sweetheart, taboo-breaking intimacy at lunch, badly scared by teenager with little more than a gesture?*

She drove through woodlands and fields, making a huge arc around the town. Driving on autopilot, speed steady, back roads, where the sky formed a blue line between treetops; if she saw anyone, she didn't notice and certainly didn't acknowledge them.

As she clicked off miles on the speedometer of her cruiser, she began to get a little distance from the day's events. She felt like she'd been at a theme park all day, now ebbing from too many sugar highs and roller-coaster thrills.

Had it really been just a week since she'd been placed in the school? It seemed so much longer. And less than twenty-four hours since she'd visited Dylan with Katie.

Her heart gave a little bump, stomach dropping out, the lump immediately constricting her throat once more.

She closed off the scent of Katie in the cafeteria; the warmth of her body when she had drawn close to whisper new rules. She would just shut the girl out of her thoughts while she drove.

Charlene traced the blue line of the sky above her, guiding the cruiser as if on rails.

Are you really that naïve?

She heard Sturmann's question, could see the pent-up anxiety on his face as if he were projected on the windshield.

No, I'm not, she thought, all the time hearing a little voice whisper that she should just stop lying.

Her conversation with Sturmann kept pushing at her. Snippets and words, gestures, facial tics. She knew this feeling, her subconscious pushing at her.

What am I not seeing? She thought, *what's missing?*

His political conspiracy paranoia; the belief that Mason and his cronies wanted to take the schools private and that it went back long before...

Long before...

The windshield seemed to blaze with white light for a moment and, without even checking her rear-view, Charlene skidded to a halt in the middle of her lane.

Bill Tanner, she thought, *no-one has spoken with Bill Tanner.*

She pulled her car over to the side of the empty road, now checking behind and in front to make sure she wasn't on a blind bend. Once parked, she keyed his name into the on-board computer, retrieving his address; a small apartment block on the west side of town, a reasonable neighbourhood, though close to a trouble-spot. She set Bill Tanner's address into her GPS system.

At the next junction, the automated voice told her to turn right, back towards the hub of her afternoon's drive.

* * *

The apartment building was low and squat; two floors only, grounds functional though not prettified in any way. Just a brick path through trimmed and edged lawn. Beyond the property, the sidewalk was cracked, and weeds grew where concrete slabs connected.

Charlene looked up and down the street; two miles out of downtown proper, another mile or so would have taken her into the abandoned industrial district, where long-empty manufacturing facilities wallowed in disrepair, and where package stores, pizza joints and porn stores were the only viable businesses. A mile to what passed as a drug trade in this small town, which lived in an uneasy truce with the police department: *keep it within your own space, don't upset the town's status quo, we don't bust you.*

As she looked up the street, Charlene tried to remember just how long she had railed against that compromise when she'd first joined the force. She couldn't do it; her past little more than a half-recalled blur.

She turned to the apartment building and walked up the path. Four apartments, Tanner's one of those on the upper floor. She thumbed the buzzer next to his name and waited for his voice to emerge from the little metal grill next to the buttons.

Nothing.

He's out, she thought, *working or getting an early dinner.*

She thumbed it again.

No response.

She tried once more, hearing the buzz echoing down the internal stairwell.

"Hello?"

A voice from the windows above her head. She stepped back and looked up, scanning the windows to spot which one he'd spoken from. Then she saw him, the tip of his head leaning out of the window on the far right corner.

"Hi, Bill," she waved.

"Hi," Tanner replied, "I'll buzz you in."

His head withdrew and the window closed.

Charlene returned to the door just as the buzzer sounded to unlock the door. She looked up and down the street once final time before pushing the door open.

* * *

His apartment door was ajar, yet she was still hesitant to push it open; some vestige of privacy perhaps, or more likely the remnants of her own fractured day.

But push the door she did.

She stepped into Tanner's living room and heard him bustling around in the room beyond.

"Bill?" she called.

"Come on through," he answered.

Charlene walked through to what turned out to be the kitchen, finding his back turned to her.

"I'm making coffee," he said, "want some?"

"Sure. Mind if I sit?"

"Nope! Go right ahead."

She did so and watched in silence as he went about preparing the coffee pot. They had met previously, when Tanner had taken on the school security job and trained with the department. She'd bumped into him a couple of times since. He seemed like a nice guy.

Yet, she was nervous and couldn't escape that itch in the pit of her stomach. The lack of conversation began to swell and she searched for some way to move things forward; looked at his back, noted his uniform.

"Just back from work?" she asked.

"Nope," Tanner replied, "heading out actually. I got a new gig at a furniture place over at the Mullen Heights mall, night shift this week and next and then back to days. Two weeks on, two weeks off."

"Oh, I didn't know."

"Why would you?" he laughed, "it's hardly a town-wide announcement, is it. Wouldn't expect to see it in *The Daybreaker*!"

He took a couple of cups from the cupboard above his left shoulder.

"Milk? Sugar?"

"No, thanks. Black's good. How long have you been working the mall?"

"About a month," he said, getting quieter, "I was drawing unemployment for a while after the school gig ended. Things were tight. Then this came along and I'm back on my feet again."

He turned, carrying steaming mugs to the table. Charlene took hers and sipped at it, blowing a little to take the edge off the heat.

Tanner sat and look at her for a moment.

"So," he nodded, "are you going to ask me what you came here to ask me?"

"Oh."

He smiled.

"I wondered when anyone would actually come out here."

"I…" Charlene didn't know what to say, blind-sided by the turn in conversation, "I'm sorry, I didn't think to…"

He burst out laughing; a couple of donkey-brays.

"Kidding!" he laughed. "How're things at the school?"

Charlene eased back. His act had been complete, but she could tell he wasn't hiding behind a charade any longer.

"Could be better," she said, deciding to stick to the facts for the moment, "we've got two kids beaten up, graffiti down-town, yours-truly stationed at the school…"

And all the rest, she thought.

"Any ideas who did it?"

She shook her head.

"Suspicions, maybe," she said, "but nothing more than gossip or hearsay."

"How's Sturmann doing?" Tanner nodded. "Still whining?"

"He's fine," she said, "at least I think he is. Pretty high-strung but seems to be in control."

"I wouldn't be so sure. I've never seen anybody wear a mask like that guy."

Charlene thought of the times she'd seen his game-face lock into place in the past week.

"Yup," she said, "it's something to see, all right."

"Did he spin the conspiracy out for you?"

She nodded.

"I'm not surprised. And, thing is, he's not that far off the mark. Mason and his crew have their fingers in most every pie they can."

They were quiet for a moment before Tanner spoke again.

"So, you gonna ask me or not?"

Charlene smiled at him.

"Okay," she shrugged, "can I come clean with you?"

"Sure."

"I mean, you're just about the only one who'd understand how weird this past week has been and what it's like…"

"Sure," Tanner repeated, making a show of looking at his watch, "but I've gotta go to work, so hurry it up, okay?"

"What do you know about Jason Liu?" Charlene said.

It was like someone had thrown cold water over Tanner. His good-natured grin flickered into a grimace before setting into tight lips, biting down. His forehead creased.

"What?" Charlene nodded encouragement.

"I…" Tanner began, but his mouth snapped shut again.

Charlene was quiet; sipping from her coffee cup.

"He's the reason I got kicked out," Tanner said, "Jason Liu. He's why I'm not there any more."

"No," she shook her head, "it was the town council, wasn't it? Budget cuts?"

He stared at her.

"That's the how," he said, "but it ain't the why."

"Go on."

"Look," Tanner said, anger rising with his memories, "when I was at the school, Jason Liu was acting out like he was lead rooster, like he owned the school. *Big-time pimping,* I heard some of the kids call it. Like he was leader of the pack."

A snippet of the classic song went through her head; but it passed in a moment.

"Did he have a gang?" she asked, "other kids involved?"

"Some. I guess. Mostly he'd be on his own, but sometimes there were other kids around. Sure."

"So, how was *he* responsible for you getting canned?"

Tanner sighed, looked at the ceiling above him and then around at the building.

"He found out where I lived," he said.

"He came here?" Charlene was shocked, hadn't imagined it could stretch beyond the school campus.

"No," Tanner shook his head, "Well, not... But... Charlene, who do you think owns this building? Who do you think takes my rent each month?"

Gears whirred, cogs clicked together.

"His father," she breathed out.

Tanner nodded.

"When I began to lean on Jason," he said, "bring him under control, just a little, nothing major, he... We were down near the gym..."

His hunting grounds, Charlene thought, remembering how she'd broken up the scuffle there a few days earlier.

"...I called him out. He was quiet while I sent the other kids away but, soon as they were gone, he squares up to me and says my address. Tells me, *I know where you live*."

"So, he *was* threatening you."

"Nah, it was what he said next that got me. He was still staring me out, and I could have swore he was on the verge of throwing a punch. He says, *my father is a powerful man. My father loves me*, he says, *he will do anything I ask. Like getting you thrown out of your apartment. Like getting your ass fired. He will do this. He loves me*."

Tanner shuddered to hear Jason Liu's words through his own mouth.

"The next weekend," he continued, "Jason and his father came here. Checking on something in the yard. I've never seen the old man here since I signed the papers, we do all the business down at his office or by email. Anyway, the old man is checking something down there and I'm watching from up here and Jason looks up at me and..."

"Does this," Charlene finished the sentence, pointing with two fingers from her eyes to Tanner's eyes and back again.

Tanner nods.

"Almost like he was saying..."

"I see you," Charlene whispered.

"Yup," Tanner said, "he was just showing that he could make good on his promise to make his father kick me out."

"But you didn't stop?"

"Oh, I stopped all right," Tanner sighed, "just kept away from him, you know? But he came after me. Every time I turned, he'd be there, watching me, making eye contact, looking at me as if he was just waiting until I did one thing that would give him cause."

"It got so as I was getting paranoid, myself. I was almost ready to go to Mason and quit but it all came to a head anyway. I was walking the halls one day, just doing the rounds, and he tripped up some kid so as he fell into me. I flipped, shouted at Jason. He looks at me and says, *gotcha*. Simple as that."

Gotcha, Charlene thought, seeing all the times she'd spotted Jason Liu watching her, culminating in that day's direct confrontation.

"Next thing I heard," Tanner continued, "was a week or so later when the town council decided they couldn't afford me any more."

Even given the day she'd had, Charlene felt herself resisting the descent into conspiracy; the kid could try to be as *gangsta* as he wanted, but he was no Don Corleone.

"Oh come on," she blurted out, "you can't believe he can make the town council..."

She stopped. Something in the way Tanner was smiling.

"*The tax-payers resent paying for you to control their kids*," Tanner said, "that's what Mason said. *They refuse to pay for you any longer.*"

Charlene was still for a moment, confused, not quite getting the leap from Jason Liu to the tax payer.

Tanner checked his watch.

"I've really got to get to work," he said, standing.

"But..."

"It's not that hard, Charlene. The tax-payers. Not the town. Not the community. Not the residents. The tax-payers."

He shook his head as he looked at her; she still wasn't getting it.

"Jason's father owns half of downtown and most of the rest of the town. And Mason owns near everything else. It's not that hard to see who he's talking about when he mentions tax-payers."

It was like a dust cover being pulled off a piece of furniture, revealing a shape which had been clear yet indistinct until that moment. Of course.

"Liu demanded you..."

"I should think Jason spun some story about how's I was getting too big for my britches, coming down too hard on the kids, that there was no need for security anyway. Probably claimed I was getting in the way of studies; that's always a winner with parents, particularly chinks."

Charlene could practically taste the venom seething within his words.

"And this parent, who just happens to be the major shareholder in this town, and who expects his kid to go off to Harvard or Yale or wherever, puts a word in with his political dog to get me pulled off the job. Meanwhile, his kid is rubbing my nose in it, strutting the school like he's..."

"Stop," Charlene interrupted him, alarmed at the rage that was rippling across his face, "Bill... Stop. I get it, okay?"

Gradually, his face eased. He stared at the floor, unable to meet her eyes.

"Why did you come here?" he asked.

"I don't know," she replied, "I just... Needed to get some perspective."

"Did you get what you wanted?"

"I guess."

"Good," Tanner said, walking to his apartment door. He pulled it open, gesturing for her to leave without once making eye contact.

"Sorry," he said, "I've got to get to work."

Tuesday

Chapter 28:
A Bitter Breakfast

The phone was ringing when Baker stepped from the shower.

He wrapped a towel around his mid-riff and ran through to his bedroom.

This isn't good, he thought as he grabbed the handset.

"Hello?"

"What the hell am I paying you for?" Mason yelled in his ear.

Baker sat down on his unmade bed, dripping on the sheets as Mason let loose.

"More graffiti!" he yelled, "all over downtown this time! On storefronts! And where were your officers? I'll tell you where, tucked up in bed! Cosy and warm while all the time my town is getting defaced by snot-nosed brats whose only sense of community is smoking dope and drinking themselves into a stupor!"

Baker rubbed at his eyes, a headache forming; held the handset away from his ear a little. Looked out the window.

Outside, the early morning light coloured the plants and grasses of his yard in soft greens. A squirrel skittered along a branch, chased by a brother, or sister, or paramour.

Baker grimaced at life going on just beyond his own private circle of hell.

"I hadn't seen it yet," he said.

"I know *that*," Mason yelled, "otherwise you would have called me. It's why *I'm* doing *your* job and calling *you*!"

Baker looked at the handset, thumbed it to speaker and walked back through to the bathroom. He pulled his toothbrush from its holder, and reached for the toothpaste.

"Are you downtown now?" he asked. "I can be there in ten minutes."

"I'm at my office," Mason responded and Baker took some small satisfaction that his own neutrality was beginning to calm the selectman.

"Meet me out front of Annie's in ten?" Baker asked.

"Sure," Mason agreed, "we can discuss your plan over breakfast."

Baker was about to brush his teeth when he had an idea.

"Have you lined up Curtis to do a piece for *The Daybreaker* today?"

Mason hesitated before speaking.

"I... Simpson reports on what he sees fit to publish. Why would I have spoken with him?"

"No reason," Baker lied, looking himself in his reflected eye. A smile ghosted his face.

"Then why ask?"

"I think we can use him to our advantage," Baker said, dropping into Mason's natural vernacular, a caricature of political double-speak, "to flush out our graffiti artist."

"Oh," Mason considered this, "Hmmm. That's good, I'd been thinking similar as soon as I saw this latest attack. I'm glad we're on the same page on that. At least."

Baker almost laughed out loud; Mason's ego was a force of nature.

"See you in ten, then?" he asked, smiling at the handset.

"Annie's," Mason said, "in ten."

The line clicked dead.

Baker's smiled evaporated in a moment.

Shit, he thought, *this is just what we don't need.*

It was a moment or two before he remembered he was supposed to be brushing his teeth.

* * *

When Baker pulled up, Mason was already pacing up and down the sidewalk.

As it turned out, the graffiti was nowhere near as prominent as he'd feared. Sure, there was some, and one store had a slogan sprayed across the display window: *My town!* Baker suspected that it was those words that had brought such a reaction from Mason, cutting as it did to the centre of the first selectman's identity. Aside from that, Baker could only count three other instances of vandalism.

He parked. After ensuring the cruiser was secure, his phone and radio on, he stepped onto the sidewalk.

Mason was on him immediately; neither man offered a handshake.

"Did you see it?" Mason asked.

On his way into town, Baker had coached himself on playing the role of zen-master when he met with Mason, bending like a reed buffeted by gale-forced winds.

"I sure did," he said, "and I see what you mean. It's a mess, all right."

This seemed to deflate Mason, who had been ready to have a stand-up argument right there in the street.

"You... Oh."

"It'll be fine," Baker took the initiative, "there's not too much to clean and, though I hate to admit it, we've had some practice."

This almost hooked Mason, who drew in a sharp breath.

"Breakfast," Baker said, "then we can talk about what we're going to do about our friend the artist."

He walked past Mason and grabbed the door of Annie's diner, which he held open while bowing slightly in welcome.

* * *

Baker's zen calm didn't last long.

For the hour, the diner was still surprisingly empty. A postman in the corner, couple of truckers at the counter. But aside from these few and Annie's staff, they had the room to themselves.

Unexpectedly, Mason chose a table right in the middle.

So we can be heard from everywhere, Baker thought, knowing that Mason usually took a corner booth for some privacy. He had that sinking feeling in his stomach once again; knew where Mason planned to take this.

"Morning, gentlemen," Annie said, stepping up to the table, "coffee's already on its way. D'ya need menus?"

Mason scanned the board, shook his head.

"No thanks, Annie," he said, "I'll have my regular, sunny side-up."

"Jack?" she swivelled to face Baker.

He sat for a moment, thinking about anything but a food choice.

"I'll take a menu," he said finally, "I'm in the mood for something different today."

"Need those calories to fight crime, eh?" Annie joked.

Mason laughed loud at this; too loud.

Annie glanced at Baker, who nodded slightly.

"That'll be just the prescription, Annie," he said.

She walked back to the counter to grab a menu and some silverware.

"Here you go," she said, "I'll be right back with your coffee."

There wasn't even a moment before Mason spoke.

"It's enough, Jack," he said, staring across the table, "nothing you've done has rid the town of its problem-children. This graffiti is the straw on the camel's back. I've tried taking it easy. I listened to your side of the story and cut you some slack."

"But you're failing, Jack. It's time I stepped in, like I should have as soon as Dylan Ford was beaten up."

Like you should have, Baker thought, feeling anger ignite within him, *like you didn't already?*

"I don't think..." he began, but Mason interrupted him.

"Keep your voice down," he hissed, *"I don't want the whole town eavesdropping on our conversation."*

Baker fought an impulse to stand up. He calmed his voice.

"Then," he said, "can we please drop the blame game bullshit, Mason, and agree that we actually want the same thing right now: an end to this vandalism. Can we at least focus on that?"

Mason sat back, chin rising as he considered this. Baker was reminded of Marlon Brando for a moment.

"I would expect that of you," Mason said, "always wanting to ignore the big picture and focus on the small-scale."

Baker realized his hands were in fists and forced them to relax.

"This is so much more than a case of reckless teenagers," Mason continued, "this is a battle for the very soul of this community! And while you may prefer to watch as the town goes into damnation, I will *not... let... my... town... be stolen from me*."

Now we see it, Baker thought, *finally some honesty.*

"Now," Mason continued, "what is your plan for a) dealing with the graffiti; and b) stamping out the violence running out-of-control at the high school?"

Out-of-control? Baker thought. *Have you even read any of Charlene's reports?*

"I hardly think you could describe it as..."

"Will you keep your voice down!" Mason exploded.

Baker was close to losing control.

"I've had enough," Mason continued. "I expect you to fix this immediately, identify the bastard kids that are doing this and bring their guilty asses to justice. Do you hear me?"

Mason leant forward a little; Baker could see beads of sweat forming in the folds of flesh on his forehead.

"And it's time that cunt of yours wears her piece when she's patrolling the school. It's the only language that will work."

"She's already wearing her..."

"No she's not," Mason hissed, "she even joked about it on her first day, at the assembly."

I know that, Baker thought. Even with Mason's anger, he refused to throw her under the bus, though.

"We discussed it when I briefed her," he said, "and agreed that it would make her introduction easier."

Mason didn't relax at all when he heard this; logical explanation had little part to play in this discussion.

"I don't care about your reasons," he spat, "I expect her to be wearing her gun. Got it?"

Baker nodded understanding.

"Good."

Baker scanned the room. Neither postman nor truckers seemed to be paying attention. He caught Annie's eye and raised his hand.

When she arrived at the table, he ordered eggs benedict with salmon.

"Look at you trying something different," Annie joked.

"Might as well live dangerously," Baker smiled.

* * *

They ate, they drank coffee.

Mason glowered. Baker, unable to get a word in, was forced to play dodge-ball.

He could feel the barb of the hook biting into the flesh of his inner cheek, digging deeper as Mason played the line.

Chapter 29:
Hola Chica!

Charlene spent most of the morning in her office at the school; Bill Tanner's words going through her head: *Oh, I stopped all right,* he'd said, *just kept away from him, you know? But he came after me.*

But he came after me.

With the door closed, she at least felt like she'd placed Jason Liu as far away as possible.

She was lost, didn't know that she could tell Baker what had happened; about Katie, about Jason, about her conversation with Tanner.

He'd think she was losing her mind.

And he wouldn't be far wrong, she thought.

No, she had to fix this herself.

But the fixing could come later; for now, she was safe in her cave.

* * *

She didn't dare the cafeteria, the risk of another confrontation, so drove downtown to get lunch.

Saw graffiti being spray-washed from the storefronts: *My town.*

Her stomach ached to see the territorial marking.

She checked again that both her cell and radio were off. She would claim lack of signal when Baker asked why she hadn't answered his inevitable calls.

* * *

She sat in the park, alone save for squirrels.

The high school lurked, a storm-cloud at the back of her thoughts, dark, black. Dancing before it, imagined threats for her own safety, her job, her place in this adopted town.

Spaces once occupied by Suzy had filled, all right.

For the first time ever, Charlene found herself wishing they would come back.

* * *

The afternoon found her back in her office; a troll, hiding out in the dark, avoiding contact, ready to club anyone who dared breach her sanctuary.

* * *

Driving home, she realized she had nothing in for dinner that night, the previous night's confusion and her trip to Tanner's having taken the place of her weekly supermarket time.

Eating out was a non-starter, the idea of being in public filled her with anxiety.

What's wrong with you, Charlene? she thought. *How has this got you so worked up?*

She was too tired and phased to chase answers to those questions.

She needed to eat.

There, the gas station and market.

Great, she thought with dismay, *pancake-on-a-stick and beef jerky for me!*

She smiled as she pulled into the gas station's lot, where she parked alongside a black Mercedes.

* * *

Charlene was still smiling as she scanned the racks of junk food available for her selection.

Suddenly, the idea of eating out didn't seem so bad, even if it would have meant working through her anxiety in public.

She allowed herself to drift for a moment or two, idly picking up packages of food which she had no intention of buying, scanning their ingredients and nutritional information.

Thoughts breezed around, through and within her.

Like how the worst foods seemed the most gaudily packaged with nutritional information so small it was near impossible to read, crunched into a single paragraph rather than the more easily-read breakdown panel.

Like how the game for food producers seemed to be how best to combine seemingly conflicting tastes.

Like what the hell she was going to find here that she wouldn't later regret having eaten.

For those moments of considering the crap, Charlene was blessedly lost.

The thought of dropping by the donut shop drifted into sight.

She became aware of someone standing off her left shoulder and fought to come back to the moment, emerging as if she'd been entranced.

She turned her head.

"Hola, chica!" Jason Liu erupted less than a foot from her face; a near manic grin stretched his mouth almost too-wide.

Charlene jumped backwards, body going rigid.

"Jesus!" she shouted.

"Not quite," Jason smiled, "but pretty *daaamned* close!"

Involuntarily, her hand dropped to her right hip, to where her gun should have been. His eyes tracked the movement, flicking downwards.

Charlene tried to speak, but found her voice had deserted her.

"How have you been, officer?" Jason asked, a mocking mimic of civility.

She stared at him; he was a coiled serpent.

"No, really," he continued, "have things been just hunky-dory since you joined our merry gathering? Or just so-so?"

"Wha... What do you want?" she asked, pulse racing, feeling like she might puke at any moment.

"Me?" Jason smiled, "something to eat."

His hand reached out and grabbed the nearest package he could reach. For a moment, he didn't even look at it.

"I'm hungry!" he laughed, maintaining eye contact with Charlene.

He dropped his eyes and realized he'd grabbed a pack of mass-manufactured mini-cupcakes.

"Ugh," he shivered dramatically.

Now he dropped contact with her, scanning the racks; junk food and candied heart attacks. He looked back at her, frowning.

"Really?" he asked. "You were gonna *eat* this shit?"

"No!" she blurted out, surprised that of all the things she had to defend, food choice seemed to be the one she'd landed on.

"Because you know it'll just end up on your hips and ass, don't you?" Jason laughed loud.

Out of the corner of her eye, on the very periphery of her vision, Charlene noticed the gas station clerk move his head.

Hope he's listening, she thought. Her eyes flicked to the door, off to the left beyond Jason. She could push past him or go backwards around the food racks.

If she needed to escape.

If he were to attack.

"And at your age," Jason continued, "I guess expansion of the old tushy becomes a *reeeeal* problem!"

Still, words deserted Charlene. All she could think of was escape, of how she could get past him, out of the gas station, out of this spiralling situation.

Jason dropped the pack of mini-cupcakes on the floor.

"Oh, whoops," he said and bent to pick them up.

It was her chance, she lifted a foot.

He stood so quickly that she was transfixed, up on his toes, his hands rising into a boxer's ready pose, or…

Martial arts, she thought, *karate, kick-boxing, something like that.*

His whole body seemed to be thrumming like a high-voltage wire and, for the first time, Charlene wondered whether he was on something.

She raised her hands in surrender.

"Jason," she said, staring at him until his jittering eyes found hers, "please… calm down. *Please.*"

He held the stance for a moment longer and then dropped his hands, again so quickly that she was shocked.

He smiled widely.

"Just playing with ya," he said, looking over his shoulder to check whether the clerk was paying any attention.

Just as he did so, the door of the gas station opened and an older Chinese man looked into the market area.

"Jason!" the older man barked, "come on!"

His father, Charlene thought.

"Sure, dad," Jason said, all sweetness for his old man, "just a minute, though. Okay?"

"Hmpf," Liu said and stepped out of the shop again.

Jason turned back to face Charlene. His face a mask of retribution.

"I hear you've been snooping," he hissed, his hand raising to punctuate each word with a point towards her eyes, "and *I don't like snoopers*."

His finger dropped and he started prodding her chest. Later, she would think of any number of self-defence moves she might have used, but in the moment Charlene was frozen by the elemental force of him.

"This..." he spat out the words, "this is my school, it's my town and she's my girl, hear me?"

"I will be respected."

And with that, he turned, grabbed a bag of gummy bears and walked towards the door.

"Put these on my dad's account," he ordered the clerk without even looking at him.

As he pulled the door open, he turned once again to look at Charlene. This time he didn't point, he just smiled that too-wide grin before sliding sideways out of the shop.

She watched as he crossed the gas station lot and climbed into the passenger side of the black Mercedes.

She didn't breathe until the sleek car had pulled into traffic.

Chapter 30:
What Does It Say?

Charlene drove for miles, searching for any escape, any chance of oblivion that might come her way; just enough for her to be away from this mess for a moment, no matter how brief. She floated somewhere beyond the windshield, retracing roads she'd taken only the night before as she circumnavigated the town; its gravitational pull.

The light faded, evening come too soon to swallow the day. She felt the sun leave with a sense of foreboding; in the growing gloom, it was all too possible to see Jason Liu's manic smile, Katie's disgust at her blundering approach.

Her eyelids grew heavy, eyeballs rolling upward, she nodded.

The car swerved, jerking her back to consciousness.

Tired, she thought, *not good.*

She brought her attention back to the act of driving, opening the windows for some fresh air, and headed home.

* * *

She got through the front door, walked through to the living room and laid down on the couch.

Her eyes were closed within moments as sleep took her.

Every so often, her eyelids flickered; forehead creased.

* * *

The polar bear stood on its hind legs, looking down at the class.

In it's right hand, it held a cane, which it used to tap the words on the ice-sculpted chalkboard.

"What does it say?" the bear teacher asked.

But all Charlene heard was a series of gruff barks.

Besides, she was distracted by the flaming red hair of the girl two rows in front and off to her right.

I wish you'd turn.

Tap-tap went the cane on the board.

"What does it say?"

Please turn.

"What does it say?"

She tasted the dead-meat halitosis of the bear's breath, looked towards the board only to find the teacher's muzzle an inch from her.

It barked once. Spittle spattered her face.

Its teeth were enormous.

"What... does... it... say?" the bear roared.

Panicked, she reached for her gun.

But it was difficult to move; her adult body squeezed under this middle school desk.

She looked down.

Found that she was naked.

Embarrassed, she shot a glance at the girl with the red hair, who kept steady watch on the frozen chalkboard.

Tap-tap.

Please turn.

"What does it say?"

* * *

The wall slammed down into the grass, displacing clumps of earth in all directions as if it were high explosive.

Charlene ran straight into it, her earbuds flying from her head.

'Silver Lady' by David Soul played soundtrack to collision.

As her face hit brick, blood flew from Charlene's nose, spraying in a bright red halo around her head.

The pain was...

Interesting.

She reached up and grabbed the boa constrictor coiled a-top the wall. Used it to steady herself as the rest of her running body caught up with her face.

She saw her breasts collide with the wall, skin squeezing into the space where mortar had eroded. Her belly followed and finally her legs, propelling her with full force into the brickwork.

Which began to bend inward; vertiginous plummeting.

"Please turn?" the boa constrictor said.

* * *

The ice plain stretched for miles in all directions, on its far edges, ridges and bergs rose to serrate the wintry sky.

Cold.

She looked down. Her uniform was way too big for her, made for a giant. It flopped and flapped in the howling wind.

Tap-tap.

She turned around.

A desk.

She walked to it and, gathering up the seemingly endless yards of fabric that she wore, bundled herself into the seat. It insulated her some from the ice kiss of the wind.

Warmer.

Tap-tap.

The bear slid forward as if on skids, standing erect, its cane at forty-five degrees to its body.

Yet there was no board.

Please turn.

Charlene swivelled her head around without moving her body.

And looked into eyes; a jury of owls sitting in a semi-circle behind her.

"Shouldn't you be penguins?" she asked.

Tap-tap.

The bear called for her attention, though when she turned it didn't seem to have moved at all.

Tap-tap.

"What does it say?" the bear teacher growled without moving its lips.

She squinted.

Saw the tip of the cane in intricate detail.

The red-headed girl sat at a desk on the tip of the cane.

Please turn.

And now she did, as she had never done in real life.

The girl turned, and her face was blurring as Charlene watched her finger point below the desk.

There was writing on the cane. Cursive.

"What does it say?" said the girl, laughing, "what does it say, lover!"

This is a dream, Charlene thought and the ice plain began to disintegrate from its far edges as she began to surface.

The cane melted into the shape of a living, breathing boa constrictor; a tattoo rippling along its undulating flank: *Even an olive branch may beat a man to death.*

Ice ruptured around her; massive cacophony.

Tap-tap.

The girl turned to face away from her again.

Please turn!

"What does it say?"

The ground shook, and she tried to stand, fighting now against the weight of the endless uniform that had trapped her in this middle school desk.

Water flooded through the cracks in the ice; Charlene knew she would drown, pulled into the depths by the water-logged cloth she wore.

"What does it say?" yelled the bear.

"Even an olive branch may beat a man to death," the red-headed girl said from just behind her shoulder.

The boa constrictor coiled around the bear's arm and body, crushing the immobile teacher.

Charlene had never seen a snake smile like that.

It's mouth was full of teeth. And wide. Too wide.

Even an olive branch may beat a man to death.

With a massive crack, the ice gave a final shudder beneath her and she felt the water surge through the material covering her legs.

* * *

Lightning painted the sky outside her living room windows; a summer storm, crackling through over-charged humidity.

Charlene sat upright, glanced at the clock on the mantelpiece. Ten p.m. A couple of hours had passed.

Weird dream, she thought, *something about bears.*

She picked up the telephone and navigated the menu to Baker's home number.

It rang four times before he answered.

"Charlene?" he said.

"I've changed my mind," she said.

"About the school?" Baker replied.

"Yes."

"What?"

"I'm wearing my piece tomorrow."

"What?" Baker said, alarmed. "Why? Has Mason spoken with you?"

"No," she said, feeling sleep pull at her again, "I don't think the olive branch is working."

"It's not a good idea," Baker counselled, "I…"

"Trust me on this, chief?" Charlene asked.

Baker paused.

"What aren't you telling me, Charlene?" he said.

"Nothing," she replied, "I'm just tired tonight, fell asleep on the couch and my neck hurts. Trust me?"

"Oh… I don't know…" he paused to think, "okay. But be careful. The last thing we need is for this to get any worse."

"I will," said Charlene, "and besides, I don't think it's that big of a deal whether I'm armed or not. I mean even an olive branch can be used to beat a man to death."

"True, true," Baker laughed.

"G'night, chief," Charlene said.

"Sure. Goodnight."

Charlene clicked the phone off, yawned, headed upstairs to bed, hoping she could get a good night's sleep undisturbed by dreams of Jason Liu.

Wednesday

Chapter 31:
Sleeping Dogs

Baker refused to mount an overnight watch downtown, even though he knew that their graffiti artist would return.

Definitely.

This had escalated.

The immediate rush of defacing property graffiti would already be losing its lustre, and whoever was doing this wouldn't be satisfied with the same old thrill for much longer.

He lay in bed, unable to sleep, turning it all over and over. Mostly, his thoughts revolved around the strange call with Charlene and how she'd changed her mind about carrying while on duty at the school.

It wasn't even her decision that gnawed at him, it was the fact that the call happened at all. There was an unwritten rule in the department: *home calls to the chief for emergency only*. Charlene rarely, if ever, called him at home. And there had been something in her voice that he couldn't quite pin down, though it might have been an artefact of not being able to see her face; thanks to the lightning storm, the line had bustled with static and electronic noise.

Maybe it had been nothing.

Still, he was unhappy with her decision to go into school armed tomorrow.

Tomorrow?

Later today.

His eyes flicked back to the glowing clock on his night-stand.

Nearly two a.m. There would be little chance of sleep now.

Baker flopped onto his back, stared at the ceiling.

I might not have been willing to put an officer downtown, he thought.

"But I'm awake already," he spoke into the silence of his bedroom, and the darkness of his house beyond.

He climbed out of bed.

* * *

The town was dark and silent. In the sodium arcs he could see clearly where the graffiti had been scrubbed just yesterday morning, cleaner patches against the greater expanse of the walls and windows.

A trucking rig rolled slowly through downtown, a cresting whale in the stillness; he felt its vibrations before he heard it coming before he saw it. It left no change in its wake, no new news.

Alone in his car, Baker stared at nothing, letting his peripheral vision expand, letting his mind wander.

He thought of Mason's insistence that Charlene be armed. The anger with which he'd responded to the latest vandalism. It had been those two words: *My Town*. Baker doubted that anyone would have dared utter those words anywhere near Mason, knowing the ego invested in shaping the town to his vision; the stranglehold manifested at any threat of change.

This must burn him in ways that he never thought he could be burned, Baker thought.

There! A shadow moving in the alleyway between two shops. Baker was suddenly alert, sitting upright from where he'd been slumped in the seat of his car.

He waited for another movement and, after a moment or two, a piece of shadow detached.

A dog. Stray, nosing at the ground, searching for food scraps.

Baker watched for a moment, assessing for rabies and then, comfortable that the dog wasn't showing any signs, got out of his car. By force of habit, he looked both ways along the street, just in case there was an oncoming vehicle.

Stupid, he thought, *I'd hear a car coming from miles away.*

As he stepped into the road, his shoes scraped on the asphalt, loud enough to catch the dog's attention. It looked up, wary.

Baker stopped walking, brought his hands up.

"Shhh," he said, "I'm not going to hurt you."

The dog watched him with suspicion.

Baker took a step forward and, in the slight shift of light and shadow, he was suddenly able to see just how emaciated this dog was, all bony ribs and scrawny muscle, its tissue skin dappled with what looked like dark blotches; burn scars, maybe.

As he took another step, the dog snarled, and Baker lifted his hand to the butt of his gun, flipping the holster open and thumbing the safety. He didn't think the dog would attack unless triggered, and he wasn't about to do that, but it was better to be ready.

"Shhh," he repeated, hearing his voice echo back from the walls, quiet and even, "you're a hungry boy, huh?"

Baker lifted his foot only slightly and the dog turned and ran up the street before darting into another alleyway.

But even in that fleeting moment, Baker had a chance to see.

The blotches weren't scars.

They were paint. Spray paint.

And on the dog's other flank, hidden from Baker until the animal had turned to flee, a single word, crudely painted: *Dog!*

* * *

He scouted the alleys for ten or fifteen minutes, but the dog was long gone.

Maybe he'd dreamed it.

Maybe he was at home asleep right now.

He looked at downtown, at the recently cleaned areas on the walls and windows; at Annie's Place, closed up now, dark save for a bug-light glowing way in back; Page Turners, the little bookstore on the corner glowing like a jack-o-lantern.

No, he wasn't dreaming.

But he hoped that he *had* imagined that someone in this town, some kid, would be willing to treat an animal that way.

He walked back to his car and headed home, deep in thought.

* * *

As Charlene climbed out of the cruiser, she spotted Brina walking from the buses; alone as always, a cloud of teenage angst and isolation. She rushed across the car park to catch up with the teenager before she joined the wider throngs entering the school.

"Brina," she said, from behind the girl's shoulder.

Brina jumped, not expecting to speak to anyone at this time of the morning; ever, if truth be told. She turned, shocked.

"What?" she snapped. "Oh, it's you."

"Yeah, sorry about that," Charlene said, "didn't mean to..."

"Well, you sure did," Brina laughed slightly, "hell of a jolt; better than caffeine!"

Charlene held up her hands; *sorry*.

"Have you got a minute?" she asked.

Brina glanced towards the school, the other kids.

"Sure," she said, "I guess."

"Walk with me?" Charlene asked.

"Okay."

They turned towards the edge of the building, beyond which lay the tennis courts and sports fields.

Neither of them spoke.

Neither of them noticed the black Mercedes pulling out of the school exit into traffic.

* * *

Jason Liu crossed the car park, followed by a trail of aftershave. *Calvin Klein* aftershave; *expensive* aftershave. Though he didn't need to shave yet, it was important to make it seem like he did; a good impression, a *strong* impression, was the first step to commanding respect.

And he would have respect.

Across the car park, he saw the dyke police officer moving through the crowds.

She's just a speed bump, he thought, *a distraction from business.*

And he was all about business.

She was talking to Brina Nelson, the weirdo goth kid from his art class.

Oh, now isn't that interesting? he thought as he watched them walk off around the corner of the main building towards the sports fields, *a little girl-on-girl action, maybe?*

He watched as they turned the corner.

Other kids moved around him, arriving for another day; pliant lambs. If he'd had time, he would have spat in each of their pathetic faces and dared them to think about wiping it off. But he didn't have time.

* * *

They walked for a while before sitting on a low wall at the edge of the tennis courts, the morning was quiet, the noise of the arriving hoards, blurring with distant traffic. Birds sang off in the trees beyond the football field; a crow cawed to its brothers and sisters.

"Something died," Brina said, looking towards the birds.

"The crows?"

"Nah," Brina looked up into the sky, pointed, "turkey vultures."

And sure enough, there were a couple of dark silhouettes circling above the woods.

"Ugh," Charlene said, repulsed as ever by the thought of scavengers picking at road-kill.

Brina smiled at her discomfort.

"They're nature's clean-up crew, you know?"

"Sure," said Charlene, "but I'd rather nature used a dustpan and brush!"

"So?" Brina asked.

Charlene was quiet for a moment, thinking.

Far-off, a bell rang; five minutes until class.

"I'm gonna have to go soon."

"Yeah," Charlene said, "okay. Okay."

She breathed out hard, feeling the heaviness of the sleep and dreams she'd had the previous night.

"What can you tell me about Jason Liu?"

Brina looked long and hard at Charlene. Finally, she nodded.

"So you *are* investigating, then."

It was a statement not a question.

"No," Charlene began, "no... not... officially."

"Unofficially," Brina said.

"Maybe."

"Well," the girl continued, checking her cell-phone for the time, "if it's maybe's you want... Maybe I know Jason Liu, and maybe I don't."

She shrugged.

"Maybe I saw him beat Dylan Ford to a pulp. Maybe I heard that he was the first to try and work out who'd done it. Maybe he's my best friend and I'm already wondering how and why you're choosing to pick on the one kid who you should be working with. Maybe I know that Jason Liu is the main dealer working this school. Maybe I don't even know who he is."

"Is that enough *maybes* for you?"

Charlene didn't know what to say.

"Maybe I don't like being pulled aside and used as an informant, *Officer Charlene Goodlow*."

She spat the title with barely concealed anger.

"Shit! Make friends with the oddball, make her think you're on the same wavelength, that she might just get along with you, then pump her for information to help your little, *unofficial* investigation. Well, fuck you, if that's who you are. Fuck you!"

She stood, grabbing her bag, tears beginning to form at the corners of her eyes. Charlene was paralyzed to make any move or sound.

"Is that who you are, Charlene?" Brina continued, looking down at the police officer, "is that why you're here? Fuck you!"

Tears breaking free, Brina turned and stormed towards the school buildings.

"Wait!" Charlene shouted, stunned by the girl's reaction.

But Brina didn't turn.

* * *

Jason pushed the lever on the exit door, and stepped out by the side of the gymnasium.

Time to check on the lover-girls.

He stepped around the building and jumped back quickly. They were sitting about five yards away, on the wall by the tennis courts, facing the other way. He risked a second glance around the corner to confirm they hadn't noticed him.

He listened to them talking about turkey vultures and was just about bored enough to leave when he heard his name.

"I thought you weren't investigating?" he heard Brina say.

He listened as they argued, growing increasingly angry at the dyke cop.

How dare you? Fucking snooping bitch! he thought, *oh I've seen you all right… looking at my baby, talking to her, touching her, and now you want to try investigate me! Who the fuck do you think you are?*

Their argument ended and he glanced around the wall to see Brina Nelson storming back towards the school entrance. He watched as the dyke cop pleaded for her to return, one hand reaching out as if to grab her.

I'm gonna deal with you right now, he thought, taking a step out from his hiding place.

But she was already walking after Brina Nelson; the moment had passed. He leaned against the wall, staring into the middle distance, his eyebrows furrowed.

I told you not to snoop on me! How dare you? Fucking snooping bitch!

Chapter 32: At The Cross-roads

Well, that could have gone better, Charlene thought as she walked back around the building's perimeter, replaying the conversation over and over.

Brina's reaction had been so immediate and extreme. There had to be something behind it. Her questions had been unwelcome, for sure. Either because Brina was scared by Jason Liu or…

"Stop it!" she said to herself.

He's just another kid acting out.

But even as she thought it, she didn't wholly believe it.

No, it hadn't been fear that had come through from Brina, it had been… what? Betrayal? She'd simply asked a question about Jason Liu and Brina had exploded with anger. Betrayal?

You've been that lonely kid, Charlene, she thought, *you've lived in that bubble. You know how hard it is to trust anyone, especially when they throw it back in your face.*

She thought of Suzy, of the arguments that had sealed the end of their relationship, of Suzy's claim that she wouldn't open fully, wouldn't let her in. Of boundaries and barriers and the needless scattering of loving bonds.

Of Charlene's seeming will to make herself an island.

"It's hard to open up," she said quietly, thinking of herself, thinking of Brina, thinking of Suzy.

And suddenly tears were coming. Unable to hold them back, she stopped walking and turned to face the wall of the school. She lent against the warming brickwork and placed her head on her forearm. All of the tension of the past few days, the confrontation with Jason Liu in the gas station, her growing infatuation with Katie, and the ensuing rejection, the latest argument with Brina, all of it welling up inside her and she was sobbing into her arm, moaning with the force of it. And she realized the moan was becoming a wail, she was ready to scream. She lifted her head slightly until her mouth was over her forearm and she bit down on the meat there, tasting the salt of her own tears, and she screamed. And screamed. And screamed.

She turned, leaning her back against the wall and, feeling gravity pull at her, slid down until she was sitting. She leant forward, head resting on her crossed arms.

* * *

The bell for morning recess echoed across the school campus.

Charlene jerked awake, startled by the noise.

She stood, disorientated, and walked around towards the front of the building.

* * *

Kids tumbled out of classes. Lockers clanked open. Voices added density to previously quiet halls. The press and movement of people, transitioning from one class to another. The organism alive.

* * *

There was a spot near the cafeteria where Brina liked to sit during morning recess, when there wasn't enough time for her to get outside and away from the others. At the end of a bank of lockers, where the corridor ended in a fire escape. A little nook in which she could nestle, in which she could disappear.

She sat there now, still smarting from the argument with Charlene, drifting in her own stream; voices and hubbub distant. The pen in her hand made shapes on the cover of her notepad yet she was only slightly aware of the fact she was drawing, looking at the ink and paper, yet somewhere through those swirls and angles.

Floating in abstract space, it took her a moment to register sneakers standing by her own feet.

She looked up into the smiling face of Jason Liu.

"Hi, Brina," he said.

A drawing compass in his hand, its pin-sharp point reflecting cold ceiling lights.

* * *

Charlene walked back to her cruiser, opened the trunk, and grabbed her purse. In the mirror of her powder compact, she could see the redness in her eyes, tell-tale evidence of tears; face puffy with her unexpected sleep. There was nothing for it, even with these blatant signals of her breakdown, she had to go to school. She would go straight to her office, close the door, wait out the day and hope to find some solution for this shitty situation.

She crossed the car park and walked through the doors into the entrance lobby, turning to head towards her office. She'd taken only a couple of steps when Sturmann called her from the entrance to the administrative offices.

"Er... Charlene!" he called. "Can I speak with you in my office, please?"

She wasn't ready to face him, or the situation, just yet; wanted to get herself together behind the solid security of her office door. She glanced back, hoping that, at this distance, he wouldn't read the signs written all over her face.

"Sure," she forced a smile to her face and voice, "let me drop this off and I'll be right back!"

"Okay."

She walked on towards her office.

* * *

"Snooping," he hissed, *"snooping!"*

* * *

She knew she should go to see Sturmann, that he'd be expecting her.

Yet she couldn't bring herself to open the door.

Not yet, she thought, *not just yet.*

She fixed her make-up once again.

* * *

But eventually, feeling chastened, feeling guilty, she stepped into the corridor. What had seemed a lifetime of avoiding this walk had been but moments and the kids were still ranging the halls.

She floated, disembodied, along the corridor, untouched by them, largely unaware of them at all.

The bell to end recess rang right above her head and she nearly jumped out of her skin; a small yelp of surprise.

She was suddenly aware of being watched and, as she turned her head, saw kids staring at her, a couple of them sniggering. She blushed furiously. Shrugged. Smiled at her own idiocy.

Did everything they would have expected her to do.

But the smile felt nailed on.

The panic felt real.

The embarrassment a bitter, tangible memory.

* * *

The students began to move off to their next class and she stood for a moment, letting the adrenalin rush and embarrassment run their course; anything to delay visiting the principal's office.

She realized her hand was resting on the butt of her holstered gun. Shocked, she let it drop to her side, hoping no-one had noticed her sub-conscious grab for her weapon.

As she was mulling this, she became aware of something awry in the movement of the students. Someone blocking their path, perhaps, or… Now she could see it, someone moving in the wrong direction along the corridor, heading for the exits as everyone else headed into the belly of the school. It was like watching an animal push through a field of corn, unable to see what it might be, judging progress only by the appearance of the path. Her eyes followed the disturbance as it moved through the crowds, catching the odd glimpse of an arm or a leg, clothing or a back-pack.

She took two steps towards the entrance lobby and was just in time to see Brina emerge from the throngs, barrelling straight for the doors. Her arms were crossed about her stomach, and she was hunched forward. No wonder she'd caused such disturbance as she moved against the flow of traffic, she'd have been near to butting her way through.

The doors opened and, for a moment, Brina was a shadow against the sunlight outdoors; a hunched Quasimodo seeking escape.

Charlene ran to catch up with Brina, the door closing before she could reach it. She pushed the handle and tumbled out.

Brina was nowhere to be seen. Charlene stopped, breathed a couple of times, thinking that Brina was highly likely to head towards the tennis courts, where she seemed to find the isolation she sought. She started towards the corner, but when she rounded it, she saw kids playing tennis, running laps on the sports field.

Brina wouldn't be there.

She turned back towards the school entrance. Movement out of the corner of her eye. She looked, saw Brina walking out of the front exit from campus, turning away from town, walking fast, still hunched over.

Charlene glanced across the car park at her cruiser, thought for a moment about grabbing it and decided not to, instead taking off at a run to catch up with Brina.

When she did, four blocks later, she was winded from running.

"Brina!" she called.

The girl slowed, but kept walking.

"Please?" Charlene called, fighting to get breath into her lungs.

"No." Brina said over her shoulder. "No, no, no."

"Whu…" Charlene tried to ask, "what did I do?"

At the end of the block, Brina stopped and turned to face her.

"I can't talk to you," Brina said.

"What do you mean? Of *course* you can talk to me!"

"No," Brina persisted, "I… can't… talk to you."

Charlene shrugged, face contorting into a *what-the-fuck?* grimace.

Brina held out her hands, turning them to display her inner forearms; small red blotches punctuating pale, ivory skin.

What are those? Charlene thought.

And then she noticed the stains on Brina's t-shirt, deep black against the dark material. Almost wet looking.

Is that blood?

"Oh, Brina," she sighed, "are those… Did he… What did he do to you?"

But Brina's face was set. She folded her arms around her tummy again, wincing as she did so.

"I can't talk to you," she repeated, turning to walk away from Charlene, away from the school, her pace increasing to a near-run

Charlene stood, watching until she was completely alone at the crossroads.

She had never felt so lost.

Chapter 33: Grabbing A Snake By The Tail

About half a block back towards the school, Charlene began to feel light-headed; sun too hazy, air too humid, shapes dancing on the inside of her eyelids. Fearing she was about to pass out, she sat on the sidewalk, leaning back on a streetlight; closed her eyes, breathed deep.

This is crazy, she thought, beginning to feel like she might vomit.

Her thoughts racing, she fought hard to calm herself.

After a few minutes, her pulse had settled, and the nausea had retreated.

She stood and headed slowly back to the school.

*   *   *

By the time she returned, morning classes were over and the kids were moving to lunch.

She stepped through the entrance doors into the melee. The sound and the bustle pressed in upon her and she began to feel her chest tightening; breath becoming shallow. Panic fluttered up within her.

Where is he? she thought, manically scanning the oncoming and passing faces in readiness for the defence.

But Jason Liu was nowhere to be seen.

Looked towards the administration offices, a ghost of a thought that she should tell Sturmann about…

Where is he?

Her panic would not let the thought go.

She moved through the crowds deeper into the school buildings.

* * *

As she walked she became aware of the energy of the students.

They were moving too fast; getting away from something.

She looked up the corridor towards the epicentre of the energy: a boys rest-room.

As she approached, she could hear laughter.

Crazy laughter.

The kids here, standing to watch the closed door of the rest-room, had a frightened look in their eyes. Some whispered, most bore silent witness.

The laughter rang from inside the restroom, amplified by tiles and cubicles.

Charlene's didn't notice as her hand fell instinctively to the butt of her gun; all attention on the laughter behind the closed rest-room door.

"What's happening?" she asked without turning to the teenagers around her.

No-one replied.

Charlene didn't slow, walking up to the rest-room door. Only then did she pause, resting her ear against the door, listening for any threat.

But there was only that laughter, peeling out… No, there was something else. Quietly, between the laughter, someone was crying. Someone obviously very, very frightened.

Charlene looked down, meaning to release the strap holding her gun in its holster, only to find that she'd already done that on autopilot. She was relieved to note that the gun's safety was still on.

She breathed deeply, waiting for the next burst of laughter.

When it came, crouching slightly, she pushed the door and stepped through into a small alcove where she leant against the wall, closing the door quietly behind her.

The laughter rang from the tiles.

"Don't!" the scared voice pleaded, near screaming.

The hard *smack!* of someone getting hit.

Charlene stepped around the corner.

Jason Liu was bending over a younger kid, who had been thrown back on his butt to sit in the urinals. His attention was totally focused on the kid, whose t-shirt he held balled in his left fist. His right was lifting again, ready to hit the kid's puffy, bruised face.

"What did you say!" Jason yelled.

The kid shook his head slightly in negation or an involuntary shudder. He closed his eyes, turned his face from the onrushing fist.

"Please?" he whimpered.

Jason started to laugh again.

"Stop!" Charlene commanded.

The moment froze.

Jason's fist dropped to his side and he let the kid go.

The kid sat paralyzed, watching his attacker.

"Don't you move!" Jason hissed.

"Jason," Charlene said steadily, "leave him alone."

Jason whirled; his face was rage.

"What are you doing here?" he yelled.

"Let him go, Jason," she fought to keep her voice level, "please?"

He looked at her, at the urinals, back at her. For a moment, confusion ghosted across his face.

"You… You can't be in here!"

"But I am," she said, "and I'm not going anywhere until you let him go."

They stared at each other; the unstoppable force and the immovable object.

Jason shrugged.

"Sure, whatever," he said.

The kid didn't move. Jason whirled on him.

"Go on, get out!"

His anger seemed to break the inertia and the kid ran past Charlene, eyes only for the exit.

"Don't worry," Jason yelled after him, "there are other days, other places!"

Charlene thought of Brina, of the pin-pricks on her arms, the way she'd huddled and cried.

"No!" she yelled.

"Of *course*," Jason smiled, "this is my school!"

The patches of blood on Brina's t-shirt.

"No!"

And suddenly Jason lurched towards her, fists raising.

In pure reaction, Charlene pulled her gun, levelled it at him.

He stopped immediately about two feet away, his fists raising to open palms above his head.

"Turn around."

He did.

"Arms behind your back."

He did.

She cuffed him in one smooth movement.

"Come on."

She marched him out of the rest-room and into the corridor.

* * *

She couldn't deny taking some pleasure in his walk of shame.

Gun holstered, she marched him slowly to the principal's office.

She stayed focused on him, wary that he might try and run at any moment, but he acquiesced silently to each of her commands.

For the first time since she'd arrived at the school, the corridors fell silent, even though they were packed with teenagers. They watched, this mute audience, as she paraded him to see Sturmann.

She didn't know whether it was adrenalin or vindication, but she had to fight the urge to smile or punch the air in a victory salute.

* * *

When Sturmann asked for details, she had a moment to consider whether she should fill him in on everything that had been happening.

She looked at Jason Liu, sat in a chair, cuffs off; hunched, chastened.

She decided to tell Sturmann only what had happened in the rest-room.

When she was done, she looked at Sturmann.

"Over to you," she said, "I'll go and check things have calmed down."

"Sure," Sturmann said, "I've got this."

Charlene stood and headed out of the office, leaving Jason Liu head down, silent and embarrassed; just the way he should be now that she'd taken him out.

Chapter 34:
Daddy Loves You

The phone rang only once before Sturmann picked it up.

All the time, reading and re-reading the email at the head of his inbox.

"Principal Sturmann," he answered on autopilot.

The email that had arrived only minutes after he'd tried to contact Jason Liu's father.

"Ah, good afternoon, Principal Sturmann," an erudite voice said, "this is George Liu. I believe you were trying to contact me?"

The email from Mason.

"Good afternoon, Mr Liu," Sturmann said, eyes scanning the email. "Yes, I wanted to let you know that we caught..."

The email.

"... there was some trouble today involving Jason."

"Trouble?" a note of panic.

"He's fine. But we do need to talk. Is there any chance you could come into school tomorrow?"

"Sure, let me just check," Liu paused for a moment, "I could make it at about eleven in the morning?"

"That's great," Sturmann said, "thanks so much for being flexible."

Written in capitals.

"No problem. Is Jason with you?"

```
STURMANN – THE CHILD OF ONE OF OUR
TOWN'S MOST RESPECTED BUSINESS LEADERS
DOES NOT GET TAKEN TO THE PRINCIPAL'S
OFFICE. NOTHING HAPPENED. DO I MAKE
MYSELF CLEAR? MASON
```

"No," Sturmann said, closing his eyes, seeing Mason's rant on the inside of his eyelids, "it was getting towards the end of school, so I let him head home. Figured we could talk about it tomorrow."

He tasted ash.

"It's nothing serious."

* * *

Katie closed her locker and walked back towards her home room, lost in thought.

Her parents had really challenged her the previous night; reflecting a decision she needed to make. Up until their conversation, she'd thought that Dylan's recovery, and this weird thing with Charlene, were the full extent of her worries.

But her parents had pointed out that she needed to make a decision which college she wanted to attend if she wanted to be in this year's application process. They'd laid it out as cleanly as that; it was her decision.

And, of course, Dylan had already decided to go to Florida where the football was...

Sudden commotion at her side and she was flying through the air towards the wall. Only it wasn't a wall, it was a door, slightly ajar.

Katie's momentum pushed the door open and she tumbled through it.

The sound was muffled; she smelled paper, marker pens.

Somebody followed her in and the door closed behind them.

It was dark for a moment before the overhead bulb illuminated the room, washing out her sight.

She heard someone breathing close to her and, instinctively, threw her hands up in self-protection.

Ever so slowly, too slowly, the bulb's after-image faded.

And she was face-to-face with Jason Liu.

"Hey, baby," he said, grinning at her.

She screamed.

"Oh, I'm *sorry*, did I startle you?"

She nodded, frightened, fighting her breath back under control.

"You take a moment," he said, allowing his gaze to drop down to her body, "I'll just enjoy the view!"

She wanted to cover herself up, to block him; this visceral sense of violation. She hoped somebody had seen the attack, or heard her screams, though knew it unlikely given his previous form.

"Stop," she breathed.

"I bet you feel fucking awesome," he said, his smile fixed, "how's about it, baby? Got a feel for Daddy?"

She shuddered, stared at him.

Beyond the door, voices echoed down the corridors; they passed without stopping.

"Please, Jason!" she said.

His anger was immediate.

"Don't you dare speak my name!" he yelled.

He pushed her back against the shelves of office supplies and let his hand drop to her breast. Instinctively, she made a grab for it but he batted her away like a fly, without even looking away from his hand.

He squeezed.

She was whimpering, distressed by the sound of herself as much as by the attack.

She opened her eyes and looked at him.

"Nice!" he smiled, anger pulsing just beneath. "Wonder how sweet your cunt..."

She panicked, pushed him hard enough that he tumbled into the collected boxes and bags, yelling surprised anger. Katie ran blind for the door and the sanctuary promised by the voices beyond.

"No!" she heard him yell.

Then she was in the corridor, running, running, running, expecting to feel his hands on her at any moment; whimpering, amidst laboured breathing.

She reached the corner, saw people, headed for them. They hadn't noticed her yet and she slowed to a walk, breathing deeply to hold back the tears.

When she was within a few yards of the other kids, she turned to glance over her shoulder.

Jason Liu was nowhere to be seen.

Desperate to find help, she walked quickly towards Charlene's office, panicking a little when she saw that the door was closed.

Please be there, she pleaded in silence, *please!*

* * *

Charlene sat in her office, fighting paradoxical emotions.

She was still coasting down from the satisfaction of having dealt with Jason Liu, the vindication of marching him to Sturmann's office, asserting her position and role in the school.

At the same time, she couldn't avoid the sinking feeling in her stomach. It was Katie's certainty that he had been involved in Dylan's beating; and if so, it was a fair assumption that he'd also had a hand in breaking Bobby Kingston's arm. It was the stab marks on Brina's arms, the blood florets on her t-shirt; what *had* he used on her? It was Tanner's warning that the kid came after him.

She had completely missed it that first day, when she'd misread him as victim.

Now she could see it clearly.

Something was very off with Jason Liu.

She sighed.

Well, at least he was with Sturmann now and, whatever the Principal's personal shortcomings, Charlene trusted his professional capabilities.

Jason Liu was out of her hair.

There was a knock at the door, and she flinched.

He got away! her panic screamed.

Another knock.

Charlene gritted her teeth and waited for her unknown visitor to leave.

* * *

She thought about walking the halls, some small part of her hoping that she might bump into Katie. Even though her infatuation wasn't reflected, she still felt an ache to spend time with the teenager, even if only moments.

As she thought of Katie's smile, the dread of returning to her house, yawning wide and empty on the other side of the afternoon, hit her once more.

She gritted her teeth against the tears that wanted to come.

No more, she thought, *I'm done. I refuse to let this get to me.*

Though, of course, she wasn't, and it did.

She sat in her office long after the sound of kids running in the halls had faded to nothing.

* * *

Finally, though, she could sit no longer; the school would be locked up around her.

She gathered her things and headed out towards the school entrance.

The administrative offices were closed and dark; hallways silent.

The car park was largely empty, her cruiser an island in the grey asphalt.

She stepped into the roadway, glancing left in memory of her chase to catch Brina; saw no-one, only passing traffic on the road that fronted the school. Even that traffic was light.

Everyone's got somewhere else to be, she thought bitterly, biting down on tears, *someone else to be with.*

When she turned to face the cruiser again, she noticed what she hadn't immediately.

That's not right, she thought, looking at the car.

She'd already taken a few steps before she realized what it was; the cruiser sitting too low on its wheels, like a low-rider or...

"A junker," she said out loud.

She rushed forward and, sure enough, the tyres on the passenger side had been slashed. She rounded the hood and found the same on the driver's side. All four tyres, slashed; the car sitting on its rims.

Her hand fell to her gun, checking it was still in its holster.

She tried the driver's door and found it locked.

Well, at least he didn't break the windows, she thought, relieved.

Charlene leaned back on the driver's door, blew air up towards the late-afternoon sky.

"Shit," she sighed out on that breath.

"Hi!" yelled Jason Liu, popping up from where he'd been crouched at back of the car, *"what say we have some fun?"*

Chapter 35:
This Is So Unfair!

Panic leaped in Charlene's chest and stomach.

She turned and ran.

"Wait!" Jason yelled behind her; mocking. *"Where are you going?"*

She didn't hear him for the blood rushing in her ears.

She ran.

* * *

The football field was deserted as she ran across the foul line.

She was flagging, muscles screaming at her to stop, breath harsh and choking. Finally, she couldn't take another step and she came to a dwindling halt. Tried to suck in air, to fight it in, force it in; in through the nose, out through the mouth, in through the nose, out through the mouth. But it seemed to be for nought, her vision blurring; firework flashes of red, orange, yellow.

"Man! That was sooooome work-out!"

She whirled to face him, finding his fists pumping the air in victory.

He started to shout the theme song from the Rocky movies.

"Please," she gasped, holding out a hand to ward him off.

But he ignored the plea, kept singing the tune over and over, dancing to his own beat, shuffling his feet as he shadow-boxed the air.

"Whu... What are you doing?"

He stopped, jarring the world to stillness.

"Isn't it obvious," he said, "I'm just getting warmed up."

He took a step forward and her hand moved like a viper, unlatching the strap across her holster. She didn't draw; this was a warning.

Jason stopped. Stared at the gun.

"Well," he said finally, "I guess that gives you the upper hand doesn't it?"

Charlene didn't reply.

Jason threw his arms to the sky.

"Why are you doing this?" he yelled, sounding every inch the whining teenager.

It's sooo unfaaaair, some small part of Charlene's thoughts laughed. The presence of that thought gave her some courage.

"Why am I doing what?" she asked.

He stared at her for a long moment before sweeping his arm in a gesture which encompassed the two of them, the football field and the school buildings beyond.

"This!" he said. "Everything was fine until you showed up and started snooping around where you weren't wanted! I had this under control! I had respect! This school was mine!"

She looked at him, wary; danger coiled in his words.

His teeth showed something between grimace and grin; skeletal.

"But now here you are trying to mess it all up. Just because you're the one in a uniform! The one who gets to carry a gun to school! Not fair!"

That small part of her laughed again, and she was distracted for a moment.

He took two steps forward, now within grabbing distance of her and she realized he was reading her in split-seconds; losing focus for even a moment could carry severe consequences.

"This doesn't change a thing!" he yelled. "This is still my school! And not you, not anyone else is going to change that. It's mine!"

"Calm down, Jason," she said.

"No! I will not calm down! Fuck you!"

"Jason," she repeated, "please ca..."

"No! Fuck you!"

"How many people saw us coming out here, Jason?"

"Huh? What?"

"How many people, Jason. How many saw you chasing me?"

She knew it was no-one; a deliberate bluff that succeeded in getting his attention, doubt creasing his face for a moment.

For a moment, he became a kid, counting on mental fingers.

He shook his head.

"No-one! There's nobody here!"

"Are you sure?" she said, glancing towards the school for emphasis, "because there sure are a lot of windows over there."

He glanced towards the buildings but his gaze snapped back as if on elastic.

"There's…"

Charlene breathed deep, ready to claim the moment, keen to be away from this, escaping to whatever space and time would give her chance to think about what she was going to do.

A hundred different openers ran through her mind:

Let's just forget this ever happened…

Take some time to think about what you've done…

Dead or alive, you're coming with me…

"I'm leaving," she said calmly, "and you are going to let me go."

He was momentarily struck dumb.

"I can't let this pass, Jason. But I need to think how best to deal with it. If you try and stop me leaving, it'll make what happens eventually that much worse."

She knew this was brinksmanship, that his detonator might blow at any moment, but she needed the time to get away from him; especially now that her cruiser was going nowhere.

I wish there was someone to see this, she thought, forcing herself not to glance at the windows, *but pretty soon he'll realize there isn't. Because there aren't any sirens. Because no-one's called 911.*

The thought was like iced-water in her veins; she was on borrowed time already.

She dropped her hand to the butt of her gun.

"Yes, Jason," she said, "this does get respect and right now, young man, you are going to turn and walk in that direction."

She pointed to the far side of the football field, away from the school.

When he didn't turn to follow her instruction, she pulled the gun slightly.

"Move!" she commanded.

This time he did, though his every move was reluctant.

"Keep walking," she said firmly, now beginning to back up herself, towards the buildings, car park and school exit, "just keep walking."

When she'd put thirty yards between them, she turned and started walking away, glancing over her shoulder every second step to confirm he was still headed towards the trees on the far side of the field.

Eventually, as she reached the edge of the bleachers, he wasn't even a speck in the distance and she was able to let loose the shuddering sigh which she'd been holding in for what felt like forever.

She sat on the lowest bench, and let the tears come.

* * *

Charlene came back to herself violently.

I have to get out of here, she thought, looking up at the abandoned windows, *how long have I been sitting here?*

She stood, feeling numbness in her legs, a potent combination of adrenalin, running and sitting.

How long have I been sitting here?

Feeling a chill, despite the late afternoon sun, she rubbed at her arms.

She turned for the car park and started to walk.

As she did so, without even thinking, she clipped the holster strap back over the butt of her gun.

She turned the corner to walk by the tennis courts, her thoughts dreamlike, verging between calm delusion and manic visions. She glanced towards the nets, half expecting to see Brina where they'd first met.

Oh, I hope he didn't hurt her too bad, Charlene thought, thinking of the pain that had creased Brina's pretty face, *I should check in with her.*

But the courts were empty; nets swaying slightly in the breeze.

She passed the end of the courts and crossed the interior road to walk alongside the buildings.

Thinking of Brina. Of how she was really much prettier than she thought of herself. Thinking of Katie. These two extremes of beauty, one to be persuaded, the other out for all to see.

She slowed a little, stewing in the mixture of guilt, desire, remorse and confusion that these images conjured within her; she ached with it, longing to let it out and be done with it.

To be able to say *'I love you'* without fear of repercussion or the crushing weight of judgement and intolerance.

To not be alone with this any longer.

To...

Jason charged from the alleyway entrance to the gymnasium. His last step was to vault off the low wall where she and Brina had talked, so that when he struck her, his speed was amplified by gravity.

The branch struck her square on the top of her head and she crumpled like a rag doll.

Unable to move, she opened her eyes.

Saw his scuffed designer sneakers as he stood staring at her.

Saw Brina's passion and pain.

Her eyelids began to droop as she disappeared.

Saw his sneaker take a step towards her, scuffing up dust in little clouds.

Saw a single tear drop from Katie's chin to bless the curve of her breast.

I love you, she thought as she plummeted into the black.

Chapter 36:
Turn Left

"There's been no change, he's stable."

There was, perhaps, no more infuriating update to receive.

Katie looked at Dylan now, those simple, empty meaningless words ringing through her head.

She could see change. She *could.*

Ah, who am I kidding, she thought, *just trying to convince myself that he's getting better?*

If there had been any change, it was limited to the colour and puffiness of the bruises that peeked from under the sheets, darkening his familiar face.

She needed so badly to speak with someone, anyone, about what had happened with Jason that afternoon.

How's about it baby, his voice hectored, amplified by memory, screeching, *got a feel for Daddy?*

She drew her arms around herself, holding tight. Still, the tears would not come.

"Oh, Dylan," she said, "please come back. I need you."

She stood, leant to kiss his forehead and then left the room.

* * *

The first thing Charlene sensed was stickiness in her hair, where her head had been resting on the ground.

Oh shit, she thought, *this is bad.*

She lay still and lifted her hand to feel her head.

The pain was immediate and sharp; her hand recoiled. A cut, a *big* cut.

She forced her hand back to the cut, through the pain, to press at her skull. She could sense no fracture.

"You're a tough old boot, Charlene," she whispered and went to sit up.

Nausea flooded through her and the horizon, growing dim as the light faded, rolled like the mighty Pacific itself.

She almost disappeared again; orange and red lights flaring in her eyes in time with her nauseous pulse.

No, she thought, placing her hands flat on the ground, *no, you are not going to pass out!*

It did the trick.

Charlene sat and breathed.

* * *

The emergency room was quiet as Katie walked through to the car park; still-frame snapshots of Sunday evening, of Charlene, of Bobby Kingston and his badly broken arm.

She shuddered at the memories, blocking them out and walking through the doors into evening gloom.

* * *

As soon as Charlene could sit without passing out, her mind burped that he might still be here. She looked about herself, panicked.

But she knew he was gone before she'd even confirmed it visually.

He wouldn't have let me sit up.

* * *

The stars, beginning to peek through the darkness, twinkled like a childhood song. She pulled the key to her dad's car from her pocket.

"Hi, Katie."

She whirled, pulse racing.

Jason Liu stood by the open door of his father's black Mercedes, parked a couple of spaces away.

Panicked, she looked around the car park.

Empty.

They were alone.

Jason lifted his right hand from where it had been hidden by the door.

The gun gleamed darkly in moonlight and sodium arc.

"Get in," he commanded, gesturing her towards the driver's seat.

* * *

She thought about running.

She thought about screaming.

She thought about rape.

She thought about whether he would pull the trigger.

She thought all this and more as she sat in the driver's seat.

* * *

I need to get help, Charlene thought.

She looked up the internal road toward the car park, but it was empty, the lights of the town far beyond.

She didn't think she could walk that far.

And the cruiser's tyres had been slashed.

The cruiser…

Wait!

She pulled herself onto her knees, swallowing down hard on the fresh bout of vertigo, and crawled towards the car, the radio within.

* * *

After moments that felt like minutes, he tapped on the glass of the passenger door. Katie looked toward the sound, confused.

He tapped again.

What does he want? she thought.

And then she realized: the door was locked.

For a moment, she felt a thrill of relief run through her.

I can lock myself in!

Another tap.

Of metal against glass.

She looked up from the door handle and lock, straight into the cold circle of the gun's barrel.

She reached over and flipped the lock.

* * *

When Charlene reached the cruiser, she realized her keys weren't in her pocket. She grabbed a rock and smashed the window on the driver's side.

* * *

He sat with the gun in his right hand, aimed sideways at her.

Tossed the keys into her lap.

"Jason..." she began.

"No," he said, staring out the windshield, "don't say anything. Just start the car and drive."

* * *

Streetlights flashed stroboscopic through the tinted windows of the Mercedes.

"Are you going to rape me?"

"I said don't speak."

"Sorry."

"Shh!"

The car crept through the quieting town.

"I haven't decided yet."

* * *

"Boss? It's Charlene."

The trees see-sawed again.

"Huh?"

Stars began to prick the night.

"Yes, I'm fine... No, I'm not."

She breathed heavily, felt the running board press into her abdomen.

"In the school car park, the cruiser..."

Closed her eyes.

"Okay, I'll wait here for you."

Dropped the handset and leant forward to rest her cheek on the seat, amidst the glass from the smashed window.

* * *

The miles passed, dark country roads, lights of the town ghosting the night sky with a glowing dome.

"This town," Jason said, "it's too much!"

"I.."

"Shhh!"

"They're all so small. So… Insignificant! They're no match for… Left."

She turned at the stop sign, headed into the black.

"They're like fucking sheep, standing around all day, chewing grass while I'm stalking… No, it's not even that. I'm not stalking them. I'm not a sheep dog, I'm the shepherd! That's right! I'm organizing their fucking lives! They don't dare take a shit without my permission! This fucking town!"

His hand stroked her thigh for a brief moment, and she recoiled involuntarily.

"It's all about respect," Jason continued, "it always has been. My father earned their respect by owning their fucking houses and shops and restaurants and just about every other fucking thing in this town that isn't nailed down! Now I'm doing the same thing!"

"Only kids respect you more when you take out one of their own, one of their heroes!"

"So, it *was* you…"

"If I have to tell you to keep your mouth shut one more time, I swear I'm gonna punch you so fucking hard! Just shut up and listen!"

"Sorry."

"Better. Yes, I handed *Captain America* his ass on a plate, of course I did. Who else would have dared? Not the pussies in this town, for sure!"

"I took out their home-coming hero! How's that for getting respect? How's that for going down in fucking history!"

Another stop sign.

"Right."

She turned. In the darkness, she sensed more than saw, as he lifted the gun slightly, seeming to feel its weight for the first time.

"And now, I'm gonna complete the pair," he said, a cat with cream, luxuriating in his satisfaction.

Chapter 37: Deep In The Silence

Main Street cooled in the early evening, asphalt radiating stored heat.

Buildings rested, freshly scrubbed of recent graffiti.

Cars passed through, others pulled over.

In the park, ducks settled for the night by the renovated riverside walkway.

People walked to restaurants and bars; their conversation having little chance of replacing the overbearing silence of the town.

* * *

Charlene leaned against the deflated front tyre of the cruiser, her head resting back on the wheel arch, drifting in and out of consciousness while she waited for Baker to arrive.

The headache had come on strong; when she reached her hand up to the cut on the top of her head, she could feel swelling. She closed her eyes against the pain for a moment, wishing she could disappear into the black again.

Something's not right.

The thought was like a jolt of pure electricity and her eyes sprung open.

What is it, she thought, *what is it?*

She looked around the car park, in case something there had triggered such a powerful intuition. But there was nothing. She was alone with her cruiser, the silent town far beyond the school exit.

The evening was still. No breeze. No clouds; stars pricked the darkening sky.

Something's not right.

She blinked, and an image of Dylan Ford flashed before her; on his hospital bed, all bruises, cuts, wires and tubes.

Something's not right.

She heard the engine before she saw the lights, revving its way towards the school. Looked over that way, saw twin headlights piercing the night as a car screeched into the car park.

He's come back to finish the job, she thought, realizing that she had no strength with which to fight back.

The car sped across the asphalt towards her. Unable to move, blinded by the headlights, she could only listen as it bore down upon her; a massive bull, charging, all heat and muscle, ready to trample over her.

"Please," she pleaded, waving a feeble hand in the hopes of warding off collision.

The bull stopped, breathing heavily a few feet away from her.

The brightness of the headlights through her eyelids, there and then gone. She heard the door click open, waited for the next blow to come.

"Please."

She began to drift.

A boot struck the ground, followed by fast steps in her direction.

She waited for the kick.

Opened her eyes; still blind with after-burn.

"Jesus, Charlene!"

Baker knelt by her side.

"What happened?"

Charlene fell into the black again.

* * *

Mason sat in his home office, scanning through emails.

Tomorrow's piece about the graffiti was waiting for his review and he clicked it open.

Haven't seen today's report from the school cop, he thought before his attention was distracted by the article opening on his desktop, its pointless headline.

"Really, Curtis?" he asked the silence of his office, "Really? Do I have to re-write everything you publish?"

With a hefty sigh, Mason went to work.

* * *

Along country roads beyond town, through the darkness of the dense woods either side, the black Mercedes rolled.

Katie gripped the steering wheel with both hands; the fear a constant, rhythmic drumbeat, punctuated by blaring horns and dissonance.

Jason continued to lay claim to the town and his demands for respect.

Eventually, he told her it was time to turn the car around.

* * *

Sturmann sat at his dinner table, reading the New York Times; between sips at his second glass of wine, he spooned cold ravioli into his mouth. Losing himself in faraway news had become the only way he could switch off the noise of the school; soundtrack to every waking thought.

As he went to turn the page, he realized his wife had been talking to him.

"Huh?" he said.

* * *

Something's not right, Charlene thought, as she felt Baker checking the extent of her injuries.

"I think it's just your head," he said, "it's bad but I really think that's it?"

Something's not right.

"How many fingers?" he said.

She opened her eyes to look, the headlights' after-burn receding.

"Three," she said.

"You're sure?"

Something's not right.

"Three."

"Okay. So it doesn't seem like concussion. Still, we should get you to the hospital."

"No. I'm all…

Something's not

… right. Really."

He paused. Thought for a moment.

You're a good man, Jack Baker, she thought, *you always stop to think first.*

"Well," he said eventually, "I'll tell you what, we'll head back to the station and see how you're doing when we get there. If you're any worse, we're going straight to the hospital."

"Me and Dylan, both," she joked, holding her hand up to him.

Something's not right.

Reality swam a little as he pulled her to her feet, but after a moment stability returned. Baker scrutinized her, looking carefully into her eyes.

"You okay?" he asked.

"It hurts, boss," she said, "but nothing more than a headache. I'd tell you otherwise."

"Well, okay," he aquiesced.

They crossed to his cruiser, Baker drawing in worried breath at the sight of the slashed tyres on Charlene's vehicle.

He opened the side door for her and she stepped into the car.

Something's not right, she thought as the door closed behind her.

* * *

Brina leaned around her bedroom doorframe, listening intently.

The sound of the Food Channel wafted up the stairs. Her mother would be watching for a while now, entrenched with cookies and a cup of sweet tea.

She stepped back into her bedroom and pulled her bloody t-shirt from under her bed, where she'd stashed it earlier that afternoon. The florets had turned dark brown now, drying to hard crusts on the material.

On autopilot, her hand travelled over her torso; the wounds had healed to tiny, hard scabs, each surrounded by an emergent bruise. She would be able to hide the damage.

She was good at hiding.

She crossed the landing and descended the stairs, careful not to disturb her mother.

Out the back door and yard to the alleyway that ran behind all the houses on her block. She looked around herself, checking no-one else was around. A glance at the houses confirmed that no-one was looking at the alleyway.

She stepped out and walked down the alleyway until she was five houses away from her own place. This was the old lady's house, Mrs Rossini; mostly housebound, highly unlikely to check her trash before it would be collected.

With one final check to ensure she wasn't being watched, Brina lifted the lid of the trash can and pitched her blood-stained shirt.

Rubbing at the pin-pricks and bruises on her arms, she could have been a proto-junkie.

She turned and walked back up the alleyway.

Inside, she trod carefully as she climbed the stairs to the safe haven of her room.

* * *

Baker was quiet for most of the journey back to the station.

As they neared the entrance, he broke his silence.

"Do you know who jumped you?"

Charlene didn't move her head from where she'd been staring at the silent town through her window.

Something's not right.

"No," she said, "he… I got jumped from behind, around by the tennis courts."

"Not by the car?"

"No, I went there afterwards, to call you."

"And you really don't know who did this?"

She could taste the disbelief in his words, and didn't know why she felt compelled to lie; some mixture of embarrassment, shame, and that ever-present doubt that nagged at her: *something's not right.*

Something.
"No," she said, and went back to staring at the silent town.

Chapter 38: Something's Not Right

"Here you go," Baker said, handing the steaming mug of coffee to Charlene. He watched carefully for any tremor or other sign of concussion, before putting his own cup down on a filing cabinet and unlocking the door to his office. He opened the door and gestured inside.

"Want to come in?" he asked.

She shook her head.

"I'll sit for a while."

And so she did, outside his office like a kid waiting for the principal; diminished, collapsing in on herself.

Charlene sipped on her coffee, the caffeine forcing her even further into that nagging doubt: *Something's not right.*

* * *

Baker watched Charlene through the internal window of his office. She sat still, the back of her head facing him.

He lifted the phone's handset and punched the autodial for Mason.

In the light of the office, it was clear that the cut on Charlene's head was a lot less severe than it had seemed in the car park; the scalp could bleed, for sure. And she had told him time and again that there were no other injuries; something he'd monitored by seeing how she moved, which seemed to confirm her claim.

The line connected and the phone began to ring.

She insisted that she hadn't seen her attacker. If she'd been attacked in the car park, he would have doubted that, but as he'd been driving out, she'd directed him around by the back of the gymnasium where she'd been jumped. In the nested shadows, it was all too easy to see how she could have been attacked without even knowing it was coming.

She sat, quietly sipping at her coffee; he wondered when the shock would kick in.

Mason picked up on the third ring.

"Baker?"

"Yup. Wanted to let you know that something's happened."

"Oh?"

"Yes, at the school."

* * *

The sound of Baker speaking was muffled through the wall, a basso rumble of indistinct syllables.

Charlene floated on it for a while.

* * *

"Happened by the gym," Baker said, "she was jumped."

"By the gymnasium buildings… What was she doing there?"

Didn't think to ask, Baker thought.

"Just making her final rounds of the day," he said.

"And she was attacked?"

"Yes. From behind. Got knocked out."

"Any idea who…"

"No," Baker cut in, "she didn't see who it was. I've asked her to think of who it could have been but she can't bring anyone to mind."

"Well," Mason paused, drew breath, "I believe this supports my instinct. Teenagers will run riot unless we control them."

Baker thought of the stray dog he'd seen the previous night; the blood drying in Charlene's hair. He had no choice but to accept that this could no longer be explained as run-of-the-mill teenage bravado.

"With all due respect," he said, "this is *so* not about that."

* * *

As she listened to the rumble, her mind began to ease back from red alert. Images began to flit across her conscious mind and she let them come through.

Brina's t-shirt and the florets of blood.

Dylan's broken body.

Marching Jason Liu up the corridor of shame.

But

A tear on Katie's breast.

But

Vindication in Sturmann's office.

But

Jason standing from behind her cruiser.

But

Chasing her to the football field.

Something

Dancing as he sang the theme from Rocky.

Something's not

Pulling her gun to threaten him away.

Something's not right

His manic insistence that the school and the town was…

"His," Charlene whispered and, for a moment, she felt her muscles let go. The coffee cup almost escaped her fingers but she grabbed at it with her other hand, causing the liquid to spill in all directions.

"Why didn't he finish the job?" she spoke to the empty office, already knowing the answer.

She reached for her holster and, this time, she did drop the cup.

She didn't even feel the coffee as it scalded her hands.

"He wanted my gun."

* * *

"I'm pulling her out," Baker said, glancing over at the drying blood on the back of Charlene's head.

"What?" Mason's anger was clear.

"We never should have put her in the school," Baker admitted, "I knew it at the time but…"

"But nothing!" Mason exploded. "This is exactly why we did the *right* thing putting her in the school!"

Baker closed his eyes, turned his face towards the ceiling tiles, tried to bite down on his anger.

"One of my team is sitting in the lobby with blood drying in her hair," he said, "and you're trying to tell me it's the right thing to have done."

"Of course," Mason fired back, "I mean, I'm sorry for Officer Goodlow and everything. But she'll heal in time and we've managed to flush out the attacker."

"Flushed him out?"

"Right."

"The attacker who we have failed to identify?"

Mason paused.

"Look," he said finally, and Baker could see him pointing his finger at the phone, "attacking an officer of the law is a serious offence. If I hadn't ordered a police officer to be placed in the school, your department would have bumbled along in a meaningless investigation for months. This way, we've... accelerated that timeline."

Really? Baker thought. *You're really going to claim that this was what you planned all along? Really?*

He was suddenly aware of how tired he was, of this day, this job, this constant pandering to egos run amok.

"Now," Mason continued, "the only decision we need make is how many *more* officers we place at the school."

"What?" Baker shouted, standing to look at the wall behind his desk; framed certificates, pictures of the many officers he'd trained and led over the years. "You're planning to double down?"

"Of course! Why wouldn't I? We've got him on the run!"

"But Charlene..."

"Has great medical! I know, I'm paying for it. She can get some rest and then get back on the job. We have to find this errant teenager and bring him to justice!"

There was a taste in Baker's mouth, bile and sawdust; he'd had just about enough of Mason's automatic use of talking point bullets.

"Are we done?" he asked.

"I hardly think so," Mason said, "we have to plan our next step."

Baker closed his eyes, tried to count to ten, only made it to five.

"Tomorrow," he spat, "we can talk about it tomorrow. I'm going to check that Charlene Goodlow hasn't got a delayed concussion."

He slammed the handset down on its cradle and whirled towards his office door.

It took a moment to register.

Charlene wasn't there any more.

Chapter 39:
Listen To Me

Jason and Katie walked across the football field towards the gymnasium's rear entrance. Though he'd stuck the gun in the waistband of his pants, it was within easy reach and, after the tension of the drive here, Katie had no doubt that Jason would use it.

The fear, a constant flow in her now, was morphing into resigned numbness.

The car was parked behind the bleachers. Jason had directed her to mount the kerb and pull into a small stand of trees. In the darkness, the black Mercedes had faded to a shadow among shadows.

Out of sight, she thought, and then filled in the blank in a cold, chilling voice, *we're alone here*.

They passed the tennis courts and crossed the internal road towards the main buildings.

"Wait," Jason commanded.

Katie stopped walking, watched him as he walked over to a low wall, scanning around him.

"What are you looking for?" she asked.

"Shh!"

After a moment of staring into the distance in all directions, he bent to kneel on the ground.

Laughter bubbled out of him; dark, worrying laughter.

Gooseflesh rippled along Katie's arms and she rubbed at them to be rid of it.

"Come and look at this," Jason said through the laughter, "you're not gonna believe it!"

She closed the gap between them, looked down, noticed that his hand was on the butt of the gun.

Naïve hope of escape evaporated once again.

He was looking at a stain on the ground.

"What is that?" Katie asked. "Is that… blood?"

He looked back over his shoulder.

"Sure is!" he smiled. "I was like a ninja, crouching-tiger-hidden-dragon-style, hit her before she even knew I was in the air!"

Katie didn't know what to say.

Jason, looked around the area by the wall.

"Ah, here it is!"

He scuttled over to the wall and took hold of a length of tree branch.

"Amazing what they leave lying around when they clear the woods, isn't it? I was like…"

He climbed onto the wall, took the pose of a warrior about to charge into battle.

"… and then like…"

He raised the branch above his head like a mighty, cleansing sword.

"… and then…"

He leapt towards Katie, swinging the branch down in a vicious arc.

Katie flinched sideways, closing her eyes against the blow.

But it never came.

When she opened her eyes, the branch was hanging by Jason's side and he was smiling at her.

"Oh, you don't need to worry your perfect little head," he said, "I've got other things planned for you. I was just showing you what I did to her."

"Her?"

"Yeah, that dyke cop that's been coming onto you," he shrugged, looking around himself.

Charlene, Katie thought and a memory of their reconciliation surged through her, their embrace, *thank God she got away.*

She knew she wasn't about to be so lucky.

"The police officer?" she asked, "Charlene?"

"That's the one," he nodded, perplexed. "Hmmm... I wonder where she went?"

He stood for a moment, like someone had unplugged his power or hit the reset button. Then, just as suddenly, he jerked back to life.

"Oh well," he smiled, "time's a-wasting. Come on!"

He pulled the gun and wagged its barrel towards the gym.

When they arrived at the rear entrance, she saw that the door was propped open by a small rock.

The bottom of her stomach dropped out.

He's planned this, she thought, *all of it.*

* * *

The high whine of a mosquito, close to her ear.

Charlene awoke with a jolt.

There was a brief moment of almost total confusion, where she didn't know who or where she was, becoming little more than an animal with neither fore- nor after-thought.

She shook her head to clear that ghastly sensation and immediately regretted it; the whole of her head singing a chorus of pain. Even wincing her eyes closed in motor response to the pain made it worse.

She opened her eyes.

Breathed in.

Looked about herself.

Breathed out.

She was in the riverside park, had walked here from the police station, desperate to clear her head enough to decide what to do.

Jason Liu had her gun.

Had attacked her to get her gun.

The mosquito whined its return and she slapped at it, catching her ear in the process and setting off another depth-charge of pain. She moaned in reaction to it, and the moan became tears.

She sat crying for a few moments; all the time, wondering why he'd taken her gun.

"Why?" Charlene moaned at the stars. "Why are you doing this?"

Because he's staking his claim, Baker's voice spoke calmly from her subconscious, *marking his territory.*

His territory.

"This is still my school! And not you, not anyone else is going to change that. It's mine!" Jason yelled in her memory.

The school, she thought, *that's where he'll make his stand.*

She stood up from the bench, waited for the head-rush of vertigo to pass, and then turned towards the school.

* * *

The gymnasium was dark, save for the emergency lights above the exit doors, and a single lamp high in the middle of the hall.

Katie sat in the tip-off circle of the basketball court, knees drawn up to her chin, arms hugging her legs. Her eyes had been blinded by the single light above and, beyond its halo, it was hard to see Jason. All she knew was he was somewhere up on the bleachers, looking down on the hall.

His voice echoed off the walls, reverberating in the empty, cavernous space, sounding at once like he was whispering in her ear, yet talking across the gulfs of space.

As she sat listening to Jason, his rage grew so total, the threat of the gun so oppressive, that she feared her end was upon her.

He ranted.

About high school kids.

About teachers.

About pointless lessons.

About how weak they all were.

About how they needed someone to look up to.

About how he was that person.

About Sturmann.

About Dylan.

About that goth kid, Brina.

About his father.

"Do you know what it's like?" he asked her, asked himself. "No, of course not, how could you? How could any of you shitheads understand what it feels like to know you'll inherit a whole town just as soon as your Father gets out of the way?"

"My father loves me, you know? He's built this whole town up from nothing and all because he loves me. Right? *Right?*"

His shouts reverberated to silence.

"Right," she whispered.

There was something in his voice, hitching and coughing and choking his words.

"Asshole," he finally managed to say, and Katie heard him sniff, sensed the shadow of his arm sweeping across the indistinct moon of his face.

Really? a sardonic voice rippled through her thoughts. *Really? All this is because he's got Dad issues?*

She almost laughed, but choked it back at the last second. This powder keg didn't need an unwitting fuse.

"What?" Jason snapped, like a dog protecting a bone. "What are you smiling about?"

"Nothing," she whispered, scared.

"Be quiet!" he yelled. *"Haven't I got through to you yet, you dumb cunt!"*

She stared warily at his shadow self on the bleachers. Nodded her head with relief, grateful to see he hadn't moved.

"I don't get it! Why won't you respect me? Fuck! I'm the one holding the gun!"

Katie saw red light glimmer off cold steel; braced herself for a shot.

Jason was silent for a moment. When he finally spoke again, his tone was calm, though rage formed a mighty undercurrent.

"Take off your t-shirt," he said.

She shook her head, partly in surprise at the request, partly in negation.

"Take it off!"

She did so, pulling it over her head and dropping it to one side.

She hugged her knees to her chest, fully expecting the next instruction to be the removal of her bra.

But the instruction didn't come.

"Better," Jason said, "very nice."

And, in that moment, Katie knew the night was never going to end, that his abuse and torture of her would spread over hours, that he was a cat with its plaything mouse, delaying the killing strike until maximum pleasure had been derived.

She hugged herself even tighter, felt tears beginning to course down her cheeks.

"Now," he wondered aloud, thought echoing around the dark gym, "where was I?"

Chapter 40:
Little Miss Perfect

Charlene limped into the school car park, head throbbing with exertion. The school buildings were little more than dark shadows against the night sky, punctuated every so often by the weak glow of inconsistent street-lamps. Between each oasis of orange light lay deep pools of black.

She eyed those deep shadows nervously as she headed for her cruiser, solitary on the far side of the car park, hunched down on deflated tyres.

He could be anywhere, she thought, *anywhere*.

* * *

"Do you know how much he's worth?"

Katie sat and stared, teeth clamped firmly to keep her mouth shut.

"In real estate alone, you've gotta say, what... sixty or seventy million... And in investments? Shit! It's a *lot* of money."

"Ha!"

Katie flinched.

"Make my own way, he said, I've gotta make my own way! Earn it myself, he said! So I... get this... so I learn the value of money! Ha!"

He was quiet for a moment.

In the pool of light at the centre of the basketball court, Katie hugged her knees tight; long beyond praying for release. The silence stretched before she heard it.

The barrel of the gun spinning until it clicked to a halt; the hammer clicking back into its locked position.

Though she fought against it, a small whimper escaped through her clenched teeth.

"Take off your bra," Jason said from the shadows.

* * *

Charlene reached the cruiser and went to grab her keys.

Only they weren't there.

She patted her pockets. Nothing save for some cash; notes and a few coins.

"Where did I…" she wondered out loud.

Only then did she remember smashing the window.

It wasn't just her gun. Her keys had been in a pouch on her equipment belt, which he'd taken as well.

How did I not notice that? she asked herself. *How the hell did I not notice?*

The pounding throb in her head and blurring sight gave reason enough; she sat down on the asphalt surface and leant her head back against the cool metal of the car; pain flared, a momentary thunder flash.

Jason Liu had her gun, her car keys, her mace spray, her notebook, her phone … He had her life.

Wait! she thought, *he has my phone!*

Finally she was able to grab at an option; something she might use to bring this terrible situation to an end.

"Talk him down," she said quietly to the night air and attentive mosquitos, "like he's on a ledge."

Whether he would listen was another thing completely, she knew. For now, just having the option of calling him was enough.

She thought about radioing the information through to Baker but her head was heavy again and the cool of the car's metal on her scalp so calming. She would radio the chief.

In a minute or two.

Her eyes closed.

* * *

Baker stared through his computer screen, hardly registering that it had tripped over into screen-saver a moment or two earlier.

The streets had been empty when he'd gone looking for Charlene; her house dark, not even a porch-light to welcome her home.

No sign of her at the school. He'd driven past her cruiser, made a mental note to get it towed the next morning.

Defeated, tired, he'd come back to the station to see if there was anything even close to resembling a Plan B.

He stared through the computer screen, lost in thought, his finger tapping absent-mindedly at the face of his cell-phone, lying to one side of the keyboard and mouse.

* * *

"Look at you," Jason spat, "*little miss perfect*. Not so perfect now, huh? Oh, I get your game, golden girl, I get it *all* too well, posing up and down the halls, making sure all the boys see just enough to get turned on but never enough that they don't want more."

"So they follow you like you was a bitch in heat."

"I could show them a thing or two. How many of them could get you naked, huh? Huh?"

He paused, raked laughter high into the gymnasium rafters.

"I'll tell you! None of them! Not a single one! But me… Oh yeah, I did it without even trying. And there you are, *little miss perfect*, just waiting for me to tell you what to do. Easy."

Katie shuddered, hugged herself tighter.

"Drop your knees," Jason sneered.

"No," she shook her head.

"I said *drop your knees, bitch!*" he roared.

Katie closed her eyes, winced, and let her legs drop into a cross-legged position, folding her arms across her chest. Tears pricked at her eyes and she felt the first streamers of snot form and dribble down her lip.

"Pretty," Jason said, "very pretty. *Little miss perfect*. C'mon girl, flash me some nipple!"

He laughed at himself.

She shook her head again.

"Do it," he said coldly.

She dropped her arms, felt the relatively cooler air of the gym tickle across her breasts; gooseflesh rippling across her skin.

"Not so fucking perfect now, huh? Just another rack, like we've all seen before," she heard something approaching disappointment in his voice, "they're smaller than I thought they'd be…"

He trailed off for a moment and she slowly folded her arms back over her chest. If he noticed, he didn't say anything. Through her tears she watched the shadows, wondered whether he was jacking off up there in the bleachers.

Suddenly, he roared laughter.

"Of course!" he yelled. "See? *See?* Of course they're smaller. It's all a fucking mirage. You and your fucking boyfriend, homecoming queen and Captain America, just made to put on fucking cereal boxes and toothpaste ads. It's all a fucking mirage!"

"I own you," he was growing manic now, putting new fear into her, "and as soon as I get what's owed me by my father, I'm gonna collect from all of you motherfucking cunts. I'm gonna line you up one by one and take aim."

Katie sensed as much as saw metal moving in the dim light.

"No!" she screamed.

"Gonna line you up and then…"

BOOM!

The gun fired; its flash and fury obliterating Katie's every conscious thought.

* * *

Charlene drowsed against the cold metal of the cruiser door.

Even the slight glimmer of hope from the fact that he had her phone couldn't bring her optimism.

She knew he was out there somewhere, but where. And why?

She thought of Brina and her blood spattered t-shirt; knew in some sinking part of herself that the answers to her questions involved Katie.

She rolled her head back slightly until the metal was directly in contact with the wound, wincing at the sharp pain, but waiting for the cool relief. She closed her eyes as it began to kick in.

BOOM!

She shot upright, eyes suddenly wide; all dilated pupils and panic, pain forgotten.

Looked both ways, but there was no sign of where the shot had come from. She waited a couple of seconds, but there was no repeat.

Maybe it wasn't a shot, maybe it was a… she began and then caught herself, *no Charlene, it was, and you know the sound of that gun.*

She stood, wavering slightly, and took a couple of steps away from the cruiser.

She turned, remembering the smashed window.

I should radio it in, she thought.

But she didn't.

Instead, thinking only of Katie, she turned back towards the school, some instinct moving her at a loping run around the corner and towards the gym complex.

Chapter 41: Twisting In The Gyre

Baker hated this feeling; his gut telling him to move, his head telling him he had no idea where he would go.

All he knew was that Charlene was missing on a night when she'd received a pretty serious head trauma, even if he had earlier dismissed it as a heavily bleeding scalp.

She could be anywhere: a ditch, a gutter, a bedroom, a car, anywhere.

But he had no clue where.

Still he sat, the confines of the police station drawing close about him, ceiling pressing down, walls closing in. His computer screen was no conduit to a different world, it was the harsh reflection of electric lights and his own troubled face.

He thought about using the community emails gathered by the department over the past few years; pretty much three quarters of the town had voluntarily given the information during neighbourhood watch week. For once, this piece of social manipulation hadn't been part of Mason's wider political schemes.

It had been Charlene's idea.

But to use the lists would be to go public about what had happened.

Excuse me, but one of my officers is missing, he thought bitterly, *if you see her, please call…*

He wasn't ready to pull the town into this mess. Not yet.

He didn't need it getting any messier.

He closed his eyes and, breathing slowly, recited the alphabet backwards; an old trick.

When he got to *'A'* he opened his eyes.

"Sturmann," he said, opening his contacts file.

* * *

"Honey!"

"What?" Sturmann looked up from his papers, annoyed at this interruption to what was already annoying him just fine.

"Phone!"

He threw the paperwork aside on the couch and stomped through to the kitchen where his wife was holding out the receiver.

"Who is it?" he mouthed, raising his eyebrows in a frustrated question mark.

"Police," she said silently, holding out the phone in encouragement, "Baker."

Sturmann stood for a moment, hands on hips, raised his chin, breathed out heavily at the ceiling.

He took the handset from his wife, who leant back against the counter to listen in on the conversation.

"Hello? Jack?"

"Oh hi, Walt," Baker said, "glad to have caught you. Hope I didn't interrupt anything."

"No," Sturmann replied, lips tight, "nothing I wasn't looking for an excuse to avoid, anyway. What's up?"

"I didn't know if you'd heard or not," Baker said, "it's Charlene, someone attacked her at the school earlier this evening."

Sturmann saw his own shock mirrored on his wife's face; she had seen his jaw drop.

"Attacked?" he whispered.

"Yup. Someone jumped her around the back of the school, near the tennis courts. Knocked her out."

"No," Sturmann was speechless.

"She was out for a while, but made it to her car to radio me. She was bleeding pretty badly."

"Shit," Sturmann shook his head, "that's serious. How is she now?"

"That's what I'm calling about, Walt. She left the station while I was on the phone."

"She left?"

"Yup. I was on the phone, talking with... Anyway, I finished up and she'd gone."

"Where did she go?"

"That's the million dollar question," Baker sighed, "I've driven around town but there's no sign of her. Her car is still at the school."

"So she didn't go back for that?"

"That's the other thing, Walt," Baker said, walking the evidence trail in his mind, "the tyres were slashed."

"No?"

"Yup. It's getting worse. So, I need you to think of anything, anything at all that happened today that might have triggered this."

"I can't..."

"Please," Baker pleaded, "anything?"

Sturmann shook his head, forehead creasing in annoyance.

"If you'd let me finish," he said, "I was about to say that I can't think of anything specific today. She seemed fine when I spoke with her after the Jason Liu thing."

"Liu? George's boy?"

"Yeah, she..."

Sturmann paused, remembering Mason's email: *Nothing happened. Do I make myself clear.*

"Walt?" Baker asked, "did I lose you?"

"No, I'm here," Sturmann confirmed, "nothing happened, just a little spat. You know how kids are. I kept Jason in my office for a while, let him cool off. Nothing to write home about."

"And Charlene was okay with that?"

"She..." Sturmann felt wounded pride rise up within him, "it doesn't matter whether she was okay with it. I'm the school principal and I'm telling you, it was nothing."

"Oh," Baker paused, "okay. Sorry. I'm just worried that Charlene's out there somewhere. She said she was feeling fine but you know how concussion can be..."

Sturmann looked around the kitchen, suddenly desperate to be out of a conversation with so many bear-traps and landmines.

"What was that, honey?" he called as if his wife were calling from another room.

She glared at him and he raised a finger to his lips, pleading for her complicity. In return, all he got were folded arms and a stare that could melt ice caps.

"Oh, okay! Look, sorry Jack, I've got to go. I'll keep thinking on it. If I get anything, I'll give you a call, okay?"

"Sure, but listen, keep this quiet at the moment. I don't want it getting out yet. If you do think of anything, I'll be here or on my cell. The number there is…"

"I have it, Jack. Good luck."

Sturmann ended the call.

His wife held out her hand and he returned the receiver to her. She replaced it and then folded her arms once more.

"Well?" she said

* * *

Baker stared at the phone.

He wasn't sure that he bought Sturmann's line about Jason Liu, but it still didn't sound like anything that would have triggered the attack on Charlene.

Oh well, at least he's got my cell if he has any other ideas, he thought.

It was like a depth charge going off in his mind.

"Oh my lord," he breathed out angry at no-one but himself, "what are you, blind or stupid, Jack?"

He grabbed his cell-phone and paged through to Charlene's contact details, selecting her mobile number and hitting the green button.

* * *

In the silence of the gym, up in the bleachers, a cell-phone trilled an incoming call. It rang once.

Twice.

Three times.

* * *

Baker sat with his phone pressed against his ear.

Heard the far end ring once, twice, three times.

Then it clicked.

"Charlene!" he said, believing it answered.

"Welcome to the voicemail service," a neutral female voice spoke robotically in his ear, "the person you are calling is not available. Please leave a message after the tone. When you have finished recording…"

Baker ended the call. If Charlene wasn't answering then it was for definite she wouldn't be checking messages.

He stood, needing to be out of the station for at least a moment.

As he walked towards the door, his cell-phone rang. An unknown number; identity withheld.

"Hello?" he said.

"Who is this?" a male voice asked.

"Jack Baker, poli…"

The line clicked dead and Baker stood in the stillness of the empty station.

He was still standing there moments later when the landline in his office shattered the silence.

Chapter 42: Amplified

Charlene hobbled across the car park, half lurching, half running; a caricature movie henchman. She didn't like the silence that had replaced the gunshot, didn't like it one bit.

She reached the entrance to the school, tried the doors; locked.

When she glanced back towards the cruiser, it seemed as if the distance had stretched. Going back wasn't an option.

She stood, breathing heavily, her pulse throbbing in her aching head.

Eventually, she was ready to go on.

She moved off towards the corner of the building, towards the tennis courts and, beyond, the gym complex.

* * *

Jason ended the call, pocketing his phone on auto-pilot.

He picked up Charlene's phone and, although tempted to smash it into pieces, chose to power it down.

Katie was curled into a tight ball, rocking back and forth in the centre of the basketball court. He could hear her *drama-queen* crying from here. The gunshot had shattered the backboard, littering the court with twinkling shards.

He was tempted to make her walk on the broken glass.

Just for kicks.

* * *

She saw light from the high windows of the gym itself.

More than emergency lights, she thought, *someone's in there.*

She stopped as abruptly as if she had been pushed back.

There were many shadows here.

She remembered his attack, the way he'd come from nowhere, waiting for her, planning it.

If the gymnasium wasn't a beacon, she didn't know what was.

Well, two could play at that game.

She turned away from the gym and across the open ground to the tennis courts, planning a long loop around to come at the buildings from the far side, where he would least expect her.

Pretty soon, she was just another shadow amongst the darker shadows beyond the tennis courts and football field.

* * *

Jason put the gun down by his side.

His hands were shaking. No, scratch that, his whole body was shaking. What a rush! Pulling the trigger and then the thud of recoil and the sheer sound and energy of the firing. It had been like every video game or movie he'd ever seen but amplified many, many times, a sheer adrenalin hijack.

He hadn't even aimed, just pointed the gun somewhere in the air and pulled the trigger. His head swam with images of how the shot might have gone.

Principal Sturmann flew backwards as the shot carried him off his feet.

That wimp, Bobby Kingston, holding up a hand to ward him off, only to have the shot tear a clear hole through his palm.

His father's head exploding.

In slow motion.

He was dimly aware of the erection pulsing in his pants.

He leant back on the bench behind him, hands behind his head, coasting down off the buzz, coming back to rest.

As he settled, he heard once again the snivelling coming from the tip-off circle.

He rubbed absent-mindedly at his pants.

"Hey, Katie!" he yelled.

She didn't respond, but he knew she was listening.
"Take off your jeans," he commanded.

* * *

Charlene hugged the treeline for as long as she could, though eventually, she would have to cross open ground to first reach the bleachers before crossing to the buildings. She looked across the field towards the low wall by the tennis courts. The exit over there was shrouded in shadow; nothing moved. Scanning the bleachers told her the same, even though she cursed the shadows for stealing complete certainty: *no-one was out here*.

Her hand wandered to the sore spot on the top of her head, checking to see whether she had started bleeding again.

While she assessed the wound, a thought raced through her.

I should get a stick!

She scanned the ground, but there were just small twigs and kindling here; turned back, looked deeper into the shadows, and there was one that would work, a couple of feet of wood with a little nodule of trunk where the branch had been rudely ripped from the tree.

It would have to do.

She picked up her makeshift weapon, feeling the weight and balance of it.

Good enough, she thought, looking across the open space to the bleachers, *it's time*.

And without giving herself another chance to rethink, she started for the gym.

* * *

In the centre of the basketball court, naked save for her final shred of underwear, Katie watched the shadows.

Chapter 43:
Haven't You Heard?

Baker grabbed the phone.

"Who is this?" he yelled, fully expecting the voice that had called his cell-phone to respond.

"Baker?" a different voice asked ,"Jack?"

Baker breathed to quiet his racing pulse.

His gut was churning, intuition firing off warning signs.

"Yes?" he said, "who is this?"

"It's me, Curtis?"

Now, he saw the caller ID on the phone.

Calm down, Jack, he thought.

"Oh, what do *you* want?" Baker said.

"I..." Simpson paused, "I... er... wanted to get the inside scoop?"

"Huh?"

Baker was confused, was Simpson talking about Charlene?

Oh shit, he thought, his gut clenching, *something's happened to her since she left the station.*

"What's happened to her?" he asked, worry gnawing at his thoughts. "What's happened to Charlene?"

"Er... I don't know... Is... er... is she involved in this?"

"In what?"

"The shooting at the school."

Baker almost dropped the handset.

Worse, he almost asked *'what shooting?'* in response. Luckily, his long experience of avoiding specifics when talking with Simpson saved him from the gaffe.

"No comment," he said.

"Oh, come on chief," Simpson whined, "surely you can tell me a little something?"

Baker remembered how Simpson had been on the phone almost as soon as they'd found Dylan Ford unconscious in the school car park; the glee with which the newsman had seemed to greet the story, and the resulting betrayal when he'd published even though he'd promised Baker he wouldn't.

"Right now," he said coldly, "I've got more important things to worry about. Goodbye, Curtis."

"But chief!"

"Goodbye, Curtis."

Baker slammed the phone down, grabbed his keys and ran for the door.

* * *

He drove out of the car park fast. Thankfully, the town was so quiet that he wouldn't need his siren or roof light. He headed through downtown to the school.

His head swam with so many questions that he chose to ignore them all, focusing only on the matter at hand.

He thumbed to the number of the ambulance dispatcher, ready to put the call in.

Maybe I should check it out first, he thought. After all, he had only Curtis Simpson's word that a gun had been fired.

But Simpson hadn't said that. He'd said: *'shooting'*.

Baker thumbed the phone to standby as he rolled past Annie's diner, its windows dark, bug lamp glowing ultraviolet somewhere off in back.

Not gunfire.

A *shooting*.

Mentally, he walked through scenarios that he might encounter on his arrival at the school.

Chapter 44:
No-one Can Stop Me

Charlene waited by the rear school exit, leaning on the wall, her makeshift club dangling by her side. Waiting, for what she wasn't entirely sure. Was it another shot? Some sign that someone was actually inside the gym?

No, you know he's in there, she thought, *you're just plain scared, Charlene.*

But even admitting it couldn't get her to move.

She leant against the wall.

* * *

Katie stared at the bleachers through dry, tired eyes. She had no more tears, this evening's crazy roller-coaster had used them all up, just as it had every reserve of hope she'd held.

Just get it over with, she thought, *if you're going to kill me, just kill me.*

She opened her mouth to say just that but found her throat so raw from crying that no sound would emerge.

Jason stepped down a couple of benches on the bleachers, emerging from the shadows, the gun in his right hand. He sat again and the light glinted off his eyes, rendering them empty; mirror chips to reflect the world.

He'll rape me first, she thought, with something approaching resigned despair, *of course he will.*

Jason studied her, head tipping slightly to one side.

He gave one short, derisive snort of laughter.

"Little miss perfect," he said, mostly to himself.

"Why? Why are you doing this?" she asked, the words emerging without a conscious thought to propel them. As soon as she heard her voice, she closed her eyes, fearful of his retribution.

It didn't come.

She opened her eyes.

He shrugged.

"Because," he said, as if everything were clear.

She hugged herself tighter, near-foetal.

"Because?" anger swelled in her; ferocious, tempestuous. "That's all you can say? *Because?*"

He shrugged again and then his attention seemed to drift, as he looked towards the high ceiling of the gym.

"Did you see it?" he asked. "It exploded. Like stars. Like diamonds."

His voice was lost in wonder.

Katie watched him.

"I did that," he said, amazement mutating into pride. "Me. I did that!"

He levelled his gaze upon her, gestured at her with the gun.

"You are such a fucking trophy, *little miss perfect*," he punctuated each word with a prod of the barrel, "I'm gonna fuck you over, have you stuffed and mounted over my fucking fireplace! I can do that. No-one can stop me."

And then, absurdly, he pulled the gun to his face and kissed the cool metal.

"No-one can stop me," he said.

* * *

Baker swung his cruiser into the car park.

Charlene's car was still there, on its rims. He pulled up alongside.

As yet, no-one from the town had shown at the school, not even Simpson. Baker hoped it was because they'd decided to turn a blind, or at least half-blind, eye to the reported sound of a gunshot. After all, if it had been a single shot it might easily be dismissed amongst the other noise of the evening; a car back-firing, someone hosting a back-yard firework party.

Maybe Simpson had made up the story, based only on such triggers, just to get under his skin.

Maybe.

Still, he would do well to tread carefully.

He switched off his car, grabbed his own gun and stepped out onto the asphalt.

When he tried the door, he found Charlene's car still locked. Each door was the same. Nothing untoward, save for the slashed tires and shattered remnants of the window.

From everything he could see, it didn't seem like she'd come back here at all.

Where are you, Charlene, he thought, *where in hell are you?*

* * *

Katie watched in mounting horror as Jason stepped down the final two benches of the bleachers until his sneakers touched the basketball court, squeaking slightly. He adopted what she thought was an absurd gangsta strut, grabbing at his crotch and rolling his shoulders.

It was only after a moment that she realized this was no act. He was masturbating through the material of his pants as he walked.

He gestured at her with the barrel of the gun.

"Open wide," he ordered.

She did the opposite, pulling her arms tighter around her knees.

He stopped, stamped his foot hard on the floor, the sound echoing around the gym.

"No!" he yelled. *"You will do what I tell you to do! When I tell you!"*

With each word, he shook the gun by his ear, like he were rattling dice ready for a crap shoot.

"Now... Drop your knees and open wide!"

She didn't move.

"No," she whispered.

The gun levelled upon Katie and she stared into its black, dark eye.

"Little miss perfect," he said, *"and her perfect cunt!"*

* * *

Charlene leant back against the cool brick of the wall, silently watching the stars for a moment. She breathed deeply.

There's no-one in there, she thought, *there's no-one...*

BOOM!

For a moment, she actually felt the wall reverberate with the shot.

But then she was moving, lifting her club, fully ready to use it yet having no idea what she might face when she got inside the building.

She opened the exit door and, as she stepped into the darkened hallway beyond, the school swallowed her.

Chapter 45: SWALK

Baker leant on the cool metal of Charlene's cruiser, wracking his brain as to where she might have gone. Maybe she'd just seen sense and gone to the hospital after all.

"Stupid, Jack," he said to himself, "that's where she'll be!"

He stood upright and returned to his car, pulling the door opened and stepping down into his seat.

The door was just swinging closed when he heard it.

A shot echoing across the car park, coming from somewhere within the school buildings.

* * *

In the gym corridor, Charlene dropped to one knee and slowly peeked around the corner into the gym. She could never have been ready for the sight that greeted her and shock pulled her back behind the door, wrestling with what she'd just seen.

Katie, naked, lying on her back, knees up.

Charlene hadn't been able to tell whether she was conscious or not.

Jason Liu towering above her, pulling at his shorts.

Laughing.

That sound. That laughter.

The gun pointing at Katie.

"Little miss perfect," Jason sneered now, his voice an echo across the basketball court.

Charlene swallowed once before peeking again.

He was on his knees, a hand reaching out for Katie's leg.

Katie's head swivelled to one side, as if to allow her conscious self to drift away from this attack, to some blank place where…

Their eyes locked.

Charlene was mortified by what she saw in Katie's eyes; numbness, resignation, acceptance, avoidance. Death.

Hardly even a plea for help.

Her heart leapt into her mouth, despairing.

Jason pulled at his shorts as he spread Katie's legs wider.

And suddenly, with neither thought nor plan in mind, Charlene was moving, running across the gym, raising the club above her head. She might have been screaming; if so, she couldn't hear it for the protective rage that clamoured within her.

In hindsight, in dreams, in the physical impossibility leant by abstract memory, it seemed she closed the distance in a matter of a few steps. The club *whooshed* through an arc, roaring with displaced air as she swung with every ounce of energy she had.

He turned, just as the club struck.

Or at least she remembered that he did.

"What?" he said, as he seemed to notice her for the first time.

The club hit him square in the middle of the forehead.

* * *

Baker sprinted to the school entrance, found the doors locked. He glanced back over his shoulder, fancied that he could see the glow of headlights coming in this direction.

On the second shot, they'd lose all inhibition.

The flood would begin.

He wished he could establish a perimeter, wondered why he hadn't called one of the others, wondered…

Then he snapped back to his instinctive, trained self.

None of that was important right now.

He sprinted to the corner of the building and, around it, towards the gym complex, from where he was sure he'd heard the gunshot.

* * *

Charlene kicked the gun towards the bleachers as she bent over Jason's prone body. He was breathing though, for the moment at least, unconscious.

She looked him up and down, this child, this teenager, previously so full of his own importance and bravado. Now... Well, he was just a kid. A kid!

It took her a moment to realize why she was scanning his body, what she was searching for: *her belt*.

Her handcuffs.

But he wasn't wearing the belt.

She took one last look; he wouldn't be surfacing any time soon.

She turned to Katie, stepping over to her and crouching by her side.

The girl looked up at her; fearful, in shock.

Tears welled in Charlene's eyes and she wiped them angrily away, reaching out for Katie and pulling her into a tight embrace, even in this moment of extremis experiencing the sensation of smooth, young skin; solidity of beauty.

"Come on," she said, "let's get you out of here."

She pulled Katie to her feet.

"Wait a second," Charlene said, and she bent to regain Katie's discarded clothes.

"Cunt!" she heard Jason Liu scream, his voice slurred.

She turned, looking over her shoulder, watching as he launched himself at Katie, barrelling into her, his momentum carrying them nearly all the way to the bleachers.

In the semi-shadow, she watched as Jason slapped Katie twice around the face before straddling her. His hand grabbed one of her breasts and squeezed tight.

Katie screamed, her hands skittering to fight his grip; he batted them away and her arms momentarily fell to the floor, her hips bucking to try and throw him.

Charlene was up on one knee, pushing off to run towards them.

Katie's hand came up.

With the gun.

She shot once, through his stomach.

For a single, isolated moment, as echoes evaporated, everything was still.

Then Jason fell to one side, leaving a trail of deep arterial blood across the white flesh of Katie's abdomen.

Blood and Beauty. These moments; forever to be frozen in Charlene's memory.

* * *

At the tennis courts, Baker's hand fell on the handle of the exit door, but it too was locked.

He carried on around the gym, toward the back door of the school.

As he ran along the side of the building, another gunshot boomed through the relative silence.

"Shit!" Baker hissed as he began to sprint.

* * *

Katie stared at the gun in her hand, looked towards Jason's dying body, back to thc gun.

"I... I..." she began.

Charlene reached her side, just as Katie began to tilt the gun towards her own head.

"No!" Charlene yelled, diving for the girl, wrestling her gun arm.

Sitting behind her, she pulled Katie into a tight embrace, hugging her as if they sat watching a campfire together. They rocked like this for a moment in soothing rhythm.

"I... I..." Katie stammered.

"Shhh," Charlene calmed her, "it's over... You didn't do anything. Shhh..."

She heard the door open at the far end of the corridor beyond the gym door.

"Charlene!"

Baker's voice.

They had moments only; this last embrace.

Katie was shaking in her arms, sobbing now, shock hitting full on.

Charlene kissed the back of Katie's neck gently.

"I love you," she whispered.

On the floor, Jason's head flopped to one side; he stared at them and, even though it was clear he was on the way out, rage still shimmered in his eyes.

"Little… miss…" he hissed between gasps of air.

Charlene took hold of Katie's gun hand, placed her fingers over those of the girl.

Aimed.

"I love you," she repeated.

Charlene shot Jason Liu in the face, a single hole opening high on one side of his forehead, blood spraying out from the exit wound.

"I love you."

Later

Chapter 46:
The Finger Points

Déjà vu sat heavy on Baker's shoulders. He'd seen this movie, read the book, ordered the poster and munched just about all the popcorn he could stand.

The room was anarchic clamour, voices raised in energy if not volume, an almost frantic level of discussion at the core of which was the shooting at the school and what the town council were going to do about it.

Worried glances; fingers of blame.

Baker scanned the room and saw only grown up adolescents, victims seeking some surrogate parent to take the pain away.

Mason entered at the back of the room, followed by the other members of the town council. They had been in closed session all afternoon; Baker had not been invited.

The council walked to the dais, each step a signal of their deflation; even Mason seemed less purposeful than Baker had ever seen him before.

The crowd took a long, long time to come to order.

* * *

There was some perfunctory business-at-hand, names and roll-call, but nobody was in any doubt. This was a special meeting.

They were here to discuss one thing only.

Once the town council were seated, Mason crossed to the podium, tapping the microphone to ensure it was on.

"Good evening," he said, "can you hear me okay? Is this thing on?"

There were nods from the audience.

"How about at the back?"

More nods.

"So, to business," he said, his usual functional smile muted by events, "before we open the floor, I'd like to read a short statement for the record."

Looking down at the hand-written page before him, he didn't wait for response.

"Thank you for coming out for this special meeting. We, the members of the town council, have been as shocked as you all by the events at the high school last Wednesday night. Our thoughts are with the Liu, Browning and Ford families, whose children have borne the brunt of these terrible circumstances. At the request of George Liu, one of the town's most respected business leaders, we will be making a donation to the ICU, where medical staff are doing such wonderful work caring for his son, and Dylan Ford. I am sure these children are in all our thoughts."

Mason looked up from the paper, his eyes glinting in the harsh lights.

"Now, I'd like Police Chief Jack Baker to join us up here to discuss how he plans to handle the violence in our high school."

Baker's jaw almost hit his chest and he felt his stomach drop out.

He's going to pin it on us, he thought, *only Mason would try and deflect this. Only Mason.*

Mason stared down at Baker, his face fit for poker, revealing nothing.

Baker held his gaze for a moment and then, shrugging, stepped up to the podium.

* * *

He looked out across the audience, saw anger, resentment, fear, all brimming at once.

"Good evening," he said, breathing deep to maintain his calm. "I have a few comments and then I'll be happy to take questions."

Some nods, but mostly they waited for him to speak.

He could feel Mason's gaze on his back and, beyond that, the fact that Mason would throw Charlene to these frightened people. Baker wasn't blind to the fact that the first selectman had neglected to mention her in his opening remarks, focusing instead on the families, one of whose kids had abducted and abused a fellow student, and threatened the life of an officer.

But Mason didn't care about that.

He needed a bad guy that he could blame without consequences.

Charlene.

It hadn't been her fault, and she didn't deserve that fate.

Honesty, he thought, *it's time for honesty.*

"Last Wednesday night," he began, "Officer Charlene Goodlow was attacked by a student at the high school, Jason Liu. After knocking her unconscious, Jason stole Officer Goodlow's sidearm, which he subsequently used to abduct a fellow student, Katie Browning. Officer Goodlow sustained a concussion, however this was not serious enough to require hospital attention and, after checking in with me at the station, she returned to the school for her cruiser, only to find its tyres had been slashed in the interim. While in the car park, Officer Goodlow heard shots from the gymnasium and, on entering the building encountered Jason Liu on the verge of committing the gunpoint rape of Miss Browning. Thanks to her training and significant experience, Officer Goodlow was able to prevent the rape, however in the ensuing fight, Jason Liu was shot twice, once in the abdomen and a second time in the head."

Baker spoke calmly, his voice level, recounting the skeleton facts that had been captured in his initial report. Though *The Daybreaker* had run with wall-to-wall coverage of the attack since Wednesday, many of the specifics had not been shared with the public. As Baker watched them now, he saw shock and surprise; his intent all along.

"As first selectman Mason just indicated, Jason Liu is currently in critical yet stable condition in the intensive care unit of the local hospital. Miss Browning is with her family and Officer Goodlow is on indefinite leave pending a full and formal investigation, which I fully expect will highlight her bravery and selflessness during these dangerous events."

He placed his hands on the podium's edges and scanned the room.

"Now," he said, hoping that he'd done enough to head off the more difficult anger in the room, "I'll be happy to take questions."

For a moment, no-one raised their hand. Baker glanced back to Mason, eyebrows raised, shoulders shrugging slightly: *want me to go on?* Mason glared at him and then turned his attention to the audience. He scanned from left to right, urging someone to start the ball rolling.

When no-one did, his gaze finally settled on Curtis Simpson, sitting three rows in from the back of the crowd. Mason nodded at him.

Here we go, Baker thought, turning back to face the inevitable, planted question.

Simpson raised his arm.

"Yes," Baker said, "near the back."

"Chief Baker, you've said that..."

"I'm sorry," Baker interrupted, "could you state your name and occupation, just in case people don't know you?"

Though he had been polite enough, there was intent to Baker's question, to both prevent Simpson getting into his flow while also labelling him for the audience; *The Daybreaker* was far from universally loved, respected and admired.

"Oh... Sure," Simpson responded, momentarily flustered, "I'm Curtis Simpson, lead reporter for *The Daybreaker*."

He glanced around the room, fixing his face in a *'hi-there!'* smile. When he turned back to Baker, anger simmered just below the surface of that smile.

"Thanks for doing that, Curtis," Baker said calmly, "I'd like us all to follow the example this evening, so that the record is clear. Now, your question?"

Simpson's lips reared back over his teeth; an unconscious animal gesture.

"How..." he began, "How does it feel knowing that one of your officers tried to murder a teenage boy? Are you proud of your department, Chief Baker?"

The venom in these questions stung Baker hard and his fingers tightened on the wood of the podium.

"I…"

Simpson glared at him.

"Hyperbolic questions won't help anyone, Curtis," he said keeping his tone even and non-confrontational, "I've just shared the specifics of what happened last Wednesday and I will await the outcome of the investigation before rushing to judgement."

"So, you're dodging the question?"

"No. I am answering your question as honestly and openly as I can. I have no comment until the investigation is complete."

"But Officer Goodlow is on indefinite leave, right? So, you must have some doubts, otherwise why wouldn't she be back at work already?"

Baker noticed a couple of heads twitch towards Simpson, he decided to ride the energy that he sensed; the turn.

"Curtis," he said quietly, gesturing to the audience, "these people have come here with questions and the hope to answer some of their concerns. I'm more than happy to help you dig for sensationalist details outside of this forum but for now, do you have a specific question?"

Simpson began to register the looks on the faces around him; the eroding ground upon which he stood.

"Yes," he said, thinking, "yes, I do. Do you regret sending an armed officer into the school, an officer whose own weapon was used to shoot a student?"

Baker's grip tightened on the podium again, he fought to bite down on his initial angry response, but its energy didn't disappear, choosing instead to seep into his every word.

"Officer Goodlow was in the school for a little over a week and, initially, didn't even wear her sidearm. Something happened on Tuesday though, something that made her decide to wear her piece."

He thought back to Tuesday, after the graffiti had returned, and Mason's insistence that she should be armed.

"I suspect, given what we've witnessed," he continued, "that Jason Liu was growing more erratic, more antagonistic; on Wednesday, Charlene… Officer Goodlow had reason to take him to Principal Sturmann's office. The investigation will…"

“So she pushed him over the brink?” Simpson nearly crowed at having found his angle, “made him take her gun?”

“No!” Baker protested. “She did not. The only reason there was a gun in that school was because we, all of us, decided to put one there. If you’re seeking to blame someone, you might as well point at each and every person in this room.”

“Not Officer Goodlow, then?” Simpson laughed.

“No, Curtis. Not Officer Goodlow. The town council demanded that we place a police officer in the school in response to what appeared to be typical teenage rebellion. However, it now seems that we had a very damaged individual who…”

“Wait!” Mason blurted out, near apoplectic. “What are you saying? That George Liu’s son was… That George Liu…”

“I’m not saying anything of the kind,” Baker said, choosing not to look at Mason, instead making eye contact with as many members of the audience as possible. “What I am saying is that whenever one of these horrific situations happens, it’s a natural reaction to look for specific cause and effect; to point the finger of blame. I’m not commenting on Jason Liu’s mental health, or his family in any way. I am, however, able to see his actions and the bottom line is that he was already heading towards some form of what actually happened. But I doubt it would have escalated so far and so fast if *we* hadn’t chosen to introduce a police officer into the school.”

“We did this,” Baker nodded, “the grown-ups in the town. It’s time we all take responsibility for what happened last Wednesday. Only Jason Liu knows why he did what he did, but Officer Goodlow did not choose or seek out Jason Liu as a target, she defended a young girl from a horrific attack. If anyone pulled the trigger as she did that, it was me, it was Bill Mason, it was each and every one of you who decided that it was someone else’s job to keep you safe.”

“There wouldn’t have been a gun in the school if we hadn’t put one there.”

Baker stood and stared at Simpson who, after a moment, sat down.

Around the room, people were nodding; quiet agreement as to their culpability.

Behind him, Mason stirred, and Baker feared for a moment, that the politician would choose to continue this debate. But the room was with the police chief, and Mason too adept at political survival to cut into that level of support.

"Now," Baker said, "noting once again that the formal investigation is getting underway, does anyone have any questions?"

Chapter 47:
These Pools Reflect Their Depth

"Are you sure you want to do this?" Katie's father asked, turning to face her.

She looked out of the car window at the entrance to the hospital.

There was no way she could put into words what had been happening within her during the restless days and sleepless nights since the gym. No way to explain that she was busily swallowing it all down into a black hole that she fully intended to top with concrete; burying it deeper than she would ever dig again.

No way to explain that visiting Dylan was no different to sitting on the couch at home, or lying in her bed; wherever she turned, Jason Liu's leering, manic smile greeted her behind her eyelids, the cool air of the gym rippling across her naked skin.

No way to explain anything without screaming as if she might never stop.

She reached out a hand and patted his arm.

"Sure, Dad," she said, "it's quiet where Dylan is. I can just sit with him."

Her father frowned; not fully buying the story.

"Want me to come sit with you?" he asked.

She shook her head.

"I'll be fine, Dad," she protested, "really."

He stared at her for a moment and she hated the sight of the tears glimmering in his eyes.

"Really," she repeated, leaning across and kissing him on the cheek.

"Okay," he sighed, glanced over his shoulder, "I'll park over there, might grab a coffee. I'll be here when you're ready."

Her smile broke through the numbness for a moment.

"I know you will, Dad," she said.

* * *

She walked directly to ICU, partly to avoid the stares which she sensed followed her everywhere now, partly because she didn't trust her legs to keep her upright if she paused for even a moment.

She stood outside the ward entry doors, gathering herself, already feeling the tears pushing to be free; her concrete not as solid as her rational mind would have her believe. She reached into her purse for a tissue, dabbed at her eyes and then blew her nose. It made hardly a difference.

Time, she thought, *let's go, Katie.*

* * *

She rounded the corner towards the reception desk on auto-pilot but then stopped suddenly.

The waiting area was full.

The Fords sitting alongside the Lius.

Katie almost ran, but then Lilly Ford was on her feet, crossing the room and pulling her into a tight embrace.

She was filled with panic, claustrophobic with the intensity of the moment and the strength of Lilly's arms.

"No," she said into the meat of Lilly's shoulder, "No."

"Shhhh..." Lilly patted her head.

"No!"

Katie pulled back and stared wildly around the room, unable to bring her gaze directly upon Jason Liu's parents.

"Katie," Dave Ford said, standing from his seat, "what..."

But then George Liu was rising, turning towards her and she wanted to scream because his face was so like his son's and it was like Jason was standing before her once again, his manic smile and crazy laughter as he bore down upon her and Charlene was holding her hand and...

George Liu stood before her, head bowed slightly.

She almost ran.

But he reached out and took her hand in both of his.

She almost screamed.

But his hands were solid, warm, reassuring.

He clasped her hand, now managing to snare her with his gaze.

He nodded slightly.

"I am sorry," he said, "for whatever my son has done to you. I am sorry."

She wanted to scream that it wasn't enough, never enough, to let it all out there and then, raining hellfire down upon this man in pure vengeance for the evils his son had done.

But she didn't.

Because she saw her own sadness reflected in his eyes, a bottomless well of hurt with no chance of being refilled. She saw her own sleepless nights in the angle of his shoulders and the sadness curling the skin around his eyes and mouth.

Katie looked at George Liu for a long time, as he clasped her hand in both of his.

Eventually, she nodded and removed her hand.

She turned towards Dylan's room and began to walk, leaving the two families behind in the waiting area.

There was a police officer she didn't recognize standing at the inner door of the ward. He looked at her as she approached, and she knew he planned to prevent her entering.

"It's all right," she heard Lilly Ford say from behind her, "she's Dylan's girlfriend."

The police officer didn't move though. His eyes flicked slightly from where they'd been looking at Lilly.

"Please," George Liu said, "let her in."

The officer nodded and stepped aside.

Katie stepped through the inner doors to visit with her boyfriend.

Chapter 48:
These Arms Of Mine

Charlene stepped out of the court-house, into the clamour of reporters and television trucks. Microphones jostled and gestured, poking towards her face as if to make a point.

She stared coldly at them all.

"Officer Goodlow!" a familiar voice rang from the back of the pack.

Curtis Simpson.

She looked at him; like staring through gauze, everything on this fall day had taken on a hazy quality, like it wasn't quite real.

And wasn't that what it came down to at its root, nothing had been quite real since that night in the gym. Not the investigation, nor the lawyers, nor the paparazzi parked outside her house, nor the ban on visiting the school, nor Sturmann's understanding yet cold shoulder, nor Mason's consideration that she be awarded a public service medal. Not any of it.

All of it was masked by the twin sensations of feeling Katie warm against her, within her arms, and the very specific sight of the bullet entering Jason Liu's head.

"What's your reaction to today's decision?" Simpson shouted, pushing his microphone towards her. She looked at him through the haze.

"I..." she began and then a hand swooped from behind her and covered the microphone.

"My client has no comment at this time," her lawyer, Joshua Goldblum, interrupted.

"But surely you didn't expect the case to be dismissed?" Simpson continued to Charlene. "That you'd get off without even a slap on the wrist?"

"I..."

And the truth was, she hadn't. She should have been charged with the attempted murder, or at least manslaughter, of Jason Liu. In the darkest times since the gym, she'd fully persuaded herself she deserved as much. At minimum, her defense team had been planning for a lengthy inquest; she had been truly shocked when the judge had ruled self-defense earlier that morning.

Goldblum stepped up to her side.

"Obviously," he said with calm authority, "the speed with which this case has been dismissed has taken us by surprise, and I'm sure you'll understand that we need some time to synthesize what's happened this morning."

"I..." Charlene continued.

Goldblum looked sideways at her, annoyed that she wasn't taking his heavy-handed hint.

"My client has *no further comment* at this time," he reiterated, "however we will be arranging a press conference in the next day or so."

He took hold of Charlene's elbow, beginning to move her through the scrum of reporters.

"I'm sorry!" she suddenly blurted out.

"Charlene!" Goldblum hissed in her ear. "Don't!"

But the reporters knew their fish was biting. The microphones jostled for attention.

For a blessed moment, the first in weeks, the haze lifted and Charlene had clarity of thought and purpose.

"I just want to..." she began, but the words failed her for a moment. She breathed slowly, closed her eyes, focused herself.

"I don't care about verdicts," she said, "I'm sorry for what happened to Jason Liu. I'm sorry for his family, for the school. I'm sorry that Kuh... Katie Browning was attacked and held hostage. I'm sorry that I... I... let him take my gun. I'm sorry... I..."

She began to cry then and, as she felt Goldblum putting his arm around her shoulders, let him lead her through the baying pack.

* * *

Later that week, all the oxygen was sucked away from Charlene's story when a hurricane unexpectedly turned towards the north east. She became no-one again, which suited her just fine.

Baker had given her time to recover, offering her the option of returning or not. Whichever way her decision went, she would always love him for his support throughout the aftermath of the shooting; his shoulder had proven strong and massive.

She thumbed through the contacts on her cell-phone, vaguely connecting that it was the handset Jason Liu had stolen along with her gun.

She waited as the call went through.

"Hi, Charlene," a female voice answered, "how're things?"

"Okay, I guess," she responded, "can we get together? The house is feeling big and empty and I need to talk with someone."

"Are you sure that's a good idea?"

"Please?"

A pause, so long that Charlene was able to fill it with the spray of Jason Liu's blood across Katie's smooth, soft abdomen.

"Okay. Do you know the overlook on Maple Street?"

"Sure."

"I'll be there at two this afternoon."

"Thank you, thank you, thank you. I'll see you at two."

Charlene thumbed the phone, ending the call.

Tears welled in her eyes. She let them flow, too tired to do otherwise.

* * *

At two, Charlene sat at a picnic table at the overlook on Maple, alone save for frantic squirrels, seeking stores for the coming winter.

She looked down on the town, its New England patchwork of capes, colonials and ranches, white-wood siding and manicured trees.

It looked like some idealist's picture postcard, some remembered perfection, a testimonial advert for a small-town America that had long passed.

She had tasted the bitter undercurrent of this town; enough to make her sick.

High in a tree, a hawk cried, piercing the afternoon's humming normality.

A rusting car pulled in through the overlook's entrance and parked next to her own rental.

Charlene smiled at the newcomer.

Brina stepped out of the car and crossed to the picnic table.

"Hi," Charlene said, feeling tears well again.

"Hi," Brina nodded, taking a moment to look at Charlene.

When the moment became too uncomfortable, she shifted her gaze to the town, walking past the picnic bench and, for a moment, presenting Charlene with her back.

Charlene stood from the picnic bench, stepped towards the teenager.

"Thank you for coming," she said, her voice cracking, "thank you for…"

But the tears stole the remainder of her gratitude.

Brina turned, and there were tears brimming in her own eyes.

She opened her arms wide, smiling a welcome.

Charlene stepped into the embrace, and let it all out on her shoulder.

"It'll be fine," Brina said, stroking the back of Charlene's head, "everything's going to be fine."

Brina kissed the top of Charlene's head while the older woman shuddered with tears.

"Everything's going to be fine."

"Do Sparrows Eat Butterflies?"
A Novel
Vincent Tuckwood

In a moving tale of one man's search for meaning in an increasingly lonely and depressing life, a washed up seaside painter embarks on a journey that will change him forever.

Bored, lacking inspiration and verging on alcoholism, Ray encounters a man burning alive as he walks the beach near his home. The painter is persuaded to visit the burnt man's home, Certainty, where a commune gathers under the spell of its enigmatic leader, Ged. Although it seems the idyllic embodiment of counter-culture freedom, Ray discovers that Certainty is far from ideal. Something insidious, something evil, lurks just beneath the surface.

As his unusual, traumatic rebirth unfolds, Ray discovers the horror of an inferno he has denied for years. To save the love that can provide true meaning in his life, he has no choice but to answer that one, repeating question: *do sparrows eat butterflies?*

'Do Sparrows Eat Butterflies?' is a deeply absorbing story of redemption, acceptance and love. A journey into the shackled heart and soul of an artist, it will leave you profoundly changed.

"Karaoke Criminals"
A Novel
Vincent Tuckwood

In *Music, Musica*, a karaoke bar on the Spanish riviera, Roxi is about to discover that her dreams may come true when Brian Ferguson offers to hook her up with his connections back in London. Roxi has no idea of the price attached to this offer; Brian doesn't do anything without good reason.

And for Miles Ashley, who thought he'd escaped Brian's clutches years earlier, a single phone call is enough to stop the song, rewinding the tape to zero.

Throw in an A&R rep under threat of castration and an exquisitely dangerous hood on the verge of a nervous breakdown and it's time to make music; gunfire drumbeats, filter sweep of cordite.

As the double-crosses, gang wars, reclaimed favours and challenged loyalties intertwine, it's clear that only blood spilled in revenge can clean the slate ready for Roxi's success.

In this part of the world, this is how business gets done.

Even the music business.

'Karaoke Criminals' is a fast-paced contemporary novel, the bastard offspring of *'The Commitments'* and *'Lock, Stock and Two Smoking Barrels'*. Music has never been this dangerous.

"Family Rules"
A Novel
Vincent Tuckwood

New York. In this city that never sleeps, anyone could make a brand new start of it. Or so the song goes.

For some people, starting again is no option.

Kenny is adrift in the city, tormented by the scars and memories of his unique upbringing as a child star in the UK, chasing any addiction that can fill the void he carries at his core.

Increasingly unable to paper over the cracks, to numb himself with street corner narcotics, or build an abiding relationship with his junkie soul-mate Ivvy, he turns to stealing cars to provide momentary escape from his increasingly desolate life.

Estranged from his parents, Kenny has no hope or vision of a better future.

Until one night he steals a car from a gas station in New Jersey and is offered an unexpected, final opportunity for redemption; a radically different role to play.

'Family Rules' is an intense personal account of an invented life, where all the rules of family life are inverted, and of the damage done when the boundary between reality and television is truly no boundary at all.

"Garbled Glittering Glamours"
Words from 2010
Vincent Tuckwood

I yearn only for now

Reminisce
Remember
Love your memory
Accept the you that was
Yet know
your now will become
your was
Is your is
all the was
you'd have it become?

'Garbled Glittering Glamours' is a collection of poetry published at VinceT.net and elsewhere in 2010.

"Team Building"
An Original Screenplay
Vincent Tuckwood

A team of naïve dot-commers have no choice but to survive the deadly Team Building.

Alex Di Staglia and her co-founders in web phenomenon, OuiChange.com, are lured to an isolated Pacific North-West island to participate in team building.

As the pressure increases to deadly ends, the team learns that their charismatic host, Jimmy McLeish, is far from dedicated to their success and survival.

Trapped on Jimmy's island and growing increasingly isolated, Alex must decide what she is willing to sacrifice in order to save her friends' lives and the future of OuiChange.

'Team Building' is a contemporary thriller.

Robert Edmonds is a designer/artist working out of Vancouver, Canada. More of his stunning art can be found at robertedmonds.blogspot.com

Boutique Empire is an artists' collective, proudly centred around the Vancouver, Canada music scene, Boutique Empire is currently home to: Sex With Strangers, Combine The Victorious, Guilty About Girls, Gilles Zolty, the graphic art of Robert Edmonds, and the fashion of Isabelle Dunlop. With the publication of Escalation, Vincent Tuckwood is pleased to join Boutique Empire. More at boutiqueempire.com.

Vincent Tuckwood is a story-teller working in fiction, song and verse. At any given point in time, he's proud to be a father, husband, son, brother, cousin and friend to the people who mean the world to him.

He is the author of the novels *"Do Sparrows Eat Butterflies?"*, *"Karaoke Criminals"*, *"Family Rules" and "Escalation"*, as well as the 2010 poetry collection, *"Garbled Glittering Glamours"*. His screenplays are *"Team Building"*, and the screen adaptation of Family Rules, *"Inventing Kenny"*.

Vince regularly connects with his audience at VinceT.net and at his story-teller page on Facebook, often writing poetry in response to their prompts, and encourages everyone to get in touch there.

Made in the USA
Charleston, SC
03 December 2011